THE CHILDREN OF SI-THO

THE CHILDREN OF SI-THO

BASED ON WHAT HAPPENED

ULI SCHMETZER

TIZULI

TIZULI

PUBLISHER: Tizuli Publishing
EMAIL: ulischmetzer@gmail.com
WEBSITE: uli-schmetzer.com

DESIGN AND PRINT MANAGEMENT: Reno Design | renodesign.com.au | R37006
DESIGN: © Graham Rendoth 2018
AUTHOR PORTRAIT: © Tiziana Turatello 2018

Typeset in 11.5/15 pt Minion

A catalogue record for this book is available from the National Library of Australia
www.trove.nla.gov.au

ISBN 978-0-9806375-8-8 (paperback)
ISBN 978-0-9806375-9-5 (ebook)

For Tiziana

CONTENTS

WHAT IS REAL?

During life you can brush against an experience that defies logic, as does a ghost or a miracle. How can you explain to others, without provoking ridicule, that you saw your body decay as your soul floated in the void of eternity; or that all your hang-ups and physical ails were cured while you were freaked out on a hallucinogenic fungus already well known to the ancients; or that you were an ignorant witness to the destruction of an indigenous culture?

Yet this is what happened. And this is how it happened.

The Author

A Debt to Maria Sabina

Sometimes, now that I am old, the past catches up with me, unexpectedly, unwilling to let go, unwilling to let me forget, always hovering in ambush, ready to pounce when I least suspect.

This happened the other day when a gust of wind carried the page of a newspaper along the beach, cart-wheeling over moles of licorice-black seaweed dumped by the last big storm. The errant page landed on the blubbery carcass of a bluebottle. I snatched at it before another squall carried it on. In this way I learned Maria Sabina had passed away and the Sierra Mazatec had been in mourning. Local bureaucrats, so the story said, estimated Maria Sabina's age at about one hundred though the Indios insisted she was timeless. One old man told the reporter his granny insisted Maria Sabina was as old as the hills, with white hair and wrinkles like old leather when the granny of his granny was still a little girl. No, he said, serious and not offended at all, Maria Sabina could not fly. But she could make others fly. And she could cure anyone with her little children.

The news of her death brought back a rush of memories, buried deep but never erased. I owed the old Curandera a debt I never paid. Her 'little children' had cured my liver, my sinus and my teenage hang-ups.

The last time I saw her was on a news reel as she walked into the courthouse, head high, surrounded by a phalanx of armed cops, a small, fragile old lady, straggly grey hair down her back. The cops forged a path through hundreds of Indios seated on their haunches in silent vigil on the lawns outside the Court House. The cops looked worried, surely wondering what might be under those ponchos and serapes the Indios humped on their backs. The report said the natives had trickled down from the Sierra and settled in front of the Court House, eating what they brought, drinking the water they carried in earthenware flasks. They had camped there for days, without a word. Protest was not in their nature.

Maria Sabina looked neither right nor left as she walked into the Court House, ignoring the Indios who stood up and bowed their heads as she passed, moving aside only reluctantly, making clear they were making room for her, not for the cops. No cries of protest could be heard. No words were either spoken or exchanged.

The report said the prosecutor accused her of witchcraft and of feeding her little children to the gringos causing one young gringo to jump off a cliff after shouting he could fly. The charge brought back the memory of my own attempt at flying. The gringo was unlucky. He landed on a rock. I landed in a haystack.

The young gringo's parents, wealthy people from Boston, convinced their local senators to pressure the Mexican government to punish the person or persons responsible for their son's fatal leap of faith.

And so Maria Sabina was taken down from her cabin on the mountain to jail and from jail to the Court House in Oaxaca City. The first Indios arrived and settled on the lawn outside the Court House soon after. Within days hundreds came, quiet, unsmiling natives whose presence made everyone nervous and prompted the authorities to move the hearing from the waiting list to 'top priority.'

The newsreel reported the case took only fifteen minutes—most of it taken up by legal preambles read out by a court clerk. Then the Judge, visible hot under his black toga, was curt and to the point. The charge of witchcraft was dismissed. Maria Sabina had to promise never again would she feed her little children to the gringos. If she did she would go to jail.

The Curandera did not say a word nor did she accept the court's condition. The stoic expression on her face never changed as if she was saying to the court 'none of this concerns me.' Besides she could not speak Spanish. So the charges read out and the verdict remained meaningless to her. She simply turned on her heels and without a word or a gesture walked from the courtroom. No one stopped her, just as no one would ever stop her again feeding the little children to her people—and to the gringos.

In this way my adventure came back to me as vivid as does a beloved chapter in a favorite book. I put the newspaper page down and looked up at the clouds. My memories drifted back to those magic nights in the cabin, Maria Sabina behind the candle—and Xochitl breathing passion down my ear.

Those nights (and I was never sure if there had been only one or if there had been many) are inextricably entangled with my guilt and the fate of one man, a man I called my friend, a man I still consider the bravest and most honest person I ever met.

His name was José Cabezavaca. The inmates called him El Tiburon (The Shark).

What I shall write down now is really his story, though a bit of the story is mine and also some of it is Maria Sabina's—and a small part is Xochitl's. And the story is also about the fate of Haberstone, that freaked-out shaman from the Bronx. And it is about what happened when I went back—forty years later.

My story begins back then, during those turbulent years when the Dirty Wars raged in Latin America and the 'longhairs' or 'ippies' invaded the realm of the Children of Si-tho, the dwarf god of the magic mushrooms, a god the Aztecs called Teonancatl and whose offspring, the mushrooms, Maria Sabina called 'my little children'.

—

"IT IS BETTER TO DIE ON YOUR FEET
THAN TO LIVE ON YOUR KNEES"

EMILIANO ZAPATA (MEXICAN PEASANT LEADER)

ONE

Teodimo and the Lemon Tree

El Tiburon approached the bench gingerly. He walked the way a peasant moves through the poultry pen, always afraid to trot on a wayward chick.

"Name?" The official asked sharply, using the harsh let's-have-no-nonsense-here tone that never fails to intimidate the illiterate and the poor.

"José Cabezavaca, Señor," El Tiburon replied, politely. The official ran a quill down the list and stabbed a name: "Ah!" he cried. "Here it is."

He ticked the name off and a second official passed the peasant a blue ballot paper and a ball-point pen.

El Tiburon carefully laid his faded straw sombrero on the bench before he studied the ballot paper. The stern, hard-eyed face of El Candidato was easy to recognize: It was framed in the national colors with the emblem of the eagle in the center. Below El Candidato's photo was the face of a man wearing horn-rimmed spectacles perched on the tip of a long nose. This had to be him. The soft-spoken informant in the market had been explicit. Besides, no one else was on the ballot paper.

El Tiburon wiped his writing hand on the side of his trousers, planted his left thumb on the face of the Long-Nosed One and ran his right index finger slowly along the dotted line to the square. He was about to make his mark when Don Miguel, standing beside the bench, clutched his wrist: "Not there, you fool," Don Miguel hissed, "the other square."

For a moment El Tiburon hesitated then he straightened up to face Don Miguel. Behind him the people of Mitzipotla stood in silence. The men, bare-headed, ran the rims of their sombreros through calloused hands as if the rims were worry-beads. The women wrapped themselves deeper into their black rebozos. All stood with heads bowed but all squinted covertly at the official bench below the Ahuehuete tree.

El Tiburon pushed back his shoulders and raised his head a little higher. He felt a lump in his throat and cleared it with a loud rasp. "Don Miguel," he said, "I'll vote for the man with the long nose." He glanced at the Haciendero just long enough to note the momentary expression of surprise, quickly followed by the flush of rising anger.

"Like hell you will!" Don Miguel snapped, taking a menacing step forward and staring down at the bareheaded Indio: "You'll vote for the Government as you've always done."

His voice was harsh, loud. He was accustomed to give orders and be obeyed.

El Tiburon rubbed the side of his trousers with one hand. The other was holding the pen, awkwardly, like a tool never used. He could feel the eyes of the people stabbing his back and mechanically squared his shoulders.

"No offense, Don Miguel," he said: "But we've decided to vote for the man from the opposition. All of us." He made a feeble sweep with his right hand to include the quiet throng behind.

"Just put your cross in the top square, dummy. Never mind what you decided. And get on with it," Don Miguel snapped.

El Tiburon's sandals dug at the sandy soil. He had heard Don Miguel's harsh voice all his life, the way his father and grandfather must have heard the voices of the other Don Miguels in the past. The voice was law. He shifted his weight from one foot to the other and swallowed. But his mouth remained dry, his legs heavy and his fingers itched for the soothing rim of the sombrero on the bench. He only hoped that furtive little man in the Market Square had known his facts.

"Don Miguel, I have the right, the right to choose my candidate," he blurted, staring at the Haciendero's belt: "It says so in article 49, clause 14. That's what it says."

He did not see the quick exchange between the men from the Electoral Board and Don Miguel, nor the bright flush of anger on the Hacienda owner's face. But their silence told him his information had been correct.

Behind him the wall of voters, backs and heads bent like wheat stalks in a breeze, stood silent. Yet he sensed their agitation between his shoulder blades. Images and sounds tumbled through his mind: The Old Man's lowered head, Don Miguel's haughty laugh, one boot on a sack of maize, smoke curling from a cigar. Mother on her knees, imploring; Anna's tears and the brutal roar of young Don Alfonso; a duck waddling and the sharp crack of a rifle; a leather boot; a kicked-over water bucket, merciless heat, parched lips and sprinklers gushing on the Patron's land; a boy's heart bursting over a blood-stained duck; line after line of lowered heads and bent backs, sombrero rims nervously running through calloused hands—and Anna's swollen belly.

The ballpoint pen was hot in his hand as he pressed his mark into the square next to the face of the Long-Nosed One. He looked up and longer than he had ever dared held the blazing eyes of Don Miguel. Then he snatched his sombrero from the bench, grateful for the comforting rim between his fingers, turned to the line of bent heads and black rebozos and announced: "We vote for the opposition—all of us."

And they did. One by one, all the men and women of Mitzipotla over the age of 21 scrawled their coarse crosses on the blue voting slips next to the picture of the Long-Nosed One. Done, they snatched a quick peep at Don Miguel's flushed face and walked away, heads bent just a trifle less, backs just a few degrees straighter, all just a little taller.

When it was all over, the officials sealed the ballot box and fastened it to the roof rack of Don Miguel's jeep. The officials climbed into the jeep and Don Miguel drove them away, the sealed ballot box bouncing drunkenly on the roof. The whole village jogged alongside the jeep in a tacit farewell, not to the officials or to Don Miguel, but to the box—their box, ballot box number 1039.

After lunch at the Casa Grande of the Hacienda de San Carlos, the three men from the Electoral Board, the Government Party scrutineer and Don Miguel leaned back and grinned at each other. Then Don Miguel picked up Ballot Box Number 1039 and sat it on his lap. He slid the sealed lid with a letter opener, delved inside and handed the sixty-eight voting slips in bundles to the scrutineer who tossed them into the fireplace and lit them with a match.

The senior official from the Electoral Board took sixty-eight new voting slips from his briefcase and the five men quickly filled them out using the Electoral List to obtain the names of the voters. Don Miguel closed the lid and taped it down. The men toasted each other with tequila, told a few stale jokes and finally embraced. Then the four visitors drove away in the Governmental station-wagon with Ballot Box Number 1039 securely squeezed between the two men in the back seat.

Two days later, three municipal policemen from Teotitlan, dressed in their faded blue uniforms and shouldering their ancient Thirty-Threes, marched El Tiburon off to jail in Teotitlan.

And that is how the story began.

In those days Teotitlan was at the end of a newly sealed road on which the recently poured asphalt still glistened licorice-black in the sun. On this road one afternoon two young men headed towards the Sierra Mazatec on foot. Behind them, front wheels stuck in a ditch, the two left a battered VW camper, a camper worn out by too many trips, too many sleep-ins and too many bad roads. The vehicle had finally decided enough was enough. First it stuttered then it spluttered and then with a final rattle the engine coughed out its life.

One of the two young men, the one better dressed, cursed the camper in Spanish and then in English, exhorting the engine to revive. When it did not he kicked the driver's door so hard he hurt his foot and limped away, still cursing, though softly now, more like the meow of a hurt cat.

The two young men were an odd pair. Each contradicted the other both in appearance and behavior.

Serge Dunlov wore his inseparable pair of faded blue jeans and denim shirt. The beige wind jacket was tossed over one shoulder the way he had seen Italian movie stars behave when they tried to appear casual. He was handsome though perhaps a trifle on the thin and delicate side. Son of a German automobile engineer he had inherited Teutonic traits of stubbornness, determination and telling others what was good for them. An English education had furnished him with that thin layer of arrogance that comes with the conviction the British Empire was a noble institution that offered independence to its colonies in a selfless gesture and bequeathed to the world the universal English language.

In a similar manner, by education and propaganda, Thad Morton had been taught America was the greatest, the champion of freedom, the defender of democracy, the leader and guardian of the Free World, a fortress rebuffing the scourge of communism. Thad might have gone along with this credo for the rest of his life had he not been conscripted to serve in Vietnam. Now he no longer believed in anything but love and drugs. Like most dropouts he wore his hair long, like his baggy trousers and flapping T-shirt. But his sandals were made of the finest Italian leather, his camera bag of suede. He had simply shrugged his shoulders when his camper gave up the ghost. Then he sat down on a grassy knoll, rolled a joint and watched his companion's futile attempts to coax life back into the engine with curses, kicks and by turning the starter key until the battery went so flat it no longer clicked.

Eventually, with no one in sight and a few necessities tugged into rucksacks, the pair started to walk on the road that bisects the cactus desert. Both agreed that at the end of this empty paved road must be the town through which they had to pass on their way to the Sierra.

Now and the two disappeared into dips on the road, reappearing between clumps of Nopal cactus spreading as far as the eye could see. For centuries the Indio weavers had milked the cacti for its dyes. Their rug-making dated back to pre-Hispanic days when their rugs decorated Aztec palaces and temples, even the Pyramid of the Sun on which captured warriors—and the odd virgin—had their throbbing hearts torn out in the belief their blood and heart would give the Sun-God the strength to conquer the night and ensure light comes back with the dawn.

The cactus desert spread from the foot of the Sierra to the banks of the Rio Grande del Sud. The river's source cascades from the cliffs of the

Sierra. Initially the river runs as a wild clean torrent before it gradually slows to snail's pace until, in the end, it vomits silt, garbage, corpses, rotted weeds and mud into the Pacific.

For the farms and settlements along the riverbanks the water is lifeblood. But Teotitlan, the town the two young men now approached, was built too far inland to benefit from the river. So the town remained dry, its people bitter and resentful, determined to extract from others the wealth nature had denied them.

Bartolomo spied the pair from his lookout: "Two gringos," he muttered. He could tell this by the way the two weaved across the road. The Indios walked in a straight line, gringos never. Not that Bartolomo had much time for the ignorant Indios. Like most petty bureaucrats and the rural nomenclature he prided himself on his Spanish ancestry and derided the natives whenever he could. He forgot, of course, Indio blood runs through the veins of most Mexicans ever since Hernan Cortez and his gold-crazed bandits set foot in Mexico, killed the men and raped the women. By the 20th century darks skins had become fashionable, at least for politicians, after the revolution had brought to power the Mestizos, the half-breed race with brown skins. Yet even today the rural and urban gentry still consider white skins a sign of good breeding and often disown their children if they turn up with 'dark' partners. But opposites attract. Many Mexican men keep a 'dark-skinned' mistress or 'hire' one temporarily in the Casa de Sitas, those up-market whorehouses where the girls sit along the wall with numbers attached to their bikinis.

Like most loners Bartolomo often talked to himself.

"Puppets," he now mumbled, watching the two minute figures pass through the cactus desert. The duet reminded him of marionettes on a cardboard stage during his childhood days. Once a year, never on the same day, the puppet master came to Teotitlan in a cart drawn by a grey donkey with a red pompom over one long ear and a blue one over the other. The puppeteer set up his stage on the Zocalo. He gave only one performance before he packed up and moved on. Bartolomo's granny always gave him a five-peso coin so he could go and see the puppet king, his queen and the crocodile monster. With the change Bartolomo could buy a lollypop. In the puppeteer's story the crocodile always tried to eat the royal couple, every year. The truth was the puppeteer knew only the one script he had inherited. Little Bartolomo liked the crocodile best because the others feared it. Fear gave the crocodile enormous power—and prestige.

Even as a child Bartolomo dreamed of being feared.

Now he held the Smith and Wesson Colt at arm's length and squinted down the barrel with one eye. An index finger curled around the trigger. "Bang, bang!" he said softly.

In the street below the dog wagged its tail.

Bartolomo holstered the old weapon without taking his eyes off the road. The two were still a good fifteen minutes' walk from the bend where the bitumen ended and the dirt road began. Once on the dirt road they were on his territory.

Where the bitumen ended, Teotitlan began.

Bartolomo pulled the sombrero down over his forehead and squatted down on the shady side of the church bell, below the engraved '1736' number, the year the bell was cast. That was not very long after the first Spanish monks, escorted by Spanish soldiers, arrived in the Sierra Madre. The monks gave the natives a simple choice: Convert to the Holy Roman Catholic Church or be burned at the stake as devil worshippers. Few Indios opted for the fire. Most converted in public but practiced the old ways in private.

The belfry was the one spot in Teotitlan where an occasional breeze, faint as the whiff of a wing, stirred the stifling haze over the cactus desert.

The belfry was also the best look-out.

Father Ignacio had protested at first and muttered about the House-of-God but Bartolomo cut off his bitching with the ominous warning: "Don't interfere with the law, priest."

And since the Church, ever since the revolution, could neither own its temples nor the land on which these temples stood the clergy survived on sufferance and kept silent for fear of being further persecuted and dispossessed. Besides Father Ignacio was an old parched man who had buried the spirit of battle long ago in the dust of his little town.

Bartolomo spun the drum of the colt and whistled three short drills. In the street below the dog pricked its ears and trotted off to alert the others.

It was the hour of the Siesta. Then the town, cowering at the foot of the Sierra, drowses behind whitewashed adobe walls. At that hour even the flies find it too sultry to buzz. After a while Bartolomo leaned over the belfry rail and glanced up and down the empty streets. The dog had returned and looked up at his master on the church tower, head cocked to one side.

"Good fellow," Bartolomo muttered: "They're coming."

The dog wagged its tail. It was a shaggy black mongrel with a white patch over one eye. Like its master, it never slept. Even at night both man and dog snoozed with one ear cocked, ready to react to the slightest sound. No one in Teotitlan had ever noticed Bartolomo or his dog until El Presidente appointed him Sheriff. No one could recall where he came from. People scratched their heads and finally admitted he may have lived among them all his life. But now he was like a weight on their shoulders. Wherever they went Bartolomo seemed to watch from below the felt sombrero which he wore ever since he became Sheriff. He hardly spoke to anyone but all knew he knew and in the knowledge of his knowledge they feared him privately but cajoled him publicly.

The Sheriff gave the drum a final twirl then stuck the colt back in the frayed leather holster on his hip, a holster he found in the attic of his granny's home. "Two gringos," he observed aloud as if reporting to a superior, though no one could hear him. With a snarl he added: "Poor lot. On foot."

Over recent times, the era of the hippy boom, Bartolomo had learned to assess arrivals by the size of their automobiles and the size of their wallets. He figured any gringo on foot had to be at the very bottom of the social ladder in Gringoland.

Down in the dusty Square the dog wildly wagged its tail.

The foreigners had arrived almost overnight, first in trickles then in ever growing numbers as word of mouth was passed on. With them came dramatic changes: Teotitlan was appointed Capital of the Sierra, in charge of the Land of the Sierra Indios up beyond the cliffs, the strip of fertile land by the river and the barren land of the Cactus Desert.

Modernization followed quickly in the wake of these promotions:

First came the sealed road, next came the electricity and then came the Post Office. Like most towns invested with sudden importance, Teotitlan's face changed, though not the face of its people. Those remained sullen and arid like the dry soil they tilled. No, it was the face of the town itself:

The onion dome of the church was painted mustard to make it look like gold. The Municipal warehouse for maize was extended into a Market. A row of shops opened. Three Señoritas learned to type. A post office was authorized. A sign outside the Post Office announced 'BUS'.

Yes, the bus now arrived twice a week. True, it was a rickety contraption with crates and baskets piled high on its roof rack, a bus that rocked like a ship in a gale. Still it was a bus.

Conscious of the arrival of civilization in his town El Presidente prohibited anyone to mount beasts of burden along Avenida Insurgentes, the main thoroughfare, and ordered the construction of a municipal toilet, just off the Zocalo, a toilet grandly labeled HOMBRES. More important Teotitlan now had a jail located in a former Spanish garrison barrack as well as a weekly market on Wednesdays to which the Sierra and River Valley Indians lugged their goods. Their merchandise was then ferried in overland trucks along the new bitumen road, a road already peppered with potholes but still paved, to Tehuacan and from there, so it was rumored, even to Mexico City.

The town now had an Attorney General, a plain-cloth Municipal policeman and an Administrator-Accountant. The trio, together with Bartolomo the Sheriff ran the affairs of the town and the villages under the new authority delegated to Teotitlan by the State Government.

Much had changed in Teotitlan, but not the hour of the Siesta.

Bartolomo burped. The dog turned its head and pointed a patched eye at the belfry. The gringos were approaching the end of the paved road. From below his sombrero Bartolomo's keen eyes appraised them expertly: The thin pallid Longhair bore the eager and enthralled expression of the gringos at the sight of the mountains. He was one of those. He would cave in at the first blow. Yet his companion seemed indifferent to the mountains. He was maybe in his mid-20s, not a man used to hard work by his slight build. He carried about him an air of arrogance. Bartolomo already considered him an affront. This gringo was visibly irritated by the walk, the dust and the heat. Even from the belfry he looked a troublemaker. Angel and his sidekicks would soon cut him down to size. Bartolomo whistled through his teeth, a soft sound like that coming from the valve of a pressure cooker. The dog below pricked its ears.

Bartolomo gave his cojones a good tug. Then he stretched.

The first afternoon clouds above the Sierra peeked into the Cactus Desert, pregnant freighters contemplating whether to nose into bay and spill their wet cargo. The clouds rarely did. So the valley stayed dry.

Bartolomo gave his colt a reassuring pad then flicked a finger against the bell. The brass hummed darkly. He smiled. At last there would be some action. The place had been far too dull in recent weeks. Maybe the gringos had been frightened away. El Presidente and Angel had overdone the campaign.

The word had spread. But thank God it had not reached everyone.

The Sheriff climbed down a spiral staircase into the nave of a church reeking of must, stale incense and the sour sweat of people. Planks hung loose on the pews and the dark velvet cloth over the altar was stained where the Sacristan had spilled the wine.

Bartolomo paused for a moment, relishing the coolness of the nave and its semi-darkness. Then, determined, he pried apart the heavy church portals. In the street the heat and the dog met him.

"Ola, Squinkla!" he muttered, booting the animal casually in the ribs and pointing towards an alley. The animal obediently trotted in that direction while Bartolomo sat down on the bench in the Zocalo—the town square. The bench was so positioned he could watch the jail entrance, the boxed-up adobe houses, the Municipal Palace and the church. All of them faced the Zocalo.

He pulled his sombrero down and dropped his jaw.

During his schooldays Serge Dunlov always walked into a new class with an air of contrived bravado. This was to hide his fear of being scrutinized and judged by anonymous faces, all craned in his direction. And since his parents were constantly on the move, Serge walked into many alien classrooms, always accompanied by the same fear. In time Serge converted this fear into brashness.

The moment he saw the first houses of Teotitlan he immediately imagined all eyes staring at him from behind slatted shutters.

"Bloody hell!" he cried: "What sort of a ghost town is this?"

The question produced a faint grin on Thad Morton's pallid face: "It's Siesta time, man," he explained, brushing back a sweaty strand of blonde lock.

"Holy shit, that's all I need," Serge cried: "First your jalopy conks out. Next we hit a ghost town with not a single watering hole in sight and finally, I suppose, we won't even find Haberstone's skeleton."

Thad smiled, sweetly, a patient smile of indulgence emanating from a head perched on a long neck, a neck adorned with a rosary of beads, a chin on which sprouted a wispy goatee all of it encased by straggly blonde hair down to the shoulders. He could have impersonated a scarecrow—had he stood still.

"Just relax, man," he now counseled.

"Relax?" Serge was determined to work himself into frenzy: "Listen, you mushy freak, I've promised the editor-in-chief an exclusive with that goofball Haberstone. That means I've got to come up with the goods or I'll be subbing cabelese on the regional desk until my gold watch days. And right now my prospects don't look so good, do they, old man? I mean here we are, stumbling through this God-forsaken cactus desert minus transport and minus water just because some mushy freak claims he saw Haberstone up in those mountains. Bloody hell, I ought to have my head read."

Thad sighed. "What'a you bitch'n about, man?" he drawled, staring at Serge with round mournful eyes from behind rimless glasses: "We know for sure that missing anthropologist is up there. So if you want to play Stanley you've got to make tracks into Mushieland, right?"

"So what you think I'm doing?" Serge snapped.

The missing man the two young men tried to find was an expert on psilocybin which was associated with the current craze for LSD and hallucination drugs. Haberstone found Maria Sabina and wrote about her.

His scientific treatise about the Curandera and her mushroom cult encouraged dropouts from Alaska to Baja California to wander south into ole Mexico to trip with that ageless and mythical High Priestess of the Mushroom Cult.

But then Haberstone vanished almost two years ago during a research trip into the Sierra At the same time Mexico, under pressure from the powerful USofA closed off the Sierra to all non-residents because Mummy and Daddy America did not want their druggy off-springs decamping down to ole Mexico to freak out on Psilocybin Mexicana in some god-forsaken mountain enclave inhabited by prehistoric Indians, all under the spell of a High Priestess named Maria Sabina.

"Don't worry, we'll find the dude," Thad said, gently extracting from his pocket a half squeezed lemon. Thad did everything gently, even squeezing the trigger of his Pentax. "Have some lemon, man, it'll cool you down."

There was something boyishly naïve and infectious about Thad: "You and your kicks," Serge cried, slinging one arm around his companion's shoulders, squeezing hard to release his own pent up anxieties: "First it was silence-not-talk, then it was sense-not-touch, next vegetables-not-meat and now finally its lemons-not-pills. Bloody hell, when are you going to grow up?"

"Don't knock the great lemon, man."

"I won't, I promise," Serge cried, pretending to be serious while his lively eyes sparkled with mischief: "As long as it makes you happy I am content. Let every man find his own way to the grave even if along the way his liver is gobbled up by lemon juice."

Thad watched him stride away, a slim handsome man, denim jacket draped over one shoulder. He liked Serge, he understood his impatience, prompted by a profession that demanded quick results and had scant compassion for failure. Right then Thad was content to be a freelance photographer: Failure only hurt his pocket not his professional prestige.

At the crossroad above the municipal palace, the one with the patch of hyacinths on the apron, Bartolomo was propped against a lamp post, jaw on chest, breathing easily. The dog lay at his feet. The colt was well hidden under his jacket. He stood motionless as if carved in wood, eyes closed.

"A human being!" Serge piped, still in that teasing mood which always covered his anxieties.

"Señor!" Thad asked politely: "Which is the road to Utla, por favor?"

Bartolomo looked at them for some time. Then, slowly he opened his jacket and pulled the colt from its holster. He pointed the weapon at Serge who stared in disbelief at what he figured was a hold-up. Then he heard the man rasp: "Mister, you're under arrest!"

Everything in the drowsy town moved very fast all of a sudden as if an invisible projectionist had sped up a slow motion reel. From the maze of adobe houses three men stormed into the Zocalo, led by Angel's stout short figure, followed by Horacio, gaunt, squinting through bifocals and wallowing in his master's wake. Trailing both was the burly El Agente, still doing up his belt.

"You are under arrest!" Angel squawked, still halfway across the Square but approaching at a trot. "You're hippies! You're trespassing!" He waved at them a huge badge with the semblance of an eagle engraved: "I'm the law, you see! I'm the Attorney General. And don't try to escape or he'll shoot you," he cried, pointing at the disheveled figure of El Agente.

The idea to run had not occurred to Serge, at least not yet. So he blinked open-mouthed at this weird quartet surrounding them. Then his temper began to flare, as it always did when he came across perceived injustice. On such occasions he also became inflated with the self-importance common to members of his profession.

"Now, just one bloody minute," he protested, holding out both hands as if to ward off this weird quartet: "I'm a journalist accredited by your Government, you can't just …"

The rest was never expressed because El Agente, from behind, slugged Serge with the butt of his pistol, right behind the ear.

The journalist pitched forward into the dirt.

The echo of El Tiburon's sermon bounced off the stone walls of a prison built as a Spanish garrison but serving as the town lockup in modern days. He delivered his homely in a conversational manner, without the dribbling piety common to men of the cloth when addressing their flock.

"I saw many sad faces again yesterday," El Tiburon began, "and eyes on the mountains far too long. I've told you before: We are here because this fine lady who speaks for you before the great father up there behind the clouds has decided to test us. She knows what she is doing, even if we do not. Like all fine ladies she does not always see the suffering since ladies often see only the fine and noble things in life. But we cannot be angry or impatient with her for she gave birth to a son and stayed a virgin—and that, amigos, as you know, is no small matter ..."

Serge could barely suppress a snigger. Was the peasant making fun of the doctrine of the Immaculate Birth? Such suspicion can be nurtured by Catholics in private, never in public. He could never understand why the Indios and the great mass of the poor swallowed the myth of religion as their salvation. Even in this miserable dungeon the prisoners contented themselves with the hope of a better after-life rather than fight the injustice of their current existence. In reality the Church was their worst enemy. It absorbed their discontent like a sponge and channeled their aspirations towards a glorious future in paradise, perhaps not in the front pew but in the heavenly balcony reserved for the plebs. For centuries the clergy and the ruling elites in Latin America had worked hand-in-glove teaching the peasants and the poor to pray rather than rebel. The symbiosis between religion and power had been profitable for both the clergy and the elites, even in Mexico where the two sides had been constitutionally separated ever since the 1920s.

Obviously El Tiburon's oratorical skills were based on what he had learned by listening to the sermons of the priests. The man was a typical indigenous product taught from childhood to have faith in God and the Virgin. But deep down he probably loathed and distrusted the clergy like most Indios, conscious the priests always worked hand-in-glove with El Patrone. Yet the peasants learned about life outside the Sierra from the priests who periodically came to villages to preach, eat heartily and collect alms. Over the years El Tiburon must have realized the priests were not his friends and their holy doctrine had a number of baffling anomalies.

"So you have lived through another night," El Tiburon now told his congregation, inmates squatting on their haunches around the courtyard: "I suppose that is something for which you can thank the Virgin whose dark image you have seen in your churches where she looks like just one of us Indios. And that, my friends, is one more miracle because the Virgin Mary of their churches does not look like an Indio woman but our Virgin of Guadalupe is dark just like us. And don't ask me to explain how that miracle happened."

The men looked at each other and grinned. Obviously it was not the first time El Tiburon had cast doubts on the miraculous metamorphosis of the Virgin Mary into the dark-skinned Virgin of Guadalupe.

"Amazing," Serge mumbled, addressing Thad while both sat on a boulder in the courtyard of the jail of Teotitlan: "This Tiburon guy is intelligent. He is challenging some of the religious contradictions the church has been feeding the Indios for generations. I mean how come the Virgin of Guadalupe resembles the very Goddess the Aztecs venerated but who miraculously metamorphosed into the Madonna after she appeared to some poor Indio shepherd on the same hill that was sacred to the Aztec Goddess? You have to hand it to these missionary priests: They knew how to weave old and new credos into a gullible mishmash of New World Catholicism."

"Want a squeeze of the lemon?" Thad asked.

"You'd live happily forever here, wouldn't you," Serge suggested, "you thought we'd arrived in Nirvana just because there is a lemon tree in this damn courtyard. But I need to get out of here and I don't intend to thank the Virgin of Guadalupe for the privilege of having slept another night in this calaboose."

Agitated Serge drummed the concrete floor with a piece of wood. Above them the lush foliage of the lemon tree formed a green dome on which the sunrays fractured themselves into glittering specks. Serge found it amazing a lemon tree should grow through cracks in a concrete courtyard in an old Spanish garrison converted into a jail. Certainly it was no ordinary tree; its branches were far too vast, its gnarled stem split into four subsidiary trunks. In its prolific foliage the inmates stored their razors and bars of soap. The tree's regenerating process was uncanny: Fruits and leaves of which it had been stripped seemed to reappear almost overnight, the lemons opulent, the leaves pungent and moist. More baffling still, no one seemed to tend to the needs of a tree grown out of concrete. No one ever watered it. In the end he figured the tree must be nourishing itself with the human fertilizers below Four Holes. It was the only logical explanation for the miracle of a tree sprouting from concrete in the center of a prison.

When Thad first saw the copious tree he clutched his companion's arm: "Sweet Jesus!" the photographer moaned: "A real live lemon tree: "Oh, man, I'm just 'gon'na love it here …"

"Well, I'm not," Serge replied.

Across the courtyard a scrawny inmate squatted over Four Holes, an opening sunk into the concrete. The man's eyes popped. Neck and cheeks puffed with effort. A spidery hand clenched and unclenched. The man obviously suffered from constipation. Serge felt nauseated and angry. The Municipality had not even bothered to provide a screen so a man could do his business in private. He had preferred holding back during the first two days before he finally succumbed to the dire necessity of Four Holes.

Now he saw the man, relieved, wipe his anus with the one lemon leaf everyone used on such occasions.

Serge shuddered and turned away.

"Maybe this fine lady is taking her time to get us out of here, but I am not angry with her because she must be fairly busy. But I am angry with those of you who do not provide their share of work to pay for food and medicine we need if we want to be real men when we leave here. And there are other matters: The two gringos have no one to bring them food and since this town provides nothing we must share what we have with them …"

"Bloody hell!" Serge muttered. He did not fancy charity from anyone, least of all from those poor wretches who had nothing, except the few victuals their families brought from time to time, or the scraps sent by a magnanimous soul to jail rather than the pigsty, a gesture no doubt prompted by the priest's promise that charity, though benefiting those scoundrels in jail, bought reductions in the length of purgatory.

It was time he tried to make a getaway.

A steady splashing interrupted his reflections. It came from the horse trough where Teodimo the Dwarf cleaned the two Kerosene tins with his bare hands. This made Serge shudder once more.

The tins were left outside the cells after the men were locked up at night. When their use was required an inmate whistled, as for a dog, and the occupants of other cells thrust their arms through the bars and pushed the tin towards its destination, a precarious task since the contents tended to slop over. A piece of guttering was clipped to the rim of the tin. Through it a man relieved himself. His task completed he banged the funnel against the tin to clear any stuck feces.

All night the hollow trickle of urine, the tin scraping concrete and the funnel's banging echoed around the courtyard.

"Well, amigos, we're not in the mountains now and the smell here is not so good because some of you still miss the tin and so you add to our suffering and our longing for the mountains and the good smell. That is very wicked and I want you to take better aim from now on. Amen."

"Amen ..." the men mumbled.

"Amen!" Serge mimicked.

A tall scrawny Indio called Ubaldo had quietly joined Serge and Thad below the lemon tree. He sat down, crossed his legs and stared at the journalist. The man's skin had the sickly grey tone of the caged. He was prone to wipe his runny nose with his hand during conversations.

The inmates paid him the kind of respect reserved for village school teachers because Ubaldo had acquired the amazing skill of reading. Months ago a friendly gringo had taught him to read and then bequeathed him a Four-Language dictionary which, ever since, he had been memorizing page by page. One could hear his voice in the middle of the night: "Casa—House—Haus—Maison ..."

No one complained about these nocturnal disturbances. Everyone seemed overawed by the educational feat in their midst.

"It is good for the heart to pray," Ubaldo said.

"Tell me," Serge asked pointing to a separate wing of the jail: "Who do they keep over there in the Damas section?

The Indio grinned. "Señoritas and Señoras," he explained: "Some pretty like doe in wood others like goat with pointed horns."

He chuckled, pleased with his metaphors.

"What crime did they do?"

Ubaldo threw up his arms: "Poo! Maybe sell magic Si-tho to young gringo looking for truth. Maybe sell feathers in Market without piece of paper, maybe not pay debt, maybe not do nothing, maybe just look silly." He bent forward: "Maybe big wolf-eye Agente he want make babies with them. Poo!"

"That's nasty stuff, friend," Serge cried, "and tell me what happens to gringos they put in jail?"

The Indian scratched his thatched head: "Maybe you stay one sun or one moon, maybe you stay two sun and two moon, maybe you stay many suns and many moons. If you pay you stay one sun. You bring girl, visit short, you not bring girl, visit long."

"What've girls got to do with it?"

"Girl good like money, amigo. She pay with pussy. Pay El Presidente first then pay everybody too. She makes men happy."

"Christ! And after that they let them go?

"No. First Horacio shave Hippy-hair.

"Bloody hell," Serge muttered.

The sun was hot on the concrete. The inmates had sought refuge in their cells. Seated on stools most of them were busy carving from wooden chunks the simplistic idols of the native mushroom God—the dwarf Si-tho. Relatives would offer these carvings for sale in the market. Truck drivers bought them and took them to the provincial capital and even to the federal capital where tourists and hippies bought these carvings of the mushroom god.

"Why is El Tiburon in jail?" Serge asked Ubaldo.

The would-be polyglot cackled.

"He tell all his village to make their cross next to the face of the man from the opposition, not the man from the government. Everyone votes for the government. Next day policemen take El Tiburon away. They say he stole two pigs from Don Miguel."

"So our friend is a rebel," Serge said, facing Thad: "An Indio with cojones."

Thad only smiled. He knew Serge loathed inactivity and he watched as the journalist crossed the L-shaped courtyard with determined strides heading for the grilled gate from where the guard cast cursory glances now and then into the courtyard.

"You!" he called roughly to the man: "Tell your Jefe I want to see him. Tell him I have a right to make a phone call. I've been in this dump for seventy-two hours without a formal charge or without the right to make a call. Do you hear?"

The guard stared blankly at this gringo then a slow grin spread over his cragged features.

"What's the matter, don't you understand? I want to make a phone call. I demand. You hear me?"

The grin faded, replaced by a frown, then an angry scowl. Suddenly the man ripped the carbine from his shoulder and shoved the barrel through the grill. "Shut up, gringo," he hissed: "You speak too much."

"Bloody hell," Serge mumbled and hurriedly withdrew, tense and aware of the gun at his back. He was no fool. No one would ever know if he was shot down in here like a dog. These bastards would find an excuse, like he was escaping, like he had attacked the guard. Whenever confronted by guns and violence Serge felt inadequate, powerless and this feeling inevitably translated into anger and frustration.

"You can't argue with someone holding a gun at your guts," he explained as he passed El Tiburon. "I'd like to put a knife to the throats of those bastards. That's the only language they understand."

The peasant looked up without batting an eye. Squat and short, his build resembled the chunk of wood from which he was now trying to carve the figure of a hunchbacked dwarf. His face, tanned as old leather on a well-used sofa, always remained partially hidden under a strand of black hair tumbling down his forehead. When he looked up a wide mouth opened to reveal uneven front teeth that had earned him his nickname El Tiburon—'The Shark.'

A pair of amber irises now stared at the gringo from deep sockets though the face remained expressionless the way the faces of the peasants had remained expressionless for centuries. The tiny metal nib tied to a pencil shaft which he used to carve the wood almost disappeared in a large paw more at home with ploughshares, ropes and pitchforks. A pulse ticked on a thick neck.

The peasant's outward calm irritated Serge. And so he launched into the tirade that would, eventually, have such fateful consequences.

"They've violated every human and constitutional right I know," he cried: "None of you have had a trial. You don't even know the length of your sentences—and then you sit here believing that some dear old ghost called God or the holy Virgin of Guadalupe intended it this way."

Serge paused. "Well, that's pretty sad," he went on: "Sitting on your backsides while other people are risking their necks all over the continent to be rid of governments and dictators who've sucked your blood for generations. You should have seen some of those riots in the capital—pure guts, stones and Molotov cocktails against teargas, guns and tanks. The world looks a better place when you see people still prepared to risk their lives for their rights and for a better tomorrow."

He walked up and down in agitation, unaware of the hush around him.

"Did you know that your Republic has laws that make it illegal to detain a man without proper trial?" he asked, still addressing El Tiburon: "Laws that grant you the right to an education, make it illegal to hit a man, laws that punish officials who abuse their power? Sure, nobody has ever bothered implementing those laws because you are sitting here content with the fairytale of a God and a Virgin who will come and save you. Hallelujah!

The men looked at each other, then at El Tiburon as if tacitly asking: 'What nonsense is this gringo blabbering?' But the peasant calmly chipped at his piece of wood.

"On an island not far from here," Serge continued, lowering his voice, "a handful of men kicked out a dictator together with his clan of parasites. Young men and women—the authorities call them guerrillas or terrorists—are fighting all over the continent for equal rights, for an end to institutionalized corruption, for land and fair wages while in your country the peasants and workers happily swallow the daily official bullshit that praises the greatness of the Republic and the glory of an old revolution, a revolution that, if the truth was ever told, has been betrayed thousands of times by a succession of thieves in government. And all the time while these liars are telling you patriotic fairy tales, they are getting fatter and richer on your backs."

When El Tiburon remained silent Serge went on: "Just look around this courtyard, there are enough knives, axes and tools here to stage ten rebellions let alone one lousy escape. Shit, after only a year in this country it still puzzles me how people put up with all this abuse … You know Mao was right when he said: "Power comes from the muzzle of a gun.""

El Tiburon sliced the wood carefully, chip by chip. His thoughts went back to his childhood, to the adobe hut in the cactus desert and Tata sitting on the porch waving his bony finger with the missing first joint.

"Never trust a gringo," Tata used to say.

Then, inevitably, his Tata would recall the day when his company, dug in on the northern plain with only a score of cartridges left, had been approached by a gringo arms trader who offered to supply one hundred rounds of ammunition for the contents of the Colonel's wallet and the three pearl necklaces Sergeant Toledo had scooped from the ample bosoms of three screeching matrons.

But that same night, while he went to fetch the ammunition, the trader had a better offer from the Federales.

Next morning the Federales wiped out Tata's company.

Armed with the gringo's bullets and his information, the Federales had no need to show mercy or negotiate a surrender.

"Eight men was all that was left of one hundred and forty-two," the old man always lamented as mist gathered in his eyes.

On those occasions his Tata recalled with malicious joy his Caudillo's words, "never trust a gringo no matter if they come from the north of the Rio Grande or from across the Ocean. Ever since their coming they have taken the land and the women by force or by trickery and have stolen our silver, our gold and our precious stones. In return they left us their seed and a breed of half casts who quickly copied their greedy ways."

Sometimes, when the old man was in a good mood, little José would pester him to tell again the story of the Great hanging when El Caudillo had fifteen of General Pershing's men hung from gleaming new lamp posts 'Made in the USA.' El Caudillo had fired a shot in the air and his men had whipped the fifteen horses on which the gringos sat.

As they dangled from the lamp posts, gurgling out their lives and shitting their pants, El Caudillo shouted to his men: "A good gringo is a dead gringo."

Everyone had roared with laughter.

But El Tiburon also remembered another time, years later.

The heat from the black asphalt road had flushed his face and numbed a brain grappling with a task it had no idea how to resolve. From time to time he reassuringly prodded the document inside his shirt. He was determined their piece of land, their ejido, should not pass into the hands of Don Miguel if Tata, his grandfather, died.

The big green car with its tinted windows pulled up and the fat driver with his red face grinned at him from under a white Stetson: "Tehuacan?" the fat man had asked, waving in the direction of the invisible provincial capital, still hours away by foot. He had nodded and walked on.

"Hey, amigo," the fat man had insisted, leaning back and opening the backdoor of the long green car the like of which El Tiburon had never seen: "Vamonos. You amigo, I amigo. OK? We go?"

And the fat man had smiled encouragingly from a freckled face. And when he still hesitated the fat man had rolled, with a grunt, out of his shiny green car and held out a huge pale paw with red dots on its skin: "I am Mike, OK?" he had said. "You?"

"José," he had replied taking the doughy paw in his calloused one, surprised at the firmness of its grip. Then El Tiburon sank into the backseat, scared for a moment he would sink forever, so soft and deep was the gringo's backseat. It was only then he noticed the woman, her powdery white face with its rouged cheeks hidden under a yellow sun bonnet. A thin scrawny thing she was.

"Lilly," she said, pointing at her flat chest and offering him, the peasant, a hand with long red fingernails. And as he took it, hesitantly, a scent of dead flowers, like the ones left in the cemetery too long, wafted towards him. And he was no longer sure if he was dreaming or if the sun had struck him crazy but as the car lurched forward, rolling on feathers, the gringo babbled in his broken Spanish, each incomprehensible phrase punctuated with: "OK José?"

In no time they had arrived in the regional capital and then, for a while, he forgot the miracle of the car and the strange gringo couple because the buildings were so tall, the roads, even the sidewalks were paved, the windows glittered with expensive clothes and shiny metal and people strolled in outfits so much more beautiful than Tata's descriptions; the ladies showed bare shoulders. And when he could not stop gaping, Mike laughed and made another circuit of the city and during this circuit he somehow managed to understand Mike's question and he managed to explain, slowly and using words the way the gringo's did, that he must have his Tata's ejido transferred to his name because if Tata died without the transfer Don Miguel would take the land.

The ejido was important because it was given to Tata after the Revolution and though it yielded not enough for all of them it was all they had and Don Miguel must not have it. He did not think Mike understood but the gringo nodded all the same and then he and his wife left their big car at the curb and together they walked to a great palace where the flag of the Republic fluttered from a pole and two guards in blue uniforms eyed them suspiciously. Mike ignored them and went inside into a huge hall where many Peones sat quietly on benches, looking as intimidated and lost as El Tiburon. The American kept walking until a guard stopped them and then Mike's voice became very loud and he spoke in a language no one understood but which seemed to impress everyone so much that an official was summoned to whom Mike explained with the use of the document that this man beside him was his good friend José who needed to have his name on the document at once, not manana, but now, today. And the official just gawked at this freckled gringo with his scrawny wife on one side and this Indio in his ballooning pants and sandals on the other. But all the same he took them to another room where more people waited and Mike marched straight past those people and into an office where a Mestizo sat behind a shiny wooden desk. Mike explained to this man in his broken Spanish everything until that official nodded and explained, also using broken Spanish so Mike would understand that it was not possible and they must come back in a week. But Mike said this was no good and took out his wallet and handed the official a crisp new one hundred peso note which made the man very anxious and friendly, asking them to sit down and calling out some orders to a stern woman wearing spectacles who had scowled at them all the time but now went to fetch some paper and told 'Signor José' to make his cross. And the official said everything would be alright and he could pick up his document outside in a few minutes. And outside Mike slapped El Tiburon's back and after they received the documents he steered him to a place with floor tiles and wall frescoes where many well-dressed people ate and Mike bought him the biggest meal of his life and all the time Lilly was smiling at him and Mike was talking with his mouth full and he was nodding and saying: "Si, Si" though he could not understand a word but was so happy because the ejido would be his. And later Mike said 'vamonos' and drove him all the way back to Mitzipotla and met there his Mama and his Tata, though the old man just scowled and refused to shake hands with a gringo while Mama brought some tortillas and fresh water from the well. And then, all of a sudden, Mike became very quiet and so did his wife and then they left, shaking his hand for a long time and as they drove away he saw Lilly wiping a tear from her cheeks and he could not understand why. Tata said he was a fool and now he was in for it because the gringo had done what he had done only to grab the land and he would soon come back with the law to take it all. And that scared El Tiburon so much he worked the fields always with one eye on the dirt track, watching for the cloud of dust from the car. He looked for weeks and months, determined to defend his dry piece of land with his machete, until he realized that maybe Mike was not like Tata's gringos, though the old man insisted the gringo would be back.

But Mike never came for the land.

Now El Tiburon sliced into the soft pine wood, his thick wrist and stubby fingers battling to control the delicate nib. And he thought about this new gringo who had spoken the things that had been in his own heart for many years.

And while he pondered this he heard the sound of Tonino's guitar and his song of mountains and springs, of yellow maize fields and green, pungent meadows, of love and hate and the sad, sad end of Pancho Villa.

The way Ubaldo told the story Tonino should have died months ago.

The doctor (who only came after his fee was paid in advance) had shrugged his shoulders: "He'll be dead soon," he had diagnosed nonchalantly. But then, maybe prompted by the kind of regret rural people feel for a healthy horse that needs to be put down after fracturing its leg, the doctor added: "Pity, the rest of him is in good order."

When the doctor turned to leave, El Tiburon had blocked his way: "What is the matter with my friend?" he had asked, fixing the medic with baleful eyes.

The doctor raised his eyebrows. He was not used to being questioned by the illiterate.

"Nothing unexpected, considering his inferior diet," he explained in his most aloof manner, adding with an exasperated sigh: "But if you must know, chamuli, he is dying of vitamin deficiency—and don't ask me to explain that because you wouldn't understand."

El Tiburon had stood his ground. "And there is nothing you can do?" he asked.

Impudent wretch, the doctor thought. But ringed by the inmates he kept the thought to himself. "Well, chamuli," he said briskly: "You could give him a daily injection. It might keep him alive, it might even cure him—not that this appears to be in the best interests of our patient."

He chuckled at his own cynical joke. "Anyway such remedies are beyond your means ... now if you don't mind I have other patients to attend."

"How much?"

"How much what, chamuli?"

"The injections."

The doctor had squinted, a merchant sensing a deal. But then he quickly recovered the patronizing air many in his profession display when confronted by lesser creatures.

"Look," he said wearily, pretending the matter was rather distasteful: "I'll have to charge you five pesos a day for the capsules but I'll throw in the syringe and I'll even show you how to use it and how to keep it clean. It's really the best I can do, chamuli."

And so every afternoon El Tiburon injected Tonino with the vitamin serum. Conscientiously he sterilized the syringe in alcohol, decapitated the glass capsule resolutely, drew the liquid, made sure no air bubbles remained and firmly darted the needle into Tonino's bared buttocks.

The capsules were purchased from joint funds after a vote was taken. The expense meant a considerable reduction in the daily cigarette rations for all the inmates.

The story, told by Tonino, enraged Serge to the point of desperation. He knew from a recent survey he had compiled that the vitamin serum which kept Tonino alive was one of the few pharmaceutical items the government supplied free of charge. But when he told El Tiburon the peasant only shrugged his shoulders. After all, he pointed out with laconic logic, only the doctor was able to supply the serum.

Serge looked up at the emaciated man tugging at his sleeve. Large opaque eyes peered from below a faded pink nightcap, its top drooping like the expression of its wearer. The man's long soiled nightgown, frayed at the hem, reminded him of the caricatures of emaciated scrooges counting money by candlelight. Nightcap's coming and going was as if a ghost shuffled across the courtyard now and then.

Nightcap tugged again, an unmistakable invitation for lunch. Yet despite a rumbling stomach Serge did not anticipate the summons. He was embarrassed being fed from the little the inmates could daily scrounge and then prepare on stoves fashioned from old tins. One side of the tin was gouged out allowing fuel to be placed inside. The opposite side of the tin was perforated with holes to provide a draft. Wood, supplied together with food by relatives, was axed into slivers, sharpened to the point of a pencil and stacked, points converging, inside the tin. The cooks used their breath as bellows.

Serge watched Nightcap squat before his soot-stained iron pot, waiting for the water to simmer. When the water bubbled he dropped in pieces of stale tortilla. Next he shuffled to the lemon tree, bare feet smacking on concrete, to strip one single leaf which he eased, with the grace of a courtesan, into a brew already milky from the lye in the tortillas. He waited, occasionally breathing fresh life into the flickering flame, for an appropriate moment. Then he extracted a black pepper nut from a pouch below his gown, bit a quarter off and plunked it into the stew. He cast anxious glances along the line of men engaged in similar culinary activities until a raw-boned man with a chin parted by a jagged scar, tossed him a fishbone. The bone, so clean it may have been ravaged by piranhas, joined the stew. Both simmered for a good half hour before Nightcap allowed the fire to gradually die. Judiciously he measured half the stew into a bowl and handed it cautiously to Serge, afraid to spill even a drop.

It tasted of yeast and bracken water, it was horrid but it was hot.

Serge carried the bowl to an upturned crate under the lemon tree to share it with Thad. Once they had slurped down this poor soup he walked across the courtyard to sit down beside El Tiburon. The peasant was carving with the concentration of people performing a task for which they are not suited.

"It is coming along nicely, José," Serge lied, smiling encouragement.

"You think so?" El Tiburon asked, examining with new interest the misshaped figurine of a gnome who might have been a replica of Teodimo. These carvings, supposedly representing the mushroom god Si-tho, were popular among young tourists in the capital.

"The nose is still a bit too long, José."

"Hmm," El Tiburon held the figurine at arm's length.

"What do you think of our plan?" "Will it work?" Serge asked: "You are not afraid?"

The peasant shook his head. "These people are too greedy to ask too many questions."

"We can practice some more if you like, José?"

"I understand how it works."

"Good!"

El Tiburon dropped the carved figurine into a haversack suspended by a nail from the wall. The sisal sacks contained glass bead necklaces and statuettes their womenfolk sold on Market Day to the merchants from the city.

"What will you do outside, José?"

El Tiburon stared at the ground: "I have thought of our talks in the last days. You are right. One has to do something. One cannot sit and wait for others to do it."

This statement, expressed with determination, made Serge nervous. So he added quickly: "But always remember, José, people have to understand first. It is important for them to understand before they fight. If they are not prepared you'll have only a repetition of the chaos that your grandfather saw in the revolution. People must realize they are only strong if they remain united and believe in what they fight for. You understand?"

"Strong, when all we have is our hands and our pitchforks. The soldiers feel strong because they have rifles in their hands, where we only have calluses on ours. Their stomachs are full while we fight on empty stomachs."

"José, the soldiers only fight for their wages. You are fighting for your families and the future of your children. The soldiers will tire quickly. You will keep on fighting even after you have little strength left. That's your advantage. Do you own your land?"

"Pah! I have a piece of paper I cannot read and a piece of land as hard as this courtyard. Nothing ever changes, hombre. My father and my grandfather worked for Don Miguel. Tata fought in the Great Peasant Revolution for freedom and for land. He fought well, but when he came back he and his son still worked for Don Miguel."

Serge nodded his agreement: "True. Your people fought long and bloody battles. But when victory was theirs each man took a piece of paper with a promise, laid down his gun and went home. But then how could they know that a revolution never ends."

"What do you mean?" The peasant asked.

Serge hesitated, pondering how to explain.

"Have you owned bees, José?"

"Yes."

"You know about the drones?"

"Yes."

"I believe a nation is like a beehive. It needs a good sweep now and then because the drones you kick out are always replaced by a new generation. The bees know it, just as they know if the drones are left in peace they'll soon run the hive. And the trouble is, José, the drones always find traitors among the working bees willing to protect the interests of the drones for a share of the loot. These are the real traitors. Beware of them."

El Tiburon stared thoughtfully at his sandaled feet.

"In Cuchla," he began: "Not far from my village, the man from the Peasants' Union told the Peones to stand together and demand more wages from Don Guillermo. You know how it ended?"

The penknife flicked in front of Serge's face. "As soon as the men refused to work Don Guillermo bought a machine. After a month the Peones took their sombreros in their hands and went to Don Guillermo: "We've been foolish," they said: "We'll work for the old wages."

Don Guillermo laughed into their faces. 'I don't need you anymore," he said: "I have a machine. It works for nothing. Go away, Stupidos."

"What happened?"

"The men went home but each day there was less to eat, until, in the end, the old ones decided the young men must go to the city to find work and make life easier for those left on the land. So the young men went away and the village became empty. A week later I saw the man from the Peasants Union and Don Guillermo with their arms around one another's shoulders."

Serge made a mental note of the anecdote. It would fit nicely into a political piece on the reasons for popular discontent throughout the continent, how trade unionists often betrayed their workers—for money. He would write about the shattered dreams of promised land, the failure of agrarian reforms, the rural mechanization which had caused an exodus of jobless peasants, those rural refugees who had found a subhuman existence in the cardboard shacks of the shanty-towns scattered along the periphery of the big cities. There most of these refugees remained unemployed because the fledgling industry could not absorb them as rapidly as the land ejected them. Slum cities of a million people had mushroomed overnight, monsters into which people were crammed without sanitation or amenities while just a few miles away the new and the old elites lived in fabulous villas, drove luxury cars and frequented the new department stores with their displays of glittering consumer goods imported from the USA. In the bowels of the cities costly new subway trains, built by France, rolled on rubber-cushioned wheels while millions lived in slums the trains would never reach.

Small wonder the seed of rebellion, sparked by Castro's Cuba and the education of the masses by bold men, ranging from Liberation Church priests to Kremlin-educated radicals, was sweeping the continent like sparks dropped onto dry grass. The old and new elites, all the way from the Rio Grande to Tierra del Fuego, were trembling with fear for their vast possessions. Serge often wondered just how long it would take before the feudal moguls and ruling clans resorted to their faithful tool, the military, to quash dissent and maintain the status quo.

"It is sad, José," Serge said: "But in the end, I suppose, power does stem from the muzzle of a gun."

"And where can one get guns?" El Tiburon asked, leaning forward eagerly.

"Well," Serge replied absent-minded, still thinking about the piece he intended to write and not the question: "I guess the easiest way is by making a deal with someone, someone who wants to invest money in your region and is willing to supply guns in return for concessions to your resources."

Seeing the puzzled expression on El Tiburon's face Serge explained, "resources are assets or goods, like a gold or silver mines, or wood from your forests, or stone quarries—something you have and they can sell. In exchange they give you guns or machines or build sports stadiums or railways for you … entiendes?"

"We could give them the magic mushrooms, no?"

Serge broke into loud laughter: "José, my friend, you have more than the magic mushroom. You have tens of thousands of uneducated people all over the Sierra who need schools. Your children have to learn how to read and write if they want to be accepted as equal citizen in this country."

The peasant looked puzzled: "And people will give me weapons if I let them build schools?" he asked.

"Sure," Serge said, flippantly.

Before dawn, when the sky was like a shroud, Diego the Jailer unlocked the cells and nudged the sleepers with the tip of his boot. While the men still yawned, Teodimo emptied the tin buckets down Four Holes, rinsed them at the water trough and swept the courtyard with a whisk. The dwarf always wore the same faded shirt, too loose at the shoulders, too long at the sleeves. An outsized sombrero perched on his wizened head in the manner of a lampshade and a pair of baggy pants, at half-mast, could not hide his bowlegs. When he was not busy water-carting, sweeping or rinsing, Teodimo squatted, toad-like, on the sunny side of the courtyard which he shared only with his own shadow since no one else sat in the sun. But even then his furtive eyes darted about to see where his service was required. Sometimes he squatted for hours in the hot sun under his huge sombrero, feet flat on the floor, biceps on his knees, hands flapping inanimately, waiting for a summons. On the move Teodimo was always in a hurry, using a peculiar kind of shuffle, not unlike that of an old woman hurrying to church, head arched forward anxiously while aged legs struggle to follow with the rump. The men never called, knowing a simple glance in his direction sufficed to activate him. When someone showered over Four Holes Teodimo ran a bucket shuttle from the trough and when the men finished the day's work, he swept the wood coils and shavings into a tin which he then emptied into a larger tin to serve as kindling wood. He never spoke, he never laughed, he never interfered. His going and coming was phantasmal, his presence so self-effacing that if his name was mentioned in conversation people looked puzzled and changed the subject. He was last to wash and the last to eat. He could neither cook nor carve. He threaded the glass beads into strange knots and burned himself on the tin stoves. And so, in time, he was charged with the unpleasant chores of the courtyard. In return the men fed him. When everyone had eaten someone would nod in his direction. Then the short legs whirled and the watery eyes focused doggishly on the benefactor. At each meal someone else provided for Teodimo. Nobody bothered when he ate the gristly tortillas without first boiling them to a palatable softness or gnawed at the week-old fish bone till neither bone nor skin remained—or that he did all this sitting on his haunches under the hot sun in that part of the courtyard which he considered his, not from any sense of proprietorship but simply lack of interest by others. Whenever possible or when there was the space available, Teodimo would sit near or next to El Tiburon. He seemed to regard the man with the kind of devotion the underprivileged and handicapped tend to show for their benefactor-protector.

No one could tell Serge the origin of Teodimo or the nature of his crime. No one ever visited him in jail to cast light on that mystery. Even the jail veteran, Xochin, admitted the dwarf was there the day he arrived.

Teodimo shared number One cell with Uloc, the sick one and Tenjon, the dying one. Uloc in his ragged pajamas only left the cell twice a day, in the morning and at night, to drag his spindly frame to Four Holes. He stopped every two paces to turn his head from one side to the other, gazing about him as if he had somehow stumbled into the wrong world. Tenjon no longer left the cell and the men said he would never leave it alive. Shriveled to a mummy, his cough echoed hollow from his chest, a sound that kept newcomers awake until they became accustomed to its periodic rasp. At mealtime Teodimo shuffled across the courtyard to carry broth, made by Nightcap, to his two cell companions. Done he returned to his spot on the wall and the wait for someone's nod.

No one ever spoke to Teodimo, for they had nothing to say to him and he had nothing to say to them. Like the wall, the courtyard and the lemon tree, he was part of the trappings.

It seemed only natural when Serge decided to remove the last vestiges of false modesty by showering naked over Four Holes that Teodimo should appear with a bucket of water. The dwarf was already hurrying back to the trough for more when the voice of one of the uniformed guards boomed from the gate: "Let the gringo fetch his own water."

The guards, peeved by the reluctance of the two gringos to part with money they surely possessed, appeared determined the two should not benefit from any of the social services available in the lock-up of Teotitlan.

Teodimo paused. He looked at the bucket, then the water trough, then the bucket and again at the trough. His poor fool's mind, jolted by the irrational order, was unable to cope with the issue.

Around the courtyard all talk had ceased.

"Put down the bucket!"

Teodimo stared at the bucket in his hand. Slowly the haunted expression of a man standing on the threshold of a new dimension spread across his pinched face. His eyes searched for El Tiburon. The peasant, seated under the lemon tree, shook his head. Instantly Teodimo's eyes lost their affliction. On stubby legs he flew towards the trough.

"Dwarf!" the guard barked: "Drop that bucket!" The little man ignored the order, shuffling to Four Holes so fast he slopped some of the water. Then, after Serge had doused himself, he snatched the empty bucket, heading back for the trough with the same air of urgency.

The keys rattled in the gate-lock. The guard, a short portly man with a hook-nose, cursed as he stalked into the courtyard, cradling his gun. Teodimo froze, halfway between trough and Four Holes. His neck-less head sunk deeper into the hunched shoulders, his gaze was fixed on the concrete floor, crossed arms clutched the bucket to his chest.

"Didn't I tell you to let the gringo fetch his own, you miserable sawn-off prick?"

Teodimo clutched the bucket even tighter. The guard stood right over him. The man examined the pathetic little figure with the air of a superior being. He held the gun in one hand and with the other suddenly slapped Teodimo's face. The blow echoed around the courtyard like a whiplash. It caught the little man by surprise and he staggered sideways, water splashing from the bucket to which he still clung.

Naked, Serge took two steps towards the scene, not intending any heroics, but to remove the bucket and with it the cause of the dispute. The guard, suspicious, wheeled and pointed the gun: "Keep coming gringo!" he cried: "And chinga Madre, I'll send you straight to hell."

Serge felt his knees turn jelly. He held up a beseeching hand and saw the guard's grimace full of scorn. In the wave of fear that washed over him Serge knew his cheeks burned and his penis had shriveled to the size of a thimble.

Slowly and glowing with self-satisfaction, the guard turned his attention back to Teodimo. He prodded the bucket with the muzzle of his gun: "Deaf, are we?" he asked, raising his brows, then lashed out with a boot, catching Teodimo in the groin. The little man catapulted a few feet across the courtyard like a ball. It seemed to Serge the dwarf had uttered a thin shriek, not unlike a child's reaction to having its finger caught in the door. But reflecting later he was not sure if Teodimo had made any sound at all.

The guard strolled over to the prone figure. "See what you get now?" he yelled: "See where it gets you? It gets you nowhere, that's where it gets you."

Teodimo was picking himself up, slowly, first on one knee and then the other until he finally stood up, head down, trembling, but still holding onto the bucket with both hands.

"Drop it. Drop it or I'll kill you!" the guard screamed, working himself into a frenzy: "Son of a puta. I said drop it. Drop it!"

Teodimo did not move and the guard gripped the muzzle of his carbine with both hands and swung back the butt. He was about to bring the rifle down on the dwarf's head when he saw, from the corner of his eye, El Tiburon stand up from his stool below the lemon tree. The guard lowered the carbine. He chuckled nervously and glanced around: "This son of a puta is stupid, really stupid, what can you do with an idiot like that?" he asked, addressing the men in the courtyard as if canvassing approval. Yet only silence met his appeal for a gesture recognizing his authority and his statement. A smirk would have sufficed, even a lowering of heads, but when he looked around he met only slatted eyes. For a few seconds there was no movement or gesture, but in that suspended fraction of time a feeling of collective power rippled through the courtyard and it must have seemed to the guard that the Indios had grown to giants and he had shrunk to the size of a Teodimo. Confused, the man lowered his head and squinting left and right, shambled away, muttering obscenities. Before he reached the gate Teodimo was back at the water trough, refilling the empty bucket.

In the courtyard the men resumed their conversations as if nothing had happened. Only where Teodimo had fallen, clutching his bucket, a puddle of water remained. But the sun soon lapped that up.

Every second market day Circuit Judge Juan Luis Ortega came from Tehuacan seated in the back of a jalopy driven by a liveried chauffeur. The circuit judge was obese and bald; he habitually wore a red bowtie and a white shirt stained yellow below the armpits. Señor Ortega perspired profusely: Rivulets of sweat slithered down his bulbous nose, trickled along his dewlapped chin and finally gathered in droplets on a thick neck the judge constantly mopped with a large silk handkerchief. Signor Ortega lived in his own constant lather. Only a few decades later air-conditioned automobiles made life more pleasant for people of his dimensions.

The chauffeur approached the Zocalo in low gear so his passenger could study the cargo of trucks parked on the main road. Their drivers lolled against the giant wheels with the pretentious air of urban detachment, straw sombreros cocked to one side, hands in pockets, ogling the Indian women as they drudged towards the market harnessed to the packed baskets on their backs. The women could neither turn their heads right or left without unbalancing their load.

Judge Ortega had a special interest in these parked trucks: He owned three of them and liked to keep an eye on the competition.

His car, sounding its horn imperiously, rolled through caravans of Indios and their women, all loaded up like mules with maize, frijol and coffee beans. They came down from the Sierra or up from the river valley. They held live turkeys, hens and suckling piglets. The livestock was carried head-down by the legs to keep them dizzy and quiet. On reaching the market the animals always collapsed on the first attempt to stand.

The Judge, comfortably reclined, observed the parade of goods with expert eyes though he gave the impression he was drowsing.

The chauffeur tooted: Two men argued in the middle of the road over the price of a fat pig which one held proudly by a rope. A small crowd had gathered around the two in a part of the world where the size of a pig is a symbol of pride and wealth. Only an affluent peasant can afford to mast a porker to a decent size.

The Judge tapped his chauffeur's back with the metal tip of a hardwood cane, its grip in the shape of an ocelot head. The jalopy came to a halt and the chauffeur leaned out the window: "How much?" he called to the man who held the pig's rope.

"Eight hundred pesos, Your Excellency," the man answered, ripping off his sombrero and addressing the Judge in the backseat. The Judge stared straight ahead. Only the chauffeur saw in his rear vision mirror that his master held four fingers against his chest.

"His Excellency offers you four hundred pesos," the chauffeur said.

The man with the rope gasped: "But Your Excellency it's a big pig," he whined, addressing the aloof figure in the backseat: "Fattened for a whole fifteen months on my best corn."

"You know his Excellency does not barter, impudent fellow," the chauffeur snapped.

The man with the rope seemed to shrivel.

"I've already been offered seven hundred," he whined.

A heavy tall man pushed through the crowd. He nodded to the Judge. "Four hundred, Enrico, and not a peso more," the chauffeur called out to the tall man then slipped the car into gear.

As the jalopy rolled on, a fleeting smile played on the Judge's lips. The pig was sure to fetch three thousand pesos in the capital. It was a bargain. He enjoyed these little forced transactions more than anything else. Besides he felt that he had paid a reasonable price. Too much money would only give the chamulis the wrong ideas. It was best to keep them on a tight leash.

The car moved at snail's pace through the thick of the market. People hastily stepped aside and moved their wares, the men whipping off their sombreros in deference to the morose eminence in the backseat. Though he pretended boredom, Judge Ortega's quick eyes absorbed every detail: The new clay jugs from Rio Bravo (he would get his agent to buy two dozen of those for the souvenir shop in the capital) the sisal bags (slightly inferior this year because of too much rain) the crates of oranges, lemons, mangos, pineapples and avocados (which he left to the competition, let them cover the rot loss of long transports) the carved bowls and bark paintings in shrill colors (his man would buy those up in bulk) the new ironmonger stand (where, he was told, one could buy a metal ploughshare now for only seven hundred pesos) the embroidered dresses, crocheted painstakingly over weeks (which his men picked up for a song) and those wooden idols of their God Si-tho which were popular these days in the capital but for which he still paid the price of five years ago.

Only once did the Judge turn his head, his senses roused by the firm buttocks of a young woman drudging along, arched forward under the weight of a heavy load. She wore the black reboso of the Indian women and from a yoke-pad on her forehead two ropes ran to a mesh-cage containing the load on her back.

The Judge tapped the chauffeur and the man, always aware of his master's wishes, drew level with the young woman, leaned out the window and whispered something into her ear. There was a flash of dark-eyed indignation but the harnessed head remained immobile and pointed forward, unable to turn without unbalancing the load. The Judge shrugged his shoulders. His interest had waned as quickly as it had been roused.

The chauffeur tooted his horn for several seconds to cleave a passage as the jalopy drew up outside the jail. Surrounded by a permanent odor of musty decay the Judge waddled through the jail gates, mumbling indecipherable phrases. The moist handkerchief hung napkin-like from his shirt pocket. Without paying attention to anyone he headed for the small annex next to the entrance where he knew Angel had made sure a full beaker of pulque was waiting on the table. The chauffeur dropped a thick file beside the beaker, tongued his lips lecherously and left, as usual without having been offered a drink.

Once his drained pores were replenished by this fermented agave juice, Judge Ortega, still mumbling, opened the file. He briefly scrutinized some pages and shouted a name, any name, for there was never any order or apparent logic to his selection. The uniformed guard, half at attention, marched over to the wrought-iron gate and bellowed into the courtyard: "Everaldo Nunez Gonzales?"

When the prisoner stood before him, nervously twirling his hat, the circuit judge drained the rest of the glass, cleared his throat and snapped:

"Have any money?"

The prisoner stared at his toes.

"Riff-Raff!" Señor Ortega muttered and with an impatient gesture of his pudgy hand, dismissed the man.

"Hernando Diaz Olivares!" the guard bellowed and another man emerged from the courtyard. The Judge filled the glass from the beaker, drained it, smacked his tongue, reclined, one arm draped over the back of the chair, the other with the handkerchief dabbing his face.

"You have the one thousand pesos?"

The prisoner stepped from one foot to the other, turned the hat in his hand this way and that way, shaking his head that way and this way, wetting dry lips, clearing his throat while all the time his Adam's apple bobbed like a yo-yo.

"Su Excellensia it is not my fault," he began: "The harvest has been bad, the cow gives little milk, the youngest has been ill, you know, it …"

"Hold your tongue, chamuli," the Judge interrupted. "You have it or you don't, but don't waste my time with poppycock. I'm a busy man, hombre, a busy man, so out with it."

The man called Hernando Diaz Olivares rotated his hat and wet his lips some more and then, head so low the Judge could comfortably see the nape of his neck, he said: "Su Excellensia, if the price would be a little less, I could perhaps …

"Don't be stupid, chamuli," Señor Ortega cut him off impatiently: "I have a list of your crimes as long as your arm. Don't barter with me."

Then, leaning forward and poking a ringed finger at the man's chest: "Listen you, it's the lowest fine I can give you. Don't forget that."

He reclined, waiting for the words to sink in. "What about the cow, why don't you sell it, chamuli? I even know someone who is interested; that cow and the pig and then you're still left with a mule. Well, what do you say, hombre? Do you want to stay here forever at the expense of the Municipality, getting fat and lazy, or do you want to see your woman again? Well, chamuli? Make up your mind, make up your mind."

"Señor … I beg your pardon, Su Excellensia, the cow, the pig, it is all we have. Without them we are nothing, we die, you know."

"Oh pig-headed oaf, so stay in there and grow fat, who cares. Your wife will find someone else to service her. Hey, chamuli, she is still a handsome woman, think about that. Now get out of here."

"Si, Su Excellensia, gracias."

The Judge's interviews with the inmates of the 'Damas' section were always a little longer and he would always ask the guard to close the door and wait outside. If the woman was reasonably pretty, he would lay a comforting hand on her arm or even pat her bosom, in a casual sort of way, making it quite clear he could waive or reduce the fine for certain favors which need not necessarily be consummated in jail. He never went too far however, fully aware of his status as outsider and unwilling to infringe on the rights of local officials or incur their wrath. After all, a code of honor exists even among crooked officials. Still, he made his propositions quite plain and dreamed, now and then, that one day he would receive an affirmative answer.

When the beaker was almost empty Señor Ortega turned to a recent page of names. This was the list of men and women arrested and required for sentencing. Angel provided this list. Angel always left off any foreigners since foreigners came under the direct jurisdiction of the municipality.

"Alfredo Hernandez Quitibecal!"

The newcomer came in looking uncertain. He was slow to take off his hat so the guard knocked it from his head and kicked him in the butt for good measure as he bent to retrieve it.

"Now, chamuli," the Judge began in patriarchal tones: "So you've been selling your oranges without a municipal license, hey? Stolen oranges too, hey? Nasty bit of business, hey?"

"Su Excellensia, it is not true, it …"

"Shut up, chamuli. Now listen." The tone suddenly became gruff. "How much can you pay for this crime? Hey, chamuli?"

A glint of rare interest came into Señor Ortega's eyes when he asked that vital question.

The man turned and twisted, staring at the dirt floor. "Fifty pesos, Su Excellensia," he finally cried.

"Ohoo, listen to this chamuli." The glint made way for a disgusted snarl. "He thinks it's Christmas, his birthday and the birthday of his patron saint all come together … now listen, muleshit, I'll be very soft on you because you are a stupid ignorant wretch and because I feel kind today, see? Because I do feel kind to dumb, stupid Indio muleshits who break the law and steal, yes, chamuli, steal, I'll only fine you two thousand pesos, no more, no less. Happy?"

"Si, Señor …" The guard kicked the man and snapped, "Address him as Your Excellency." The condemned man hastily bleated, "Si, Su Excellensia."

After the man left, the Judge wiped his nose, then, mumbling some more, drained the rest of the pulque. He looked inquisitively at the guard. The man nodded and walked out.

"José Cabezavaca!" he shouted into the courtyard. El Tiburon rose from his stool under the lemon tree. He picked up the knotted bundle containing his few possessions and walked briskly across the courtyard looking neither right nor left but straight ahead at the gate. The men went on doing what they were doing, not looking at El Tiburon, pretending, as they always did on such occasions, it simply was not happening,

All, except Teodimo. He seemed in shock, turning his head one way and then another as if asking someone for an explanation. He trotted behind El Tiburon to the gate and stood there as if nailed to the floor when the gate opened and then shut behind the peasant.

Serge watched the departure. He was nervous for the peasant took with him his own chance of freedom. He had no misgivings about El Tiburon. There was an aura about him that cast aside suspicious thoughts; no, he was more afraid of the bureaucracy on which their plan might founder. Yet he also felt the kind of pride mixed with anxiety a tutor feels when sending his favorite pupil out for his first test.

In his cubicle the Judge leafed through his files: "Cabezavaca," he muttered, "there" he added with satisfaction: "Four thousand pesos, four thousand little smackers, hmmm."

He looked up at the serious broad-shouldered man in front of his desk. El Tiburon's sombrero stayed on his head and he stood legs apart, gazing firmly at the Judge.

"Well?" the Judge muttered, mopping his face but burying his irritation caused by the man's air of impertinence. The guard, usually so quick to knock off sombreros, now pretended to be busy adjusting his belt. For a moment the Judge considered sending the prisoner back into the courtyard with the acid advice: "See me when you've learned how to behave in front of a judge." But his greed was bigger than his pride. Four thousand pesos was nothing to scoff at. It was a fat little sum though he would have to split it with Angel. Still, the money was enough to buy his wife that new Paris model for which she pined and the new American talking doll for his little Carlita. In the end, enough would be left to enjoy a few nights with Conchita and her girls, those naughty little tarts at the Cantina del Pajarito, who knew how to make a man happy. The Judge shivered involuntarily with ecstatic premonitions. He looked down again at the file. "Hmmm,", he muttered. "A troublemaker this Cabezavaca." Fine, they would find some pretext to put him back in jail. Anyone who could raise this kind of money must have access to a gold mine somewhere. "Let's have it then," he said gruffly, not looking at El Tiburon, pretending to study his file, so that he would not see the man still wearing his sombrero.

El Tiburon set down his bundle and pulled from his shirt pocket the wad of notes Serge had taken from his socks that morning. Without a word he laid the wad on the table, picked up his bundle and not waiting for the judge to count the ransom, walked from the annex, trailed by the guard who hurried past him into the corridor to unlock the main gate.

In the annex, Judge Ortega's pudgy fingers flicked greedily through the wad of notes. After he had counted the wad for the second time, he snapped: "He can go," quite unaware no one was listening.

Darkness always leapt into Teotitlan like a beast of prey leaving the streets instantly deserted. Only a mangy dog wandered across the Zocalo, nudging garbage with a probing snout in search of something edible, sniffing at the light pole, pawing at the caked earth. In the end, the dog hoisted a leisurely leg and trotted away, disgusted at the stinginess of the two-legged ones who left not even enough for a dog's accommodating stomach.

From the open church portals, like voices from a cave, came the mumbling of the faithful, the shopkeepers, petty bureaucrats, the municipal workers but mainly the old people of the town. Caricatured by candlelight two altar boys in angelic white tunics handed Father Ignacio the Good Book, then made faces at each other behind his back. The pews were filled with the women of the town and those men old enough to worry about their imminent departure from the cactus desert and now eager to salvage a place in that promised land. As the years passed their church-going became more regular, until, with the Great Reaper at the door, their attendance record became faultless and Father Ignacio could not hold enough masses to satisfy their sudden piety. Each year the rosaries tumbled more frequently through the gnarled, rheumatic fingers and the mumbling from cracked, bloodless lips grew louder and more insistent as if by the mere repetition of prolific prayers and long spells on wooden prayer benches, they could claim a place in the Land of Plenty, which they knew deep in their hearts they had long since lost. Their perseverance was borne by knowledge of the inevitable. Like people sinking into quick-sand the flock clutched at the priest's much-hawked straw of salvation while both their fears and their hopes filled the pews every mass.

When Father Ignacio scanned his faithful flock he closed his watery cataract eyes and gave thanks to his Creator for the piety of the town and its loyal service to Holy Roman Catholicism. In their make-belief world of incense, rosary-turning and prayer-mumbling, both the shepherd and the sheep were content.

Had the withered little priest opened his eyes he might have seen across the Zocalo three men bundle the gagged Indio girl through the jail gates. One of El Agente's arms was wrapped from behind across her breasts, the other, buried in the cascading hair, had pulled back her head until the long slender neck was arched like a bow. Horacio weaseled around the pumping legs, both off the ground, attempting to catch the girl's bare feet; Bartolomo was holstering his gun and Angel, standing apart from his three companions, glanced anxiously up and down the Zocalo. He hated witnesses.

Having carried his slender burden half across the Zocalo El Agente removed the gag, cuffed her twice then set her down. She stood there meekly enough, head bent. And so El Agente released his grip around her chest.

At that moment the girl must have seen the church portals, ajar, and heard the saintly singing from inside. When she leapt forward, she surprised everyone. She ran gangly-legged like a fawn, black hair trailing in distress, tearing Horacio's black neck scarf from her mouth. El Agente wasted time cursing her mother and her mother's mother before his own legs went through the motion of gathering speed. She had a good start by then and the portals were close. She ran through them, down the central aisle, arms rowing, gasps of despair breaking from her throat. She threw herself in front of Father Ignacio and clutched the folds of his gold-embroidered chasuble with both hands. She was a slight girl, no more than fifteen years old.

"Help me, Father, please help me," she sobbed, imploring the priest who was standing before the altar. Her dark velvety eyes floated in tears.

Father Ignacio gave his chasuble a vain tug and with the puzzled eyes of a child emerging from a dream he looked down at the girl. The chanting had ceased and through the sudden silence, El Agente's boots stomped down the aisle, his dark Mestizo face twitching with anger, his hands balled and kneading. Near the altar he lunged, snatching the girl's hair with one hand. But she held fast to Father Ignacio's chasuble.

"Slut!" El Agente snarled into the quiet church.

The girl lifted her face towards the priest whose hands were tightly folded while the quivering lips mouthed an inaudible prayer. She turned to the pews. Only blank faces met her. The faithful clutched their prayer books and rosaries.

"Save me!"

The scream echoed off the cupola ... "Save me, save me ... me, meee."

An old man blew his nose, his eyes on Father Ignacio just as they had been before this strange girl burs into the sanctuary of his dreams about a better world in which he was trying to win a place. In the front pew a young woman, a jagged scar across her cheek, spat: "Sacrilege!" and instantly the congregation crossed itself as if to ward off the evil that had invaded the citadel of their hopes. And all the time, high up on the altar, the serene image of the dark-skinned Madonna bestowed her wane and mystic smile upon all of them.

"Get up!" El Agente ordered, "El Presidente wants to see you."

The girl rose obediently. She brushed the last tears off her cheeks and with lowered head followed El Agents down the aisle towards the portals. Those she passed kept their faces pointed towards the altar where the thin voice of the priest, clinking like broken glass, now intoned the Ave Maria.

A century before the road was laid and the mushroom seekers arrived in Teotitlan, El Presidente's great grandfather built the Hacienda de las Flores on the hill above the town and above the cactus desert. He knew how to set himself apart from the town. Like his great grandson, he was a big man in all ways. The town looked up at him and he looked down on them. The Hacienda's name does not figure in any of the guidebooks which the gringo tourists buy. Viewed from a distance it resembled more an overgrown barn than the rustic showpiece of a dynasty of landowners and caciques. Still the gates were made of good oak, though without the decorative copper studs of which the Spanish were so fond. No family emblem adorned the architrave, no ivy crept along the whitewashed walls yet these walls were freshly painted and the gates had been scrubbed, their hinges greased. Despite an illness which had kept him away from the town for some considerable time, El Presidente did not allow his roost to degenerate.

The four men were propelling their prey over the last rise towards the oak gates when from an alley a man scurried towards them, clutching his straw sombrero respectfully to his chest.

"Buenas noches, Señores," he greeted them, bending his neck in deference. "I've looked everywhere for you because I must tell you …" he rasped in a nasal voice before he was cut short by El Agente shouting "scat" as he steered the now submissive girl passed the intruder.

"Sorry, Licenciado," the man said, addressing himself to Angel rather than the Attorney General's rude sidekick: "I thought you'd be interested. It concerns the foreigners."

"To hell with the foreigners. Those swine will beg to pay yet," El Agente called over his shoulder.

"What about the foreigners?" Angel asked, ignoring his associate.

The little man became immediately officious: "There I was, working hard when this Indio came in, you know the type from the Sierra, the ones with sandals and the confused look of people who've never set foot in a Post Office. He spoke Spanish though and that surprised me, since you know these people usually …"

"Get to the point you jabbering jackass."

"Of course, Licenciado." The little man bowed.

"Now this Indio, would you believe it, he wanted to make a phone call to the capital. Now what business would a fellow like that have calling the capital, I asked myself right away. And then Licenciado, I remembered how you had said: 'Ernesto since you're in charge … I'm coming to the point, Licenciado, I'm coming to it. Well, I placed the call. He had the number on a piece of paper, neatly written down. Strange, what? And him surely not able to read and write. Well, it took about an hour, the call that is. It's always difficult in the afternoon since the girls in Tehuacan take their break. Well, I listened, just as you told me, and what do you think I heard, now what do you think that silly man was saying on the phone? I ask you, what do you …"

"What, you idiot?"

"Well, Licenciado, first I couldn't understand too well, you know how it is with these people, they really never learn the language properly, do they? And then I found out they couldn't understand him either on the other end. You know why? He was talking into the earpiece and shouting too. So I went over to the phone booth and I said to him … Oh, Licenciado, you're hurting my arm … He talked to someone about the foreigners, I heard him say they were in jail and then he gave the name of the town, six times he did before they understood and then he gave them your name Licenciado, your name and then he hung up all red in the face and walked away without even saying thank you. It was a very long call. Forty pesos it cost. And now listen to this, he paid with a hundred peso note and so I said to myself, Ernesto, I said …"

"Shut up! Why didn't you tell me before?"

"Couldn't find you," the man whined.

"Get lost."

As the man hurried downhill, El Agente banged his fist against the gate.

"Come on!" he shouted: "Let's get on with it."

"Quiet! Use your brain," Angel snapped back: "You don't make calls to the capital to nobody. If you drank less, Compadre, your brain would occasionally function and if you thought more with your head, and less with your screwer we'd all be better off. That's it. She goes back. And no argument. I don't want to take any risks."

Horacio and El Agente looked at each other in dismay. Bartolomo remained impassive.

"Get her back into jail," Angel ordered.

Peeved, Horacio and El Agente pushed and elbowed the girl downhill, so ventilating their disappointment. Cursing, they discussed the lurid details of what had been in store for her. The girl said nothing. She peered through the dark at the distant lamplight in the Zocalo next to the jail. Its sight had never been so reassuring.

The sky was clear and stars blinked like myriads of miniature coins. A startled dog slunk under an awning where it shivered with hunger and fright. Near a patch of unoccupied land El Agente tugged his companion's sleeve. Both looked into each other's eyes. El Agente pointed a thumb at his chest and Horacio grudgingly nodded agreement. The two men pounced on the girl near the patch of land the widow Lopez had bequeathed her grandson, a young man who preferred to live in Tehuacan. Horacio's spidery claw closed over her mouth. The hand stank of old salsa and chile. The girl struggled valiantly, kicking, wriggling, trying to bite. She managed one choked-off squeal before the two men wrestled her to the ground and Horacio covered her face with both hands while El Agente raped her.

Once the burly mestizo had hitched his trousers, Horacio took his turn. It was all over quickly and with the minimum of fuss. El Agente saw the blood on his pants only when the trio passed below the street lamp in the Zocalo. "Dirty little slut," he growled and slapped the girl's face. By then the girl no longer cared.

The two men locked her into the 'Damas.' As Horacio turned the key the church bell struck three times. It sounded like three belches from the belfry.

The call from the capital came through at 10.45 next morning. Angel snatched the phone from its hook while Horacio and El Agente anxiously studied his face. The call was an event. The old crank-handle phone rattled rarely.

"Speaking. Yes, it's him speaking," Angel said into the mouthpiece on the wall: "Yes, a great pleasure indeed, Señor Secretario. We have. Bad people, bad ... of course, Señor."

A lengthy silence followed during which Angel's face visibly sagged.

"But Señor we found marijuana in their possession and they carry diseases into the mountains and you know it is our duty to prevent anyone from ... si, Señor, of course Señor ... I assure you Señor, it is not necessary. Of course, Señor, it shall be done ... Immediately ... My pleasure, Señor, always at your service, Señor. Adios, Señor."

Angel replaced the phone on its hook reverently, as if an abrupt click might annoy the party at the other end. He wiped the perspiration from his brows with the back of his hand, moistened his lips and vaguely gazed at the two expectant men.

"The Minister's Secretary himself," he croaked.

"The foreigners?"

Angel nodded mechanically, wetting his lips.

"I felt it, I felt it all the time," he muttered: "One of them is some foreign journalist. The government wants no trouble with the foreign media." He paused. "Holy Virgencita, now we're in for it. He said there would be an inquiry."

The men stood silent, no one dared to look at the other.

On the wall behind Angel hung the portrait of the Lord of Teototlan. El Presidente was dressed in his white charro suit with the two silver-plated revolvers dangling from his hip holsters. His leonine head was thrown back and the expression on his face was that of a man who knows what he stands for and enjoys that knowledge.

On the nose of El Presidente a firefly buzzed.

In the capital, the Minister of the Interior, a tall athletic man who tried to manipulate the complex threads of a complex bureaucracy to the satisfaction of all, especially those who one day might hoist him to the Presidency of the Republic, looked pensively at his secretary and junior minister from behind tinted green glasses set in a frame of gold.

"It's always the same," he said. "Incompetence, ignorance, stupidity and yet we need them, we need them all, Arnaldo, we need them for all the campaigns that are not campaigns and all the campaigns that are campaigns. They are our system, these self-styled licenciados with their small pockets of power whom we ordain with more power so the thin ice on which we skate won't break and drown us all. Their excesses and their megalomania are the pillars of our power. Their intemperance makes them pliable tools in our hands.

"As always I have frightened them with an inquiry, an inquiry we will never launch because it would be like opening Pandora's box. We would be sure to discover what we might not be able to hide."

The Minister looked at his junior sternly: "Remember, Arnaldo, it is the system that is important. The small individual cases, the small fry, are irrelevant, irritating maybe but inconsequential. Always remember maintaining a system is a war and in war there are casualties. But in a successful war the system achieves its aims with a minimum of casualties. That is the essence of sophisticated administration."

The Minister observed a window cleaner on a winch-chair half way up the skyscraper across the road. "You know," he went on without taking his eyes off the cleaner, "in the end some political good might come from this incident. At least it will show los Americanos, if it is ever published, how tough and ruthless we are in our pursuit of drug addicts. You know the Yankees are not interested in individual cases, they want results. This journalist, this Serge Dunlov has already been in trouble. He was caught during the revolt on Tlatelolco and we released him with apologies to his agency. Maybe we should let his agency know, in a diplomatic way mind you, he may not be suited to work in the Republic since he seems to have trouble respecting our laws and staying away from areas we have marked off-limits or areas being used for protests. I am sure his agency will understand. After all our newspapers, our ministries and our banks are good customers of their service. See what you can do, in a friendly but firm way, of course."

He waved a tired hand in a dismissive gesture and the young man walked somberly across the beige carpet. The minister watched the window cleaner's precarious task for a few more seconds, then sighed and pulled up the blue folder marked 'Progress Report Paramo Two.' The reports came once a month from the army camps where political detainees were being 'reeducated'. The minister flicked over the first pages. 'Pereda Sanchez' he read, skipping the biographic details and the terse report of the case until he came to the bottom of the page, marked by a small black cross and a date. The Minister sighed again just as the buzzer on the Made in the USA inter-con sounded and a soft female voice announced: "The ambassador, Señor Ministro."

The Minister flicked up the connecting speaker switch and reclined in his high-backed leather chair: "Dear Mister Dixon," he exclaimed, "A great pleasure. What can we do for you?"

Angel went to El Presidente's Hacienda alone.

He tiptoed through the stately mansion as if afraid to disturb the lord of the manor. Stooped, he entered the austere study with its heavy oak desk, its bureau of drawers and the huge portrait of the man himself painted by a well-known artist. Angel walked up to the desk, still ill at ease after all those years as El Presidente's right hand man.

"The two foreigners have left town, Señor Presidente," he reported, haltingly, the way a schoolboy recites his homework: "We had to apologize to them and in spite of our advice they headed for the mountains. People will want to know why we did not stop them. You know the Minister himself ordered their release. His Secretary said the Federales would come to start an inquiry into the case and I am afraid their inquiry might cause lots of trouble for us. I'm sorry."

He added the last phrase hastily, as if the apology might mellow the wrath his performance had merited.

The impassive figure behind the desk remained silent and motionless. So Angel continued: "We all make mistakes and I've been a trusty servant for many years. Have I not always carried out your orders? Have I ever questioned your judgment? Have I ever lacked in my duties? Did I not marry your daughter, fat and ugly as she is, when the honor of your family was at stake?"

Angel began to pace up and down in great agitation.

"I was obedient. I ran the town for you. And in your name. When you fell ill it was I who fetched the Gringas so you could still watch. I forged the papers when the Federales came to investigate the death of the one with the flaming hair. We have been a good team. We have done well: There is money, there is power, the people are grateful; your word is law; they fear and love you as they should. You have become more powerful than your father or your grandfather. But I helped."

A wan smile crossed Angel's gaunt face: "Remember how you thought of the gold mines that brought the electricity? But it was I who planted the fake nuggets and it was I who went to the city and persuaded the merchants after you had the brilliant idea to set up a market."

"And what of your brother, the idiot dwarf?" Angel's voice dropped to a whisper: "Only the jail and I share your secret."

He threw up his arms: "Now what shall we do? What shall I do, Señor Presidente?"

In despair Angel leaned across the oak desk. His haunted eyes sought those of El Presidente who sat, as always, on the tall fauteuil with the carved ocelots for armrests. He sat stiff and erect, dressed in his white charro suit, the gold-braided sombrero on his head. The two loaded Colts dangled from his belt. He sat facing the window so people in the fields far away could see his silhouette and pass the story that he was always working at his desk.

El President was still well preserved, a work of art by the man who did the job.

But he could not speak and he could not see.

El Presidente had been dead for nearly two years.

—

"NOW THE MUSHROOM SPEAKS ENGLISH.
IT NO LONGER SPEAKS TO US.
THE LONGHAIRS HAVE PROFANED IT..."

APOLONIO TERAN, SHAMAN

TWO

Inside Nirvana

"Most of us have exhausted our own capacities and those of the world around us. That's why we are here. Maybe this cave is a return to the womb and a desire to be reborn …"

"You're in check, buddy."

"If you close your eyes for a moment and reopen them you can pretend this is an art gallery with sculptures in calcium. Use your imagination. Over there, two Rhine castles facing off across the Lorelei, an excellent example of impressionist art. It is unfortunate the artist left no record …"

"… It's always them fellows what's got heaps of shit outside their own doorstep what's worried about the bird-shit on the neighbor's lawn …"

"Oh life was pleasant enough until that Sunday morning. It started: We deeply regret. And there was something about duty to the end, something about credit to his country and some idiotic promise of a posthumous award. I never did find out if they gave Marty that silly medal. I just wondered who would take me trout-fishing now and if I would ever go up those hills again. I guess I decided I would not. Sometimes I wonder if someone finished the annex to the hut that Marty started. Someone probably has …"

"You're still in check."

"Sweetie, stack it like this, packet it and roll the paper, two-fingered, easy like but firm. You pad it like this. OK? Now light it. Inhale. Deep. Swallow it. Right down. Let it fill your lungs, let it swivel around. Keep it down as long as you can. That's it. You've got it. Now just relax. You've got all the time in the world here."

"Aphrodite in repose. A masterpiece of the classics. No, no people not over there, over here, behind me. Note the superb curve of the breast. The indentation of the demon's hand on her left buttock, surely copied later by Bernini in his celebrated Pluto and Proserpine ..."

"I'll take a draw."

"Man, he wore skintight slacks and no briefs and them girls was just going nuts about the rock and jerk action the way Big Arnie had taught him. And one night through the sweat, the heat and beat he kind of realized them girls were not absorbing his music, but man they was watching his big stick. And that brought on the same embarrassment he felt when his older sister watched him while he showered. So he stalks off the stage and that was great too only he didn't come back and so they figured they was entitled to some fun, having paid for their tickets and all, and so they made firewood of the furnishings. And that's how Wally hit the road ..."

"Sorry can't accept a draw."

"Thad is a cute name. You're a camera freak?"

"Baby I've tried everything, acid, speed, grass, mescaline, Nam, the System, Jehovah's, the peace brigade, and right now its lenses and lemons."

"Garde!"

"Don't get your knickers in a knot, mate."

"Maybe we are all drawn by the hearsay of a mushroom paradise in which a fountain of wisdom bubbles ..."

"Do you know a guy called Haberstone, a Professor? Here is a photo of the man."

"Only professor I knew was Irish, a guy called Dinky Watson who used to hustle coke across the border in marmalade tins. Made a comfortable living of it, he did, then got greedy and used gallon drums. He is doing time now. Couldn't be him, could it?"

"We're all freaks, in different grades, of course. But then who isn't? Take Xavier over there, bell-bottoms a la mode, red polka-dot shirt, blue scarf, broad buckled belt, suede cowboy boots, still with the original sheen, sleeping bag army disposal from the officers' mess, fingernails manicured, velvet jacket with a London tailor's label. Arrived with a kilo of grass, some acid and rations large enough to keep a company fighting for a week. And then the kid says—and man get this: 'Mummy thinks I'm in Acapulco.'

"Take a draw?"

"And at seventeen she thinks drugs are better than men anyway."

"I mean the world is full of crap. I mean anything you get involved in turns out to be crap. I mean it boils all down to someone's Reichian megalomania or Freudian kink. I mean I still go for Jung if there has to be a motivation, which I'm beginning to doubt."

"Two months later he died leaving as legacy four months of unpaid rent and a cheap collection of hypodermics. Shit."

"So what do they call you then, out there in the square world?"

"Serge Dunlov. And you?"

"Twangy."

"Twangy who?"

"Twangy Nobody."

"Oh in the daytime you can sunbath nude by the river. The Indios are so sweet. They tip us off if that mad Lieutenant Garcia and his troopers are on the prowl. If it weren't for that Lieutenant you could vegetate here forever."

"Checkmate, mate!"

"Fuck!"

The cave, burrowed into the limestone, was cool but not humid. Once through the narrow entrance it opened up like a concert hall. In the old days people stored fruit and vegetables inside. But with the coming of electricity in Utla the cave became deserted. Its stalactites almost reach the floor in places though the stalagmites never quite managed to grow bigger then seagull droppings. Yet it would take another two decades before cave explorers discovered the entire Mazatec region was the largest Cave System in the Western hemisphere, endowed with an abundance of water in sinkholes as deep as one thousand meters. In the days Serge and Thad trekked to Utla the cave was unknown to the outside world though it had turned into a favorite hangout for young foreigners, people the locals called 'ippies' and the media called drop-outs, junkies, bohemians or just bums.

Margasitho sat cross-legged on a white pillow behind a votive candle, its flame flickering in the occasional draft. In the pale glow of candlelight his face was stern and immobile like the face of a Mayan deity cast in stone. The face was intimidating if one remembered the Mayans, like the Aztecs, had the bad habit of sacrificing people, even infants to their deities, casting them alive into wells. Yet it was more than this image of evil that made Serge feel an instant dislike. There was something contrived about the man, the way he swaggered, his studied aloofness, the split caftan he wore like some oriental potentate, the dismissive way he fobbed off questions. During their trek to the cave where Serge had expected to find Haberstone people they had met dismissed Margasitho as a charlatan. Yet in this cave the hippies and dropouts treated this fake shaman with awe and reverence and referred to him as 'The Master.'

"Young people adopt fake icons so easily," Serge complained to Thad. It was a pompous remark since both were of the same generation as those in the cave. Thad only smiled, aware by now Serge often elevated himself above others due, perhaps, to his profession which leaves its members often with the belief they are part of a superior order.

In the fading light from the cave's entrance the two could make out the silhouettes of the mushroom seekers huddled together for 'the trip' or what the Indios called 'la velada.' All faced The Master, fledgling birds waiting for father's handout. Had he been asked to describe these young people, Serge would have resorted to one of those ready-made media clichés 'hippies', 'flower children', 'freaks' or 'drop-outs.' In reality most of them were young people nauseated by the Vietnam War, the witch-hunt for communists and the brutal crack-down on campus protests. Student resentment and escalating hostility for the education process had toppled sacrosanct educators from their pedestals world-wide in bloody student protests. Teachers were no longer considered sage gods but defective mortals pontificating from positions of power bestowed by Academia. With the values and idols of their parents dismantled, with communism discredited and no fresh idols on the horizon (except a flock of folksingers crooning about love and peace while high on drugs) the disenchanted young generation turned to alcohol, drugs or gurus. Marijuana soon became blasé. Everyone smoked it or baked it into brownies. In the constant search for novelties the recent fable of the Magic Mushroom of the Sierra Mazatec had captured the imagination of the adventurous in search of new experiences.

The cult of the mushroom god Si-tho, a cult practiced among the Mazatl people (Deer People in the Aztec Nahuatl language) quickly became the Holy Grail once it was publicized by an American amateur anthropologist named George Haberstone. The mushroom's psilocybin was soon sold in pill form by a Swiss scientist, but the pills were quickly debunked by expert druggies as second rate.

The real thing, mushroom Nirvana, was up there in the Sierra.

Cults need a supreme being or guru and Haberstone, wittingly or unwittingly, had chosen Maria Sabina, an elderly Curandera (healer) who used various types of mushrooms during 'veladas' (healing ceremonies) to cure both the physical and psychological problems of her Mazatl people, those who came to seek her help. Maria Sabina, unlike other shamans or curanderos (who all jealously guarded the secrets of the mushroom) allowed Haberstone and other 'outsiders' to participate in her veladas.

The stories of 'psychedelic comas' in which personal truths were revealed prompted thousands of young people to head for Mexico to 'trip'—if possible—with the famous Curandera in her mountain-top cabin. Maria Sabina's fame snowballed quickly, nourished by reports that celebrities like Bob Dylan, John Lennon, Mick Jagger, Keith Richards and even the Beatles had visited her.

Yet many of those who came eager to 'trip' with Maria Sabina became trapped in Margasitho's cave, half way to the remote mountain roost of the High Priestess. Those caught in this cave cult, so the puritans argued, would never reach true mushroom Nirvana. They would be forever condemned to the improvised orgies of fake shamans like Margasitho.

Serge thought 'The Master' was unusually tall for a native of the Sierra. A flat nose split mousy eyes the way a sewage canal can split a beach. The missing upper canines gave him a deceptively mild and idiotic look. The flowing kaftan, slit and long enough to resemble a cassock, exposed hairy thighs, an exceptional phenomenon for a race virtually without body hair. He was grubby. He may have been thirty or sixty but age was irrelevant in the Sierra where grandmothers passed for fifteen and Maria Sabina was said to be nearly two hundred years old.

"You ever tripped with this guy before?" Serge whispered to the girl called Twangy. She nodded while she brushed her auburn hair with a silver-handled brush.

"And he doesn't make you feel uneasy?"

"If you were a scorpion," Twangy replied contemptuously, not changing the rhythm of her brushstrokes, "you wouldn't ask. Being a Virgo you can't help being cautious."

"Bullshit!" Serge snorted, irritated by her condescending tone. She had all the makings of a snob. Somehow in this squalid cave she had managed to remain well-groomed and scrubbed, her jeans clean, her blouse pleated.

He was spared a caustic reply when he saw Margasitho move among the cave dwellers with the confidence of a majordomo, picking his way through a busy banquet whose guests had traveled for weeks on circuitous routes to avoid the terror of Angel's minions. Some had arrived in rags, scrounging among the Indians for food and shelter. When the patience of the natives ran out, the cave became their home. Others, more affluent, came fitted out as if they were on an African Safari, including a four-wheel-drive jeep.

Angel and his boys were simply paid off. Money was no obstacle. Daddy, having been sold the lie that this was a boys outing, furnished lots of greenbacks, the best of all passports in Ole Mexico.

Margasitho held out the clay sombrero into which the revelers deposited whatever contribution they could afford. From a second basket dangling from his left arm which also held the clay sombrero 'The Master' dropped into outstretched palms a number of small peak-shaped 'pajarito' mushrooms. Their number, it seemed, depended on the amount of cash the recipient had dropped into the sombrero.

Serge, who received three fungi for the ten pesos he dropped into the hat, could almost touch the disdain of the man as he handed over the mushrooms to his 'disciples.'

With his round completed the Curandero went back to his lotus position behind the candle.

Serge was certain the man had used carbon to blacken the skin around his eyes, adding a diabolical touch to his face. Although Margasitho pretended to meditate, his eyes were only half closed. In reality he watched the revelers as they gobbled the raw mushrooms, swallowing also the tiny clots of dirt that still clung to the stems.

The steady munching of the disciples crackled like popcorn and Serge took advantage of the dark to quickly slide his mushrooms under his denim jacket. Then he watched as Thad, cross-legged on the floor like the rest, gobbled his four long-stemmed pajaritos with the same devotion that guided all Thad's actions. Thad reveled in communal events. These compensated for a sterile childhood during which his mother, afraid he might be infected by bacteria, forced him to wear tiny boxing gloves, big enough to prevent his hands from entering his mouth. She took Waldo, the Plexiglas unbreakable chamber-pot, on holidays, even left the pot conspicuously under the bed on his wedding night. True, his mother did have some justification: Thad's father fatally ruptured himself on a chiffonier he straddled while stumbling intoxicated to the toilet in the dark of night.

Not far from Serge a frail freckled waif was among the first to collapse, sliding backwards onto the floor with an ecstatic sigh. Next to pitch was the trendy dude from California, a favorite among the others thanks to his large supply of canned food and his equally abundant supply of cash. He toppled slowly forward, as does a statue from a pedestal. His face came to rest squashed against the limestone floor. One by one the revelers keeled over, in slow motion, fluttering earth-bound as do cherry blossoms in a faint spring breeze. Their eyes remained open, staring into space as if seeing but not really seeing, the puzzled expressions of people trying to come to terms with a strange environment not of their normal world.

Not to be conspicuous Serge joined the general collapse.

Some time elapsed and then he noticed the fallen figures began to stir, groping for support in their immediate vicinity, grasping at extraneous limbs, testing surfaces and textures, all the while gurgling with infantile wonder at this new virtual reality into which Si-tho had projected them. Having reassured their senses, they seemed to drop off into an uneasy slumber, open-eyed, chests heaving as if running a race.

A steady coo-coo-si-thoooo-si-thooo spilled from Margasitho's lips and the slumbering figures adjusted their heads, harking for this monotonous lullaby which soon enveloped the cave and rowed them on silky oars through their own mental labyrinth. There they obviously encountered weird visions, one after another, all running as if on a film reel judging by the haunted and changing expressions on their faces.

Serge was fascinated. The revelers appeared to writhe at the bottom of a pit on the threshold of death, some mortally wounded, gasping out their last breaths. Hands described circular movements, puffed lips mumbled inaudible sounds; open eyes, pupils dilated, gazed in wonder, or was it horror, at what must be astonishing visions. A quavering hand cupped a breast; a body rolled log-like across another; a buttock gave an instinctive thrust; an index finger trapped in a shirt pocket, a toe stuck between someone's legs; a tongue lolling on a belly; a visionary raised finger; a thumb being suckled; snot dripping … and all of it in slow motion.

Beside him Twangy gaped at a toe sticking from a sandal. Her lips tried to form a word and Serge, leaning across, heard her say: "Scorpion!" and saw her fingers curl into claws.

And then just as abruptly, Margasitho changed his tune to a seductive cooing, its volume gradually rising, worming its way into the consciousness of the listeners, rowing them on its monotonous course.

From the tangle of flailing limbs a sweet angelic head rose. It was the waif who had fallen first. She was half propped up, her childish face puckered with expectations, a teenagers' anticipation, perhaps.

Humming the Curandero weaved through the imbroglio, nudging inert bodies aside to breach a path. He knelt down beside the waif and parted the cascading blonde hair, moist with perspiration. Nuzzling his mouth against her cheek he gurgled softly down her ear. Instantly she became more agitated, wriggling in rhythm with his purr.

Serge was fascinated. Obviously The Master was about to offer a personal lesson, rowing this pretty little waif on a river of ecstasy of his own making. His cooing down her ear went on for a while and then Margasitho hitched his cassock and pushed the blonde head closer until it rested against the inside of his exposed thigh. With two fingers he pried apart her lips, swollen by the alkaline content of the fungus. And through this gap he guided his near stiff manhood. Then his fingertips tickled the sluggish tongue until it suckled of its own accord.

It took Serge a moment to realize how the Curandero gratified his lust and then he was instantly torn between a heroic impulse to smash the perverse rogue's face and his natural reticence and motto to 'live and let live,' his convenient policy of neutrality. After all he was closing in on Haberstone. Twangy had identified him from his photo as the man who stayed overnight at the cave no more than a week ago. Why covet problems? Surely this girl was familiar with the consequences of a trip on Si-tho. Why, he might even spoil her fun. This did not concern him. Everyone had the right to be kinky in their own way.

Having pacified his conscience with the logic of such argument he turned his head away only to hear the girl retch, cough and vomit. Turning back he saw the Curandero push her limp body aside discarding her the way a toddler discards a used toy.

Then the man brushed down his caftan, straightened the slits and calmly returned to his place behind the candle. Only then did a belated compassion stir Serge and he felt the need to expunge his lingering sense of guilt and inactivity, a guilt that had pursued him ever since, at the age of six, he stood by, head down, watching a bunch of boys pelting little Liesel with clots of dirt while yelling at the frail redhead "witch, witch, witch."

Now, in the cave he stood up, feeling awkwardly conspicuous among the sprawled corpses and aware of the Master's blazing eyes. He propped the girl up, turning his head to avoid the saccharine stench she exuded and the sight of semen trickling down her chin.

"Love!" she lisped. "All love!" Then her head rolled, guillotined, against his chest. He stroked her hair the way his Mamma had before her career and post-work fatigue relegated him to a secondary role. He picked her up in his arms, marveling at the feathery weight of this limpid slip of a girl. He carried her towards the entrance, ignoring the angry hum of the Curandero who realized Serge had not consumed the fungus and thus was a witness to the abuse of the girl.

He had to bend low to avoid the pointed stalagmites, dragging more than carrying his burden to the entrance above the river where a cool breeze and clean air flooded his lungs. He laid the girl down gently on the grass, making sure she was comfortable, her head on a hillock. It was a balmy clear night with a half moon and the stars close enough to touch. A faint breeze rustled the leaves of the Ahuehuete trees. The cicadas chirped. Shame and compassion made him clasp her hand. Instantly he felt her fingers curl around his in search of a bond. He looked at her thin insipid face and watched her sleep untroubled.

El Tiburon picked his way through the mist and the slushy moss, wet with morning dew. As always at dawn, sheets of mist floated off the gorges and wrapped the mountains in a wafting white veil. Many travelers would have been lost in this steam bath but El Tiburon could find his way even through the dark guided only by the territorial instinct of his people. If he stopped at times, it was to change the jute sling-bag from one shoulder to the other, each time reassuring himself the object protruding was still covered by the rags. He was anxious to keep it dry, afraid humidity might damage its mechanism.

He cradled the sling-bag in his arms as he arrived in front of the cave where he was told the foreigners were camped.

Serge jumped off his seat next to the girl at the touch on his shoulder.

"José!" he cried: "Man, I didn't expect you here. What happened? Did you find Haberstone?"

The peasant placed a cautioning finger on his lips: "I need to speak to you," he whispered. "Come with me."

"Why are you whispering," Serge asked, looking around. No one else was there except the girl. And she was asleep.

El Tiburon beckoned and Serge, grudgingly, followed him down to the river bank where he set the jute bag down and slowly unwrapped the object inside, not tearing the strings around the rags but untying them painstakingly, one by one, in the manner of peasants who break nothing, waste nothing and discard nothing since it can all be used again.

Finally he held the gleaming object awkwardly in his hands.

Serge whistled softly. He was no expert on weapons but this was a modern weapon, at least semi-automatic, probably standard issue and with considerable firing power, judging by the size of the magazine.

"Where did you get this?"

El Tiburon looked down at his toes: "Power stems from the muzzle of a gun," he muttered: "You said so."

A chill ran down Serge's back.

"Bloody hell!" he said: "You didn't?"

"It is not important," El Tiburon said gruffly.

"So what do you want me to do?" Serge asked, uneasy, his mouth already dry.

"I want you to show me how to use it."

Serge cackled. It was one of his saving graces that in uncomfortable situations he always managed a laugh. That habit had defused many an awkward moment.

"You won't?" El Tiburon asked, frowning.

"Listen," Serge said sternly, taking the gun in both hands, feeling the cold of the metal and the weight of the stock. "Even if I wanted to, I couldn't. See I haven't got the faintest idea how to use one of these gadgets. I really don't know where you got this blasted cannon from but you might as well take it back and forget whatever you had in mind. Hombre, these things need training, they are no damn toys."

El Tiburon's brows contracted and he bit his lip.

His mind was obviously trying to cope with this unexpected setback. And then a thought must have struck him for his face turned up eagerly: "One of your friends in there might know?"

Serge shook his head. "Listen, first they are not my friends, second I doubt if any-of them are capable of thinking straight right now. Hombre, take this confounded cannon back to where you found it or stole it. Tell me, you are not about to start your own revolution, are you?"

The peasant scratched the back of his head and stepped from one foot to the other, the way the peasants always did when something unpleasant confounded them or confronted them. Suddenly his head lifted and he looked Serge straight in the eyes the way he had looked Don Miguel and the Doctor in the eyes: "Something has to be done," he blurted.

"What, what do you mean has to be done?" Serge asked, superfluously, since he already knew the answer by simply looking at the peasant's face. It bore the stubborn expression of the peasants who, once they make up their minds, embark on a course with the irreversible thrust of a crazed bull.

He became anxious. This might prove a new obstacle to the Haberstone project. El Tiburon might go and pop off this confounded gun, be caught and end up blabbering Serge's name. A nice mess that would be! With some luck the Government would boot him out of the country but more likely he could end up behind bars for years. One way or the other the editor wouldn't like it. Santomoro had a healthy aversion to correspondents getting mixed up in political incidents, especially incidents associated with leftist ideals or proletarian violence. Correspondent had to dread cautiously in a news agency which survived on selling its service mainly to a media towing the official line or to government institutions, all of them clients, quick to terminate a contract and sign with a competitor in case of 'unfair' criticism or involvement in nefarious activities considered harmful to the nation.

"Sorry," Serge said, panic making his voice colder than he intended. "I can't help you."

El Tiburon's eyes narrowed: "El Señor forgets quickly." The voice carried just the right note of bitterness and accusation.

"I tell you I don't know how to use this blasted gun. I know as much as you do about it."

"It is easy to forget a helping hand when it is no longer needed."

"You're being unfair José," Serge whined, using the familiar form deliberately to bridge the gap that had suddenly grown between them.

But El Tiburon only cast him a mocking glance. "I don't ask you to join us," he said. "All I ask you is to show me how to work this gun. I remember it was you who talked of revolution. It was you who said we were doing nothing about the way we were being treated. Yet when it matters you behave like all the gringos, you turn your head away and go back to your nice home and your good life, and maybe sometimes, not very loud, you say: 'It's not right what they are doing to those poor peasants'. But amigo it is not enough to speak, it is more important to act. I know little, you know much, but I know in my heart that to be a man is to act like a man. So I shall take my gun and be a man. Adios, amigo!"

As the mist began to swallow the burly peasant, Serge felt the kind of panic and remorse people feel when someone has struck at the core of their weakness.

"Wait!" he shouted, afraid the wafting sheets of vapor might take the peasant away forever. "Let's talk it over for a minute. Maybe I can help. By the way, what the hell are you up to anyway?"

El Tiburon allowed Serge to catch up. "There are five of us," he said quietly: "Who think like me and are prepared to die. Soon we will be more."

"But what do you want to do?"

The peasant kicked the wet moss with his sandal: "First we shall open the jail," he said: "For it has become a symbol of what they do to us. After that we shall fight for what is right. That is all I know. I will think about tomorrow when tomorrow comes."

"Jesus Christ, the whole country will be after you, José. You'll find yourself on the run permanently. And this damn single popgun is not going to get you very far. Be realistic hombre, for God's sake, you can't just go around blasting off your gun. First you need to be organized. Don't become just another adventurer who thinks all he has to do is fire a few shots and the peasants will flock to his cause. It just doesn't happen that way. A revolutionary called Che Guevara tried it in a country called Bolivia recently and he failed, miserably. People have to be convinced first before they risk their lives and their livelihood. Hombre, it all needs to be properly prepared and organized."

The peasant looked down at his sandals: "I know nothing about being organized, but I can learn how to use this gun. It will speak for me and many will listen. I am not a man of clever words, amigo, but this gun speaks a strong language."

"Bloody Hell! One Gun?"

"There are more guns. The man who gave me this gun promised to give us more as soon as we start the revolution."

Taken aback, Serge asked: "And what did you promise to give that man?"

"Nothing. We made a deal. He gives me more guns and we will allow him to build schools for our children. I think it's a very good deal. You said yourself unless we are educated my people will never be taken serious … didn't you?"

Numbness was creeping through Serge. He was responsible for what was going to happen. He had given El Tiburon the money to buy himself out of jail. In return the peasant had called his office and his office had called the minister. But at the same time Serge had stimulated the idea of revolt, even that of education. He must make a last effort to halt this nonsense before it ended in bloodshed.

"José," had said slinging his arm around the peasant's shoulders, "to make a revolution you must prepare the people! That takes time. They have to understand because they will not follow you just because you have a gun …"

"Oh, they will follow me, amigo. My people get angry very slowly but when they do there is nothing that can stop them."

It was a valid point, Serge thought, remembering the gory descriptions of the great peasant uprising, the vivid accounts of plunder and rape, and the wholesale massacre of the feudal aristocracy and the priesthood. A passage from a book came to mind: 'The campesinos can patiently endure virtual slavery for generations but once their dormant fury is unleashed only death or utter exhaustion can curb their destructive fury …'

Still in the end all of them would be wiped out. The system would defend itself with the blind rage of a man who knows if he doesn't stop the first stone sliding down the mountain the whole mountain will come down and bury him.

"José you're a bloody fool. They'll kill you for this. You want to die?"

The peasant smiled. "There are many deaths, amigo, I prefer the quick one as a man to the slow one on the hacienda of Don Miguel. You do not understand, you gringos will never understand, because for you life is 'precioso.' But for me, José Cabezavaca, a peon, life is like the wind. It comes and goes. But what stays, amigo, is in the heart and the heart lives on in our people. It is better to be a man of heart than to live forever with your sombrero in your hand, in silence, while others step on you. I tell you, amigo, if they kill me it will mean nothing, but I will die knowing that I have lived. Others behind me will pick up this gun and use it and they will die too and then the ones behind them will take up the gun—and so it will go on until the day when my people can walk with their heads high and look straight into the eyes of anyone. Maybe after that we will become like you. Life will then become 'precioso' and we will start to rot inside and we will no longer want to fight. For when life is 'precioso' there is nothing left to fight for ..."

"But why can't you wait a little, José, discuss it. Make plans."

"You, amigo, are like the man I met in the market one day who told me about my right to vote for the candidate I choose. You both talk too much, you think this way and that way, you want to fight and then you are afraid of it and you change nothing because you are always talking. We have talked too much already, adios."

"Wait!"

Later, much later, Serge could not explain what had changed his mind. Maybe the peasant's speech had touched him, maybe he was prompted by an old journalist's dream not only to chronicle events but to shape them and participate in them, just once. Maybe he could not let him go because the waif had been perversely mistreated and Liesel had been pelted with dirt and he did not want to shirk so quickly another responsibility. Whatever it was, it made him place an arm around El Tiburon's shoulder and guide him back to the tree where they sat on a knoll of grass.

"And José, remember, when you raid the town you must get into the Post Office right away to cut the telephone wires. You do remember the telephone switchboard?"

The peasant nodded.

"Well if you cut all the wires they can't make a call for help to Tehuacan and this will give you an extra few hours or a day's start on the Federales. And José, for God's sake, don't make a massacre of it, just get the boys out of jail, try not to kill anybody, killing is bad publicity and doesn't bring you any sympathy. Don't let your men go wild with their guns or their machetes. And for God's sake, don't forget the post office, will you?"

Serge paused then he added softly. "Now let's see about that bloody gun. Well, there is a guy in there who might know how it works. Wait for me, I'll talk to him. Do you really want to go through with this?"

El Tiburon laid a hand on Serge's arm and nodded. Serge sighed and headed for the cave.

He knew Thad would be of no help. He had been a photographer and hated guns and would refuse to show anyone how to use them. So he approached Bruce who seemed to be recovering from his mushy trip. He told the lanky Australian one of his native acquaintances wished to sell a gun but the buyer was not interested unless he was also given the instructions on how to use it. His friend had no idea how to fire the blasted weapon. Bruce, having been in 'Nam, would surely know.

The Australian stroked his square jaw and winked as if to say 'who you kidding, mate'. But he said: "Not to worry sport if I know his little peashooter I'll have him get the hang of it in next to no time, you bloody well see."

But when Bruce saw the gun he clacked his tongue: "Great Kanga's shit, where did you get this little beaut?"

And as he fingered the weapon expertly, rocking his head with admiration, he mechanically rattled off the army manual's description: "M14—a hand-held, gas-operated, magazine-fed semi-automatic shoulder weapon. Efficient for long and short range. Standard issue for U.S. troops in Vietnam … that's her, mate, Yank gun, shit I sure hope yer know what yer doing with this little bobby-dazzler."

"He just wants to sell it," Serge explained lamely.

"Yeah?" The Australian drawled and looked at Serge as if to say: 'ooooh yeah?' But then he shrugged his shoulders. You could always count on an Aussie not to ask too many questions. The British and the Americans discovered this long ago when they first co-opted the Australians for help to fight their wars. Aussies went to fight wars for the British and the Americans without asking questions because, after all, the Brits and the Yanks were 'mates'. Australian soldiers died like flies at Gallipoli in the First World War and died in the Second World War and in Vietnam and Iraq. It all had something to do with not letting your mates down. When a mate was in trouble you didn't ask whose fault it was, you jumped into the melee and supported your mate, even if the silly bugger had done something bloody stupid.

Without further ado Bruce began his course of instructions while El Tiburon's eyes almost popped out of their sockets with concentration.

"Now see this here little donger? It's the safety catch. Got it? In this possy the gun's blocked. It won't fire. That's so as not to shoot yourself in the flam'n dick when yer's walking along. Now in that possy it's ready to blast. Got it? Righty-o. Now this little beaut allows you to fire single shots in this possy ... and automatic fire in ... that possy. Got it? Righty-o. Now the magazine here—that's where the bullets go, got it? Well, this here magazine ..."

The walk to Maria Sabina's cabin was an arduous climb and required a guide, a morose Indio who set the price at a hefty fifty pesos before he agreed to take the two men up to the Curandera's wood cabin high up on the mountain slope.

At the beginning the track snaked through maize fields, maize being staple food for man and beast as well as a source for brewing the local moonshine. Then they walked along orange and lemon groves, tended by women wearing huipil smocks, each with colorful crocheted patterns. The women waved and sniggered at the sight of more 'ippies' heading for Maria Sabina's cabin. Then the track ran along sunflower fields their thin stems quivering in a light breeze. Above them a red-tailed hawk circled leisurely on a thermal. Once a clucking pheasant, feathers ruffled in flight, scampered from the cornfields. Then the track rose sharply through a meadow. Above them towered Nindo Takoshi, adorned with the golden halo of the afternoon sun. Broken light beams cascaded over the mountain's sloped shoulders as if nature had decorated the father of all mountains with the epaulettes of a General.

Below, pasted on slopes, the adobe houses of Utla sat speckled in haphazard clusters, their thatched roofs like coolie hats above a rice field.

Across a last ridge, their guide became nervous and fidgety and finally pointed towards a distant log cabin: "Maria Sabina!" he whispered, pointing up the slope. Without an 'adios' he turned and fled down the path they had come.

"He looks scared," Serge chortled. "No wonder he wanted to be paid in advance. Poor bugger. He had no intention to run into the witch."

Thad smiled. Unlike Serge who considered emotions un-manly the mountains had worked their magic on the photographer. Their beauty in the dusk of the day brought tears to his eyes. Without saying so, Thad believed he had arrived. This place was going to be Home. Here he could forget the three years he had spent photographing the dead, the dying and the mutilated in the tragedy that was the Vietnam War, photos shunned by a media afraid of being labeled unpatriotic—until the day a naked little Vietnamese girl, mouth open in horror, napalm flames bursting behind her, made the front pages. By then support for the war had eroded and an editor could take a risk. Following that brutal image of the panic-struck naked girl tell-all photography became fashionable. But by then Thad had left 'Nam, sent home to Chicago and two months of rehab for drug abuse.

From the summit of the ridge, from outside the simple cabin, Xochitl watched them approach, hands on hips, her plaits dangling over her breasts. She studied them, her delicate head, perched on a slender neck, cocked to one side. Two naked children, one a baby, clung to the hem of her thin shift, a shift that traced her full breasts and rounded belly.

Just then, as they climbed the last slope, she called out something in the melodious sing-song language of the Sierra, a sound which resembles the high-pitched call of the muezzin and carries across dales and valleys.

Later on Serge realized she had called her grandmother, Maria Sabina, witch, healer, sage and prophet if one listened to the hype of the Longhairs, known in the world below as 'ippies.'

As always when people are about to meet a living legend Serge and Thad were caught by anticipation of an encounter with a woman, a witch to the authorities, a saint to her people. If nothing else, Serge argued, it would be a great story. He would gobble a few of the 'holy' mushrooms or 'Children of Si-tho' and as long as he didn't believe in the hocus-pocus surrounding the cult he would be safe. After all it was mind over matter. If you kept your head no cultish fairytale could harm you.

He had already decided he would have to sample the fungus to describe its effects to his readers, lift the myth of the Curandera's growing fame and dismantle the mystery of the Magic Mushroom, a mystery Serge dismissed as 'hippy hustle' or 'juvenile folly' just as he dismissed religion as a crutch for those unable to stand on their own two feet.

Still he was curious to meet Maria Sabina. After all, his interview could make the front page. Besides she might also know the whereabouts of George Haberstone.

The mist now billowed from the valley as it did nearly every evening, as if steam was rising slowly from boiling water in a kettle. Its wafting upwards brought a touch of magic as their surroundings gradually vanished into fog, though not thick but more like a silken veil.

Once arrived at the cabin Serge immediately asked the young woman for Maria Sabina. Xochitl pointed into the mist. The Curandera was obviously away so Serge and Thad sat down on a bench to wait for her. Immediately Xochitl sat down next to Serge and without inhibition, as if this was only natural, she took his hand in hers. The hand felt warm and comforting. It was calloused from hard work and it held on to him firmly, as if she tried to transmit the belief he was now hers. For a moment Serge wanted to withdraw his hand but then he found the unexpected relationship titillating. Xochitl was a handsome young woman and when she smiled at him, as she did now, her lips quivered like petals in a breeze. He was aroused and realized this may only be the beginning. There would be more, if he let it happen, though he felt some trepidation. Was she, like her mother, or was it her grandmother, also a witch? Was she bewitching him now? Was her hand gripping his hand taking over his willpower?

As happens when one comes across the unknown and the mysterious Serge was both excited and apprehensive. Neither he nor she spoke the others' language and the locals had told him Xochitl had two children and it was suspected their fathers had been demons she had captured and had bent them to her will. People credited her with the ability to cast spells and sent men mad. At the time Serge figured the warning was intended to ensure he steered clear of the beguiling young wench.

But now, watching her sideways, he had to admit she was beautiful in an earthy, some might say erotic way. There was an enormous intensity about her which transmitted itself. All of a sudden he didn't care anymore if she was the devil incarnate. She made him feel good. Waves of warm sensuality flushed his body. He squeezed her hand and she moved one thigh up against his thigh and it felt as if a hot iron had singed his leg, though there was no pain, only pleasure. He knew he would be unable to stand up without being embarrassed just as he knew the two would soon know each other more intimately.

And then Maria Sabina arrived on the crest of the mist.

Serge, not easily spooked, felt something akin to awe. Thad gazed open-mouthed. What the two of them saw coming towards them was only a head, an old head, two grey plaits on either side of a scrawny neck, wrinkled skin like tanned parchment, black eyes like burning sparks, drilling them. This head without rump, a spooky image, approached above a swirling mist while the rest of the body was buried below. In this disjointed head two eyes burned through Serge, threatened to penetrate him, his thoughts, his intentions, his very soul. He was stripped by the intensity of this stare and shivered involuntarily, unable to wrest his eyes from her gaze, mesmerized by this uncanny spectacle of an autonomous head sliding towards him above the mist, an unnatural spectacle, a weird prelude to what was sure to come.

When the veil of mist finally ebbed away she stepped into the open, an old woman in an ankle-length robe of coarse cotton, a robe hitched to carry what both later realized were the mushrooms she had gathered along the slopes. She did not take her eyes off Serge, totally ignoring Thad who stood in awe, frozen into a living statue by her presence as if some god had descended from the Olympus to permit him a glimpse of divinity. Thad was instantly under her spell.

The Curandera mumbled something in the language of her people and brushed past Serge. He wanted to talk to her, muttered questions but she replied only in the strange language of her ancestors. He turned to Xochitl but she shrugged her shoulders—and smiled. So nothing was explained, as it never would. And there was no interview and there never would. Everything was on feeling, already then.

Without being asked but without hesitating, without clarifications or even gestures of welcome, the two young men followed the Curandera into the cabin where she immediately busied herself in one corner arranging her mushrooms on a small altar of grey basalt stone. She beckoned the two men to sit in front of her while she dropped the pajarito mushrooms she had taken from her gown into banana leaves. Then, without asking per-mission, she rolled up Serge's shirt sleeve and rubbed a mud-colored nut, later identified as 'the leaf of Saint Peter' into the crook of his right elbow. She did the same to Thad who had closed his eyes and had already settled down to the experience with complete resignation. If she had asked him to strip naked he would have done so without questions. He was spellbound.

Serge, initially always anxious for explanations, made several attempts to kindle some verbal interaction, without success. He finally gave up, even on his demand to explain why she rubbed the nut into the crook of his elbow.

He too joined the unconditional surrender.

Unlike in the cave where he felt threatened the moment he entered he felt safe in her cabin, safe in her presence and prepared to drift along with whatever she had in mind. It occurred to him, only later of course that she had not even asked if the two foreigners wanted to go on this 'trip' with her. She had initiated the 'velada' with the logical assumption 'what else would bring two young gringos to her cabin?'

When she handed him the mushrooms offered on a banana leaf, Serge munched them, raw with the soil still clinging to some of the stems. For a moment however he wondered why she had offered him so many and Thad so few. But that too was only a fleeting reflection.

As the mushrooms passed his lips they left a velvety alkaline taste and the dirt-crusted stems reminded him of the days when he ate raw potatoes as a little boy to still his hunger. That was in the days after the Great War when there was nothing to eat except what one could forage from the forest or dig from the fields.

On a chair in the far corner Xochitl lit a candle. Aware of his attention she smiled at him. Before the mushroom took Serge into its power he saw her unbutton her dress and scoop out a hard brown teat, glistening with sweat. He saw the naked toddler with his long curved penis nudge the breast, saw his mouth greedily milk the nipple.

By then the mushrooms were sliding down his esophagus, fiery like Mescal and he wondered for a moment why Maria Sabina was handing mushrooms also to Xochitl, her child and the baby, the boar and the sow, the rooster and the hen, the dog and his bitch. All of the animals had settled in the cabin which Xochitl had locked by dropping a heavy wooden beam into two iron brackets, blocking the door. The same way she locked the shutters on two small windows. The only light now came from the candle and right then, before the mushroom commandeered his senses, Serge realized everyone inside the cabin, human and animal, was now in couples, the positive of male and the negative of woman. By instinct he realized Thad was coupled with the Curandera, he with Xochitl. He felt good about that. It all made sense though he could not explain why.

Every living creature in the cabin was now under Si-tho's spell.

Xochitl blew out her candle. On the altar Maria Sabina lit two candles.

A few feet away he heard Thad's wheezing breath. Then the cabin rafters started to slide in and out of focus, a zoom lens run amok.

Maria Sabina throttled her candles.

In the darkness Serge heard his own breath and the wind rattling at the batted-down shutters. Then he coughed—a deep hoarse rasp. His teeth chattered and icicles pricked his flesh. His blood seemed to coagulate, his throat contracted. Snot dripped from his nose like from a faulty faucet. His eyes burned then flooded with tears until his face was awash. A handkerchief he begged, inaudible apparently since no one replied or came to his aid. With numbed fingers he found the edge of the zarape on the floor and fumbled it somehow across his face.

"God, I'm freezing to death!" he stammered, shocked by the tinny nasal tone of his voice.

He sat inside a cupola of strings of pearls in gloriously bright and pristine colors, red, blue, green and purple color variations he had never seen. But he had no time to marvel at this psychedelic novelty because his lungs prickled, then burned as if on fire until he spat onto the floor dark licorice like ooze, tasting of carbon and nicotine and drooling from his lips in long adhesive fluffs. He wondered if his lungs were being purified of all the cigarettes he had smoked over the years or if he was going to choke on their dark extract. But before he could ponder this torture further his bowels seemed to explode with cramps and he was still wondering if there was a toilet when his liver ached and painfully throbbed for what seemed a long time, so long he thought he would die. And then his kidneys hurt as if someone had punched them and his duodenum wriggled, his scrotum prickled and every muscle in his body ached as if he had run many marathons and played many games of tennis, his chest burning worse than the day he sprinted to claim third place in the regional cross country run. He had a sudden great urge to pass water and held it back desperately, afraid to soil the serape. Then came a stinging pain in his heart and he panicked for the first time, harking to its frenetic thumping and watching, in terror, phosphorescent blood spurt through his veins, his body transparent, arteries packaged inside Plexiglas-like tubes, a system of inter-connecting pipelines, bubbling liquid, a boiling angry sea with the heart pumping … thump … thump … thump …

And then just as he thought he was about to pass out forever and quite unexpectedly the torture ended. The aches and pains abated, slowly fading away as pain does after an injection. In its place, slowly, energy rushed through his limbs, his muscles, gushing into his head. Waves of thoughts crashed through his conscience unable to be detained, like butterflies caught in cupped palms which fly away as soon as one inspects them.

And then Maria Sabina lit a candle.

Now the cabin was aglow in rusty red. Thad sprawled on his back before the Curandera's stool, grinning, sheepishly: "We, we, we're on the move!" he stuttered and Serge caught the note of excitement before Maria Sabina choked the candle.

Darkness.

Her chant, now a soft distant hum, filled the cabin with its monotonous melody. Only much later did he realize he had become addicted to her cooing as one can become addicted to a song on the hit parade.

EI Tiburon's men filed down the mule track before dawn, stealthy and careful to avoid any noise as if their mission could fail on an unusual sound picked up by someone in the distant town below. The men held their machetes by their side and El Tiburon cradled the M14, its muzzle pointed over his right shoulder into a gray sky streaked with the yellow ribbon of first light. The faded headscarf around his neck was stained with yellow Sierra sand. He once saw a painting of Emiliano Zapata in which the peasant leader wore a similar scarf. A straw hat was pulled deep down over the broad brooding face and the ends of a newly sprouted moustache had been twirled into rat-tails. On his belt he carried the spare magazine. All together he had 40 rounds of ammunition, all the man had given him as a down payment for the right to build schools and run them.

Ernesto, the potter, led the way. He knew the track well. Since childhood he had carted earthenware down into Teotitlan. Used to heavy loads, he felt awkward now, burdened only by a machete. He pointed out the potholes on the track with gestures and the men, walking Indian file, passed on his warnings with similar gestures to the ones behind.

On the fringe of the town El Tiburon raised his right arm and then sat down under a gnarled chestnut tree. His four companions did the same. All wrapped their ponchos tighter, pulled their sombreros down over their faces and sat chins dropped on their chests in silence while the ribbon of light spread along the night sky in the east.

Chalchiuhlicue, goddess of the dawn, was spreading her gown.

The hollow echo of the rap returned. After a few moments shuffling steps approached, a bolt slid back and the gate opened far enough to reveal the puffed bad-tempered face of the guard. El Tiburon gave the gate a swift kick and it flew back into the man's face.

"Not a word," El Tiburon hissed as the man let out a startled wheeze at the sight of the M14.

Beppe, one of El Tiburon's new companions in arms, scurried forward and propped the tip of his machete against the guard's neck.

"No, please," the guard sobbed.

"No, please? How polite we have become all of a sudden,"

Beppe hissed. "You were never polite when I was in this pigsty of a jail some years back, you piece of old mule shit."

"Psst!" El Tiburon whispered. Turning to the guard he added: "One word and zack ..." With that he ran a thumb across his throat. The guard wriggled his neck. His eyes popped.

In the guardroom the second man was still asleep on his bunk, curled against the wall, both hands between his thighs. El Tiburon lifted the 30-30 carbines from the racks and passed them to Oswaldo and Emilio, his other two recruits. Both immediately examined them curiously, oblivious to the sleeping man. El Tiburon held the muzzle of the M14 against the sleeping guard's head and kicked him hard. The man rolled over with an angry grunt: "Hijo de la …" he began, then shook his head the way a dog does after being dowsed.

"Shshsh …!" El Tiburon whispered, tickling the fellow under the chin with the muzzle of the rifle.

The gate to the courtyard was ajar.

Diego the Jailer was passing from cell to cell, prodding the sleepers with the tip of his boot, his daily routine to wake them up. He was so engrossed in this task he did not see El Tiburon enter the gate or notice his approach from the rear.

"Now be very, very gentle," El Tiburon whispered.

Diego wheeled and his mouth dropped open. As much as he tried he could not utter a word. He took two steps back: "What the devil you up to, chamuli?" he finally hissed.

"Paying you a visit," El Tiburon answered, still grinning because it had been so easy and the knot of anxiety he felt at the jail gate had now dissolved to be replaced by a wave of euphoria. "Just checking out how you treat my friends," he added, carelessly lowering the gun. "It's Freedom Day," he shouted to the astonished inmates, also gaping with open mouths or rubbing sleep-drunk eyes. "Everybody can go home. Vamos!"

The men looked at each other as people do who are not quite sure whether they understood what was said.

"Where did you get the gun?" Tonino asked.

"It was a gift," El Tiburon cried, elated by their astonishment. Then he waved an encouraging arm: "Come on, let's get out of here … everyone move, come on … amigos the mountains are waiting. You're all free. Get your things and then …"

The rest of the sentence was cut short because Diego had lunged to clutch the rifle. His surprise assault almost succeeded to wrest the weapon free, but El Tiburon's hands quickly locked around the barrel. The two men grimly wrestled for possession while the startled inmates looked on, not quite able yet to grasp the situation.

The peasant was more powerfully built but Diego's strength was doubled by the knowledge of being alone and on the brink of death. Desperately he butted his opponent with his shoulder but El Tiburon only grinned, baring his long carnivorous teeth, lifting the jailer off the ground as he yanked at the rifle. And then Diego lashed out with his knee. It caught El Tiburon in the groin and the pain made him relax his grip for an instant, long enough for Diego to wrest the rifle free. The jailer staggered a few steps back and triumphantly pointed the barrel at El Tiburon's chest: "Now say your prayers, bandito!" he cried.

Half crouched El Tiburon spat back: "Shoot me then, you miserable spittle-licker!" He felt more shame for his failure than fear of death.

Livid with fury after his close brush with death, Diego squinted along the rifle sights: "You big, stupid oaf!" he squealed … and pulled the trigger.

Once the guards at the gate had been overpowered Oswaldo and Emilio, two of the recruits, rushed across the Zocalo to the Post Office to carry out El Tiburon's plan. But the Post Office was locked so Emilio rammed his shoulders against the heavy wooden door. The hinges only squealed. "Let's do it together," he barked at Oswaldo who was an ashen-skinned youth with deep set eyes, a cowherd on the Rancho Grande. Both hurled themselves at the door and felt it come adrift; the hinges splitting their wood supports.

Inside Emilio found the light switch. The arc of the naked bulb lit two telephone cubicles, a switchboard and a ball of spaghetti wire.

"Give me your blade!" Emilio demanded, taking hold of the familiar machete. With zest he hacked indiscriminately, determined to carry out El Tiburon's orders to leave nothing functioning. He knocked dents into the heavy metal casing of the switchboard and split the wooden phone cubicles. Oswaldo used an iron rod to break whatever he deemed ought to be broken. Both worked earnestly in tandem, not for any joy of destruction but with the fervor of men fighting for a cause. Soon the Post Office was littered with the debris of their work.

"That should do it," Emilio finally called, surveying the havoc with the pride of achievement. He gingerly lifted one of the phones from its cradle and reeled back: The thing buzzed.

"Look!" Oswaldo called, pointing to a red light on the wall. "Santissima Virgencita!" Emilio mumbled: "It's still alive!"

El Tiburon's orders had been precise: Destroy everything so no one can call for help.

With redoubled vigor both men wielded their machetes.

Finally, when nothing was left to destroy they tore out wires, piece after piece, and chopped them up, each blow of the machete accompanied by grunts of satisfaction. They pushed the heavy telex off its table, leapt up and down on it, not in anger, but workmanlike in the way of professional wreckers, then for good measure, dropped two paperweights onto the keyboards. They found a wall box, opened its lid and found themselves confronted by shiny metal clips in glass tubes traversed by silver threads. Resolutely Emilio struck at them, only to recoil in horror when the box hissed and spewed a rainbow of sparks.

"It's bewitched!" he cried and dragged his equally startled companion out into the street where both debated what to do next.

Obviously the gadgets defied their destructive efforts. Emilio felt there was only one alternative: The place had to be burned down, the telephones and their wires had to be incinerated. There was enough paper stacked around the shelves to start a forest fire and if you opened the windows the draft would fan the flames into an inferno.

Both men went to work.

El Tiburon hastened to the Post Office as soon as he saw the billows of smoke. He realized something had gone terribly wrong. Burning down the Post Office had not been part of his plan. But then so many things had gone wrong. Still he had been lucky. He still marveled at his miraculous escape from Diego's deadly intentions. The jailer had pulled the trigger. But instead of the bang he expected he heard only a click. The safety catch was on. Angrily Diego had inverted the gun to use it as a club; but by then El Tiburon had taken advantage of his reprieve. His fist exploded in Diego's face a fraction before the butt of the M14 descended on his skull. Then, having left the inmates to gather their scant belongings he hurried to the Post Office, alerted by the smoke.

Behind him the inmates had trickled through the jail gate one by one.

Each man carried a knotted haversack over his shoulder; each stepped to freedom bewildered by having their sights suddenly extended across the walls of their jail to the edge of the horizon. They stared at each other as if expecting any moment someone would tell them it was all a terrible joke or maybe a dream. The Axeman, his hatchet in one hand his belongings in the other, checked the guards were unarmed and Diego was laid out on his back. He was breathing but he was still unconscious. The Axeman kicked him hard in the ribs, to make sure the man would stay down—and to repay him for past indignities.

Nightcap, wearing his flowing gown and beanie cap, was among the last to totter forth into the square, pin-eyes darting, nostrils sniffing. He bent down and snatched a fistful of dirt, rubbing it between his fingers. He hadn't touched dirt for years. Rocking his head he seemed satisfied it was real.

Behind him Xochin, the murderer, supported Uloc with one arm and Gregor with the other. Between them the trio had spent more than forty years in jail and only joined the escape because the others did, rather than from any desire to be free. Long ago they had attained a sense of freedom no walls could ever contain. Last to emerge was Teodimo, sheepish, a pail in one hand a tin can in the other, not quite sure what to do with either or why everyone had walked away through the gate. Like the inmates he stood there lost, turning this and that way. No one really knew what to do without El Tiburon. Beppe, the man El Tiburon had left in charge, paced up and down, cradling one of the appropriated carbines, nervously picking at his teeth with the edge of his thumbnail.

When Bartolomo came around the corner everyone jumped. Bartolomo did not. He simply pushed his sombrero out of a furrowed forehead with two fingers, stuck out his jaw and neck, raised the colt in his right hand and shouted: "Back! Back inside or I'll shoot the lot of you."

Instinctively the men huddled together, heads lowered, indecisive, seeking comfort in each other's proximity, waiting for someone to act, someone to give orders.

"Move! Move! You damn cattle and make it snappy or I'll send the lot of you to bloody hell!" Bartolomo screamed, accustomed to being obeyed. He watched with satisfaction as the men mechanically, though step-by-step, retreated towards the gate.

"Faster! Faster! You bunch of miserable dogs," the Sheriff yelled, now certain he had them back under his control.

The prospect of real trouble had never really bothered him when Anselmo arrived stuttering out the news of the jailbreak. These peasants were a servile lot who did as they were told. No, Bartolomo was not preoccupied about possible resistance but he was irked because he considered the escape an affront to his authority. And that made him livid with indignation.

"I'll teach you damn lot to take the law into your own hands," he yelled, waving the gun at them: "I'll blast away your thick chamuli heads."

The men glanced at each other and over each other's heads in search of El Tiburon. But the peasant was nowhere to be seen. At last Beppe, summoning all his courage and aware of his role as deputy commander, extracted the requisitioned carbine from below his poncho and pointed it in the general direction of Bartolomo: "Everyone is free now," he shouted, not very loud but loud enough to be heard by those closest. "We're all going home," he added, spreading his legs to give his stance additional menace.

"Nincompoop!" Bartolomo puffed: "Wouldn't know how to use this thing, would you?"

Beppe looked at his feet, covered in frayed sandals. He had never fired a gun.

"Don't provoke me!" he said bravely.

Bartolomo simply pointed the colt at his belly.

"Drop it, Fat-Head, and get with the rest," he ordered.

And Beppe obeyed.

The men had lowered their heads the way they always did when something unpleasant occurred.

"Now!" Bartolomo cried: "Into your cells, all of you and make it snappy!"

Again the men moved back, casting lingering looks around the Zocalo, maybe to catch a last eyeful of a world they were unlikely to see again for a long time.

"Move, move you bunch of cretins!" Bartolomo shouted.

Whipped by his orders the men almost hurried towards their cells, with the exception of Uloc and Gregor both sick and unable to move faster than snail's pace.

Determined to make everyone obey and unaware the two men were sick and unable to move faster Bartolomo turned on them: "You two. Move it or you'll be carried out of here in a box."

It was then that Uloc turned his bald shriveled skull and stopped dead in his tracks. Nobody could explain later why he did this. Perhaps he was tired, perhaps Bartolomo's face stirred a memory, and perhaps he felt he had reached the end of the road. No one would ever know.

Irritated the Sheriff lifted his gun: "You'll be a dead hombre if you don't keep moving."

But Uloc stood his ground. The hairless skull rotated and two sad eyes, deep in their sockets, stared at the source of the command. The men had come to a halt to watch their sick emaciated companion defy the Law.

"Get going!" Bartolomo hissed, instinctively aware he would have to remove this obstacle to his authority if he wished to maintain control. But the watery eyes inside their deep sockets remained sternly on the Sheriff.

"Go to hell, then," Bartolomo shouted and fired.

The bullet struck Uloc high in the chest. He stumbled one step back, still staring, then fluttered gently to the ground. A red blotch quickly saturated the bleached shroud into which he had wrapped himself for years.

A mutter of anguish ran through the men and Tonino ran forward to bend over the fallen man.

"You!" Bartolomo snapped: "Get back there or you'll be the next to go to hell. That's where the lot of you chamulis belong anyway."

Tonino's hand still rested on the twitching body. In the grip of death the old man looked even more emaciated, his body the size of a child. Tonino looked up and his combing gaze found the Axeman standing among the men. For a moment the big man looked puzzled, his gums working as they always did when their owner was perplexed by something in the world around him. Then he seemed to understand.

Flicked underarm, the hatchet came so swift and unexpected no one saw it, not even Tonino who had willed it. Its broad blade bit deep into Bartolomo's right shoulder and stuck there, cleaved.

The Sheriff gave a startled yelp, more in surprise than pain. The colt dropped from his disabled hand. He stumbled back and tried to smother the spurt of blood from a severed artery with his good hand. But blood still squelched through his fingers. He was so preoccupied with the task of stemming the flow he did not see Xochin until the sharp pain in his abdomen made him realize he had been stuck with the man's penknife. He groaned and doubled over, a look of utter surprise on his gaunt face.

"Murderers! Rotten rabble! Murdering dogs!" He shouted.

He might have gone on insulting them until the loss of blood shut down his ravings but the Axeman severed his good left arm using the same hatchet he had hurled.

In that instant Bartolomo must have known he was lost but his lips pursed for a final snarl: "Rabble! Rotten Indio Rabble," he rasped.

And so, even as he died, he lost none of the malice he had borne them all his life.

The men swarmed quickly around the dying Sheriff, plunging their small knives into the body now twitching with the last gasps of life. Only Teodimo took no part. He squatted by the dead Uloc, clumsily stroking the inert figure of the man he had fed for so many years. Someone said later they saw a tear rolling down the dwarf's cheek.

When El Tiburon arrived, alerted by the pistol shot, he found a raw heap of flesh and bone awash in a red puddle. At the sight of the flannel sombrero, a symbol in Teotolan for many years, he guessed the thing was Bartolomo, though he was aghast, not even the sombrero had escaped their fury. Hacked apart it had been trampled on and spat upon.

The men stood well back from their ghoulish handy work, sheepishly rubbing at the spattering of blood on their clothing as if to erase the evidence. Some already looked puzzled by their own burst of violence.

El Tiburon's neck scarve choked him all of a sudden and he pulled on it, desperate to loosen the knot.

"Animals! Bloody animals!" he moaned while the men lowered their heads and kept fiddling with their clothing.

"He had it coming," someone said. But El Tiburon's eyes blazed. No more was said. The raid had not gone well.

And worse was to come.

Bartolomo's shot had roused the town. Heads peered cautiously from windows and startled by what they saw withdrew. From the streets off the Zocalo they could now hear the shouts: "The prisoners have escaped!" followed by the squeal of frightened women, the urgent orders of men and the weeping of children. People chased livestock, humped sacks of maize and beans back into their homes, all the time glancing over their shoulders. Doors were bolted, shutters clanged and from inside the houses came the scraping of furniture maneuvered against doors.

The noise and frenzied activity appeared to the prisoners a sure sign the town was preparing for battle against them. Caught in this fear the inmates dashed aimlessly about the Zocalo like men who have lost all sense of direction in their search for a hole to swallow them. Finally, smitten by panic himself, El Tiburon dropped to one knee in the middle of the Square and aimed the M14 above the roofs of the nearest houses. He made sure the safety catch was in the firing position, the clip on automatic, before he triggered off his first volley. The unaccustomed recoil made the rifle jump in his hands. The barrel arched left and right before his fingers released the trigger.

A stray bullet hit Eugenio Galvon, the town butcher, just above the Adam's apple as he hurried across the far end of the Zocalo to reinforce the lock on his shop with an iron bar. Eugenio stumbled three more paces towards his precious shop, clasped his throat with both hands, gurgled and collapsed, spitting out his lifeblood on the pavement like the goats and bullocks whose gullets he had slashed for years in the back of the butchery.

Still, the burst of gunfire had the desired effect. The people of Teotitlan ran for the nearest houses. Shutters banged, doors slammed. Then the town became silent in fear, a fear stoked by guilt and the unspoken suspicion the prisoners' vengeance might be justified.

Near the church a child wailed, infected by the anguish on the faces of its parents. Somewhere in the maze of houses the thin voice of a woman mumbled prayers.

Prostrate before the altar of his church Father Ignacio's bloodless lips mechanically murmured prayers to a God in whom he had long ago lost faith, while his mind assembled vivid visions of his youth in the 'twenties' when the peasants had strung priests from the nearest trees and disemboweled them for good measure. His earthly life was suddenly very precious to Father Ignacio, aware he may not have earned a place in heaven, if such a place really existed.

On the Zocalo, El Tiburon stared at the rifle, fighting back the impulse to hurl it into the gutter. It had seemed such a harmless piece of metal until a few moments ago when it had dealt out death in such an imperious manner—and without his consent. By the Holy Virgin of Guadalupe he had not intended to kill that man. Eager for absolution, El Tiburon glanced at the faces of the prisoners but found reflected on them already the traces of fear and respect inevitably due to a man who metes out death. It occurred to him then that he was very much alone now. In that instant the peasant died and the caudillo was born. So be it, he thought and gripped the gun with both hands. Holding it above his head he cried: "Follow me."

And still his initiation was not over.

Only Tonino remembered the women. Locked into their cells the women had made no noise nor called for someone to let them out during the escape. The women had learned long ago it was best to keep quiet when men fought.

Tonino cut the key ring from Bartolomo's belt and unlocked the Damas section. The six women emerged slowly, uncertain if this new situation was in their favor or not. One of them was still a teenager.

Not asking questions, the women tagged behind the men as El Tiburon led them out of the Zocalo heading for the massive rock faces of the Sierra, now fully visible in the growing light of day.

But as the men turned onto the forked road, the one where the hyacinth patch grows, the first row of the escaped prisoners walked into El Agente, still hitching his trousers and hurrying towards Angel's house.

El Tiburon reacted first. He pointed the M14 at the man's belly, standing back far enough to leave a good gap between them. He had learned by his mistake.

"Hands up!" he snapped and the startled official obediently stretched his arms above his head.

Standing there, without his habitual swagger, El Agente seemed stripped naked. The thick sensuous tongue nervously flicked over thin lips and the little porker's eyes widened as the rest of the jail population trickled around the bend: "Don't shoot!" El Agente squealed: "I'm not the one you want. You won't have any trouble from me."

"What a pity," El Tiburon replied with sarcasm, though he was relieved there would be no more shooting.

The men, scowling, formed a semicircle around their prey. "It's not me you want," El Agente whimpered, fear making him unusually garrulous: "It's Angel you want, he's been the brain behind everything. I'm just a tool, just doing a job and getting paid for it very little. I'm a nobody. You understand?"

El Tiburon stepped closer, carefully. He lifted the chrome-plated revolver from El Agente's holster and handed it to Beppe. Without his gun the man looked even more naked. But he kept his hands obediently in the air.

"Believe me I'm not going to cause any problems," he blabbered: "I'm on your side. It's Angel you want. I'm just a paid messenger boy. It's him you want. Look, he just lives up there … I'll show you …"

He was about to take a step towards Angel's house when one of the women spotted him: "Santa Maria!" She exclaimed: "Look! It's the pig!"

The rest of the women craned forward to see whom she meant.

"It's the mujerijego," a second woman cried. The others pushed forward, through the ranks of the men.

"Not so brave now, is he?" The first woman hollered. "And she only a girl. The bastardo; we should send him to hell where he will roast for all his sins, all his sins of the flesh, of which there are that many.'

The other women chimed in: "Send him to hell! The rapist!"

As the women surged forward El Agente backed away towards the wall of the house where Don Esteban, the grocer lived with his family of five. Don Esteban, a thin, gaunt man would later describe the scene in all its details to the Federales. He had seen it all through a peep-hole in the kitchen. He had seen El Agente's eyes cast around for an escape route.

"For the love of God," El Agente screeched, turning to El Tiburon: "Keep those bitches away from me."

The peasant grinned: "That's a new tune for you. You couldn't get close enough to them before."

The men laughed and made space for the women.

"Let's get the swine!" shouted a long-limbed woman wrapped in a black reboso.

Spread against the wall El Agente's fingers clawed for a miraculous opening behind, an opening he knew could not be there: "Mercy!" he whispered. "Don't hurt me, please!"

"Oh listen to the brave macho now," the first woman bellowed: "Listen how he sings. When did he ever show us any mercy?"

The women moved in closer.

"Not me!" El Agente winced: "Not me. I'm just a tool."

His whole body shook and a little rivulet seeped from his trouser cuffs onto freshly polished leather boots and from there onto the ground where it formed a small puddle.

The fat woman pointed to it: "Look he's opening his bladder, the coward."

Women cheered or guffawed.

The fat woman sniffed the air: "By the nose of Huetzin!" she cried: "He's also losing his meal."

More cheers. Even El Tiburon smiled, unacquainted as he was yet with the wrath of women wronged or the depth of their savagery.

"Let him be," he said, turning away, already nauseated by another man's villainy.

So he did not see the fat woman lunge with a knife she had pulled from under her reboso. Nor did he see it vanish, up to the hilt in El Agente's belly. But he heard the squeal, piercing, followed by the cry: "Die, Pig!" and the weak plea, gurgled: "Please! Please!" Right then he knew the man would be cupping his testicles. But he was still rooted to the spot, not reacting, unaware of how far women can go in their wrath. He heard them screech and squawk and partial phrases reached him: "Down with it ... pull it ... out, out, out with it, all of it ..."

He finally turned, in time to see the knife flash above the bushel of heads and hear the chilling scream: "Nooooooo!" which faded into a terrible moan.

The knot of heads floated apart and the Fat One emerged, holding high above her head, triumphantly, the blood-soaked severed genitals.

He stood aghast, gaping at the women as if he had seen them for the first time, watching them turn away, snuggle deeper into their rebosos, walk off, fury spent, sobbing now as women ought to at the sight of death.

He hugged the gun tighter and walked through the town, looking neither right nor left, face set, not caring whether anyone followed but knowing no one had a choice. Past the school he walked and the typing pool and only a dog crossed his path. And all the way up the mule track the throng behind him remained silent while down below, in Teotitlan, a black plume of smoke floated above the Post Office and a dog howled.

He had not intended it this way.

Suddenly and without warning he was being ejected from his warm bubble bath in the womb, down a long dark tunnel gliding on a wet slide until he suddenly burst into glaring bright light.

It was a shock, this birth of his, the glare, the assault of different smells and different noises, the scare of being abandoned, cast out, no longer snug but severed from the comfort, the security, the protection, now left alone to fend—for what?

His first recollection as a child was the peculiar smell of burning houses and explosives, unforgettable. The red flickering flames of his grandparent's house, hit days after the war ended when an allied plane ditched its last bomb over the small village to which his mother and his grandparents had been evacuated. He was running down the street in his nightgown, on bare feet, a little boy with blonde hair, yelling his head off, stumbling over hoses spouting thin sprays of water from cracks in the worn rubber. From then on fire would always scare him. Then he wetted the tip of his index finger with the tip of his tongue to trap the last crumbs of bread below the table during those post-war days. Fear of starvation, he now understood, was the reason even now in the years of plenty he always ate up what was on his plate even if he was not hungry. Then he saw the fat man, the one he accidentally bumped while running, dressed only in bathers, through the galleys of the cruise ship chasing other boys. The fat man, annoyed, bellowed: "Watch it, damn Chicken-Chest." He was thirteen years old, fragile about his looks like all teenagers. From then on he would not bare his chest in public, stung by that remark. He would wear shirts while sun-baking on the beach, pretending he had a sensitive skin. He bought shirts and jackets two sizes too large to fill out his chest. And for years he made love in the dark.

Next he was on a trail between cornfields where stalks danced in the balmy breeze of a summer day. The air was pregnant with the pungent scent of freshly cut grass drying into hay; a host of sparrows fluttered overhead and he humped his school satchel lightly, elated by the importance of walking to school alone. The boys pounced from the apple orchard, sturdy little peasant lads, stumpy-legged, rosy-cheeked, rock-headed, the future tenders of the land. Shovel-like hands, so much bigger than his own, bombarded him with clots of dirt. "City slicker!" the sturdy lads chorused. "City slicker go back to the city!" They left him on his knees covered in bruises and fighting back tears. A pair of soft green eyes bent down from a strawberry-freckled face framed by flaming red hair. Two thin arms helped him to his feet, then brushed the mud from his hair and his overcoat. Hand-in-hand they walked between the corn stalks. He smiled gratefully at Liesel, whose mother, so the villagers whispered, was a witch. The peasants shut their stable doors when Liesel's mother passed and burned her in effigy each time a cow miscarried. Once the corn was harvested and the fields wore crew-cut stubbles he and Liesel walked to school again. This time the gang swooped from behind a barn. "Witch! Witch! Witch," the boys screeched and danced around Liesel, showering her with clots of dirt and pebbles. She clutched his hand tightly. Together they would face the ordeal. "She's a witch, a witch," the boys clamored and nudged him, pushed him, teased and hit him until he trembled, afraid their sadistic whim would soon be directed at him. He dropped her hand. The boys took him in their midst and whirled jubilantly around the girl, now alone. She didn't look at him. She looked at the ground. One of the boys handed him a clot of dirt and ordered: "Throw it. Throw it at the witch …"

Maria Sabina lit a candle.

He sat under a bell-shaped spider web; each fiber laced with peacock-eyed jewels, purple and yet not purple, of shapes he could not define, a web not of this earth. Beyond this luminous cupola, indigo and yet not indigo, he saw the darkness of a starless night, impenetrable, a night when fear rattles at the throat. And he heard Thad murmur: "Solid, Man! The Mother of the Universe!"

The girl leaned placidly against the car bonnet and watched as he dumped out the backseat. She was built awkwardly with a milky face ravaged by pimples but a reputation for being easy. And he had just twenty minutes to do it and get back. Then he was due, he figured, for his next table tennis-match at the church hall. He had slipped out and sped down to the Park in his father's old Ford. Thank God she was waiting for him by the ghost gum as arranged. But taking the backseat out of the car had wasted a good five minutes. Still, she'd have to lie on something comfortable; he couldn't expect her to do it on the wet grass. She seemed to know all about it though, stretched on the upholstered seat, legs apart, hands behind her head, looking at him a trifle amused while he was already covering her face with kisses and one hand crawled furtively under her dress. Her placid composure was oil for his smoldering passion. She wouldn't stop him now, wouldn't brush away his hand, wouldn't pull away her face and plead: "No, please, no, I'm scared, what if ..." This one was for real. Good old Phil had not exaggerated. Shaking with eagerness he managed to roll up her skirt until the belly gleamed in the half-light. Black knickers, he thought, bloody black knickers, already tugging at them clumsily until she helped by lifting her buttocks. He rolled them down to her ankles. His fingers ran into a furry brush and he was both startled and excited by its extent. The first pangs of an approaching orgasm threw him into panic. Quick, he thought, fingers fluttering down to his fly where the damn buttons seemed cemented into their holes. He ripped. Two popped. Never mind. Hurry, hurry! He delved inside, wrestled it free, horrified it might not get there in time when it had taken so much courage to set it all up. But where was it supposed to go? Desperate he hurled himself across her belly, hoping it would find its own way, and jerked until it was all over. She was still looking at him curiously, her belly covered in sperm. He felt a great desire to run. He started heaving the seat back and hoped in the dark she wouldn't see the shame on his face. "Bit of a mess," she observed, rearranging her dress: "Got a hanky?" God, how he had wanted to run. "Ping-Pong match", he muttered: "Important, championship. Must rush." She looked at him, a sorry grin on her lips.

"Got me all wet you have," she said.

God how he wanted to run.

Maria Sabina chanted.

Was it a rap at the barred door? An insistent rap. Someone desperate to gain entry. Maria Sabina lights a candle and shuffles to the bolted entrance. From inside the web he sees, far away in another dimension, the Curandera lift the pole from its tiepins and yank open the door spreading her arms as if to embrace the world outside. Swirling vapors billow around her feet and through them shadows scurry inside, clucking and grunting. Emerging from this imbroglio the figure of a man, hair down to his shoulders, ascetic, emaciated. Haberstone! Good Grief! A shadow of his photo, a wild mad-looking Haberstone who falls into her arms the way a drunk drops anchor on a lamp post. She strokes his cheeks, mumbles soothing words and he, grateful, slides down her waist, encircling her knees, head nestled against her lap. The pigs gobble Si-tho, smacking, the hens peck Si-tho, clacking. The pigs grunt. The dogs growl and then Haberstone—if it was Haberstone—is gone, the pole back in place, the hut dark.

A flame bursts through his psychedelic world and in its glow, on the bed, Xochitl feeds the child on her breast again. The top part of her dress is rolled down, exposing breasts and shoulders that sparkle in the pyramid of light, a Pieta on a slab of red marble. The child suckles carnally, its head thrown back, one possessive hand upon the flesh, crinkling the smooth dark skin, the greedy mouth enlarging the nipples as it draws.

Xochitl observes the child fondly through a curtain of hair cascading down to her waist. When he looks again the child has vanished, its place taken by a piglet, nudging the breast with its snout to coax forth more liquid. She holds the piglet in the crook of her arm gazing at it with the same fondness she dedicated to the child. The animal's tail curls over her elbow and one hoof rests, snug, in the dale between the teats. She sits, cross-legged, Buddha-like, the suckling piglet in her arm.

And the smacking of the sucking beckons like a lure.

The long forgotten odor of mother's milk mixed with the tartness of sweat. A hot sirocco blows down the tympanum then nibbles at blistered lips. Warmth, sensuous warmth; a balloon inflates, explodes, gushing forth an ocean of tadpoles which float on a soft cushion rocking in rhythm with the spasms, long lingering spasms, lasting forever it seems, until all is drained and only the tip of the shoot still quivers.

He thought he heard her whimper and the softness below his belly wriggles, then lays still. Xochitl! She is warm and pliable and moves with the rhythm of his thrusts, or is he imagining it all and has he shot his bolt too early—again? But she wants more and he wants to contend her, more and more and she is breathing slurping sounds into his ears and their lips are hot on one another and it goes on and on, one climax after another, one wave after another, ecstasy … and more and more and more of it.

Maria Sabina's chant changes. Now it seems angry.

Faces, so many faces, rolling by like marionettes on a string, manipulated by invisible hands; he suddenly knows their accusing stares mean he used them, charmed them, exploited them, then discarded each, once their usefulness had been exhausted, once he had extracted all the information; others had simply been replaced by new paramours.

He feels the years passing, rushing by like flotsam on a river.

He is aging.

Now his thoughts are slurred, confused, his body racked by arthritis; the toothless head has shrunk, small enough to fit the totem pole on some exotic Oceania Island; his fingers are stiff, cold and curled like talons. Sometimes he sits tacitly for weeks, maybe years—who knows—watching his body age. He listens to the wound-down beat of his own clock, feeling the sluggish passage of blood bogged down in the sewage of bygone years, his breath coming in short bursts. An icy cold creeps into his toes, rises along the wasted calves to tottering knees, no longer able to support the gaunt frame, into thighs that lost their suggestive roundness, through the sex organ, two shriveled sacks and a dead stump, now only objects of gender identification and relief; up through a concave stomach, coddled by large doses of medicine, into a chest racked by fits of painful coughing, and, in the end, towards the clock, which, in a last stroke of defiance booms loudly one last time before it stutters, stumbles, misses a beat, two beats, rattles out a mad double beat, grinds, titters—stops. He tries to mouth a final protest but only manages a feeble: "I want to live."

Then fireworks explode, then darkness.

Lieutenant Efren Garcia Sanchez wore the dress uniform, the one with the metal buttons and grey shoulder wings, the trousers kept under the mattress to keep the creases sharp. His boots, sheened on polish mixed with spittle, were toweled to a velvety gloss by Private Hernandez, a man with vast experience as 'bolero' in the Capital. Faced by his own splendor in the mirror that morning, the Lieutenant regretted it would be wasted on the ignorant wretches of Utla in this primitive capital of the Sierra. He yearned for the Parade Ground where his trim figure inevitably drew appreciative glances from the ladies.

During those moments when Lieutenant Garcia stood wrapped in his dress uniform, he completely forgot his own humble origins and promoted himself to the membership of a class which, had he ever reflected, considered him no more than a handsome piece of cannon fodder.

Seated in the center of his guests on the Garrison Balcony, the Lieutenant watched, with fake detachment, the pilgrims meander through the festooned streets to the Shrine of the Virgin as they did on every Anniversary of her Apparition, an event he ignored since he was far too preoccupied with his own importance. Their melancholic songs and radiant faces, marked by the fervor of faith, did not stir his soul or impress his eyes. Besides, as a son of the Military he was taught to consider the church an institution destined for women. Men, chosen to transform society, could not waste time on the foreign gibberish of effeminate priests whose hocus-pocus only represented the efforts of an alien power to usurp an authority exclusive to the State. That's how his Maestro at Military College had expressed it.

Still their piety this morning suitably adorned his new status as virtual dictator of the Sierra following the High Command's declaration of martial law. Of course, he had immediately made extensive use of his new privileges. First he dissolved the Municipal Police, next he occupied the office of the Municipal President and then changed the market hours from 0600 to 0830 so his sleep would no longer be disturbed by squawking vendors. He also changed the route of the annual pilgrimage to pass below the garrison balcony where he sat, enthroned on the only upholstered chair in town and flanked by the elite of Utla, all ordered to appear in homage to the new rule. He was, however, peeved by the deliberate manner in which the pilgrims ignored the dais.

To disgorge his displeasure, he beckoned to Feliciano, seated on his left. The Municipal President dutifully inclined his head. "You have been far too lax, my dear man," the Lieutenant complained: "People have forgotten how to respect authority."

Feliciano bit his lip. "But there'll be changes now, believe me," the Lieutenant promised: "Did you know the Cubans were responsible for all the trouble?"

When Feliciano remained obstinately silent, Lieutenant Garcia added gravely: "It came over the radio this morning."

But Feliciano's face remained expressionless as it always did when he failed to fathom the depth of any information, so hiding his ignorance behind a wall of silence.

"Yes, Castro's stooges supplied the weapon," Lieutenant Garcia blurted.

When neither the information nor its delivery caused any reaction, the Lieutenant frowned. This man was highly uncooperative, probably still sore about taking orders from the military. Maybe he knew more than he admitted. He would have to be watched.

But that morning Lieutenant Garcia was far too euphoric to let his mood be spoiled by suspicions. The news on the Two-Way had revamped his career, which he feared had taken a dive after he was dispatched to this god-forsaken Sierra region, a place of no interest to anyone except a bunch of illiterate Indios. Utla was the most unlikely place in the Republic to ignite a revolution. But if the Cubans were involved, he might yet come across one of their platoons seeking a safe haven in the Sierra from which to launch their raids. He might yet win a Captain's epaulets.

Garcia had listened to the transmitted message with increasing glee: The Republic's crack Olympic Battalion under General Plinio Plutarcho Pereira y Sallende had been mobilized and the Latino ambassadors in Havana had lodged protests with the Castro regime and the Organization of American States. At least one American Aircraft carrier was standing off the coast.

"The Cubans are going to be taught a lesson this time," he suddenly announced to his perplexed guests who knew nothing about Cuba. "You watch. We'll make them show their tails."

Since the Municipal President retained the same non-committal air and the rest of the guests barely managed a polite smile, the Lieutenant thought it time to devote more attention to the neighbor on his right, a plump young woman wearing her long braids entwined with the red, pink and blue ribbons used on festive occasions.

"I have the best view in town," he mumbled ambiguously.

Anna Maria Gonzalez ignored the remark as she imagined a lady of standing should. She felt important on the dais, flattered by the attention of this strapping young man who was feared by everyone. And his invitation had been delivered in style, by two armed soldiers. Now everybody had to look up to her, Anna Maria Gonzalez, the fruit vendor's daughter who was being courted by the most important man in town.

"I've kept my eye on you," the Lieutenant whispered and when Anna Maria still ignored the remark he dropped his hand on her knee and squeezed the pliant flesh. She brushed the hand away, but not abruptly, having been taught by her mother that a man's ardor is best stimulated by resistance, but not too resistant.

"I like a girl with spirit," the Lieutenant breathed, elbowing her thigh. He felt invincible that morning and like most men suddenly endowed with power his ego demanded a woman to complete the success.

"We would make a handsome couple," he suggested.

When she tilted her nose, remembering her mother's advice, he chuckled.

On the other side of the Lieutenant, Feliciano quietly repeated his oath for the sixth time that day: 'Two Bolivar candles, Holy Virgin, the tall ones with the costly strips on the tallow, if you help them."

His prayer was interrupted by the Lieutenant:

"The Army should be running this country," he announced. "Then we'd have some order. We'd be rid of these idiotic and uncivilized traditions. No one would dare stage protest marches, attack officials or import guns and Cuban mercenaries. Civilian governments are too lenient. It's their downfall."

Instead of commenting Feliciano pointed down into the street. "There goes Casimiro Arundez," he said, not addressing anyone in particular: "His son was jailed for selling Si-tho."

"The enemies of the State must be dealt with," the Lieutenant proclaimed.

"The circuit judge asked for two thousand pesos. Casimiro did not have the money."

"We must cooperate. I expect your full cooperation in this hour of national crisis," the Lieutenant demanded.

Feliciano sighed. "The laws are very harsh."

"But just," the Lieutenant added quickly. "Just and wise. Remember it is not important for the people to understand the laws but to obey them."

Feliciano remained silent.

The Lieutenant felt encouraged. "We are not your enemies but your friends. We do what is best and for that we are prepared to die, yes, to give our lives so that your children can live in a better world."

The Lieutenant paused. "One does not always expect gratitude from those one saves," he added.

"Casimiro's son was a great help to him in the fields," Feliciano continued stubbornly. "Casimiro had no way of paying the fine without the boy's help."

"Nonsense! The laws must be respected. It is the State that's important not the individual."

"Casimiro will thank the Virgin for his son's escape. Had you set him free he would have thanked you. But the Government wants money, the Virgin only flowers."

"Poppycock" The Lieutenant snorted: "Let the Virgin take care of your souls and let us take care of your bodies."

The procession passed below the dais in groups, each group preceded by a wreath held up on two poles, identifying the origin of those trotting behind: Hacienda de los Angeles, The Peasants of Oro Negro, The People of Monte Castillo, Rancho de las Joyas, Union Campesina Utla, In Memoria de Jorge Blanco.

Behind the pole-carriers came the bands, each thrashing out its own merry tune which gave the procession the musical harmony of an orchestra pit during warm up. Those from Oro Negro hauled an oxcart with a marimba aboard. Four men tickled the instrument with their hammers. From Rancho de las Joyas, Matteo the hunchbacked woodcarver, had walked eight kilometers bearing a crown of thorns. His face was awash in coagulated blood. He was honoring a pledge made to the Virgin that he would wear the crown if his cow calved safely. Erico the Whistler stumbled towards the Shrine doubled under the weight of an enormous cross, his Calvary. Albina, the Curandera from Los Lagos, had herself flagellated by a son as penance for a sin only she recalled and young Ulba, the green-eyed one from Rancho de los Rios, childless after six years of marriage, came on her knees for two days, sleeping on the roadside. Her husband and two sisters laid cushions for her all the way. By the time she reached Utla, the cushions were threadbare, her knees raw as the meat on a butcher's hook. But she had kept her vow—and expected to be rewarded with a child.

Each year these processions were entertained by the Red Devils. These masqueraded figures danced through the ranks of the procession making donkeys' ears at the faithful. Their antics brought a touch of comedy to the solemn occasion. Usually the devils, their faces behind grotesquely painted carton masks, their bodies gloved in patched red tights, danced through the columns light as feathers. But this year some of them carried sacks on their backs and their dancing was more like that of the brown bears led on chains through the villages before Spanish hunters exterminated the species, long ago.

The soldiers hung from the windows of the garrison mess hall and merrily bantered about the physical assets of the female pilgrims. Their uncouth comments were kindled by sexual frustration and the knowledge of their new status as the lords of the manor.

"Ola Chula!" Lance Corporal Guzman called out to a robust maiden. "What about a little love for a brave soldier?"

Egged on by the encouraging chortles of his companions he continued: "Hitch your skirts my little beauty and give us a look at your pins."

"Why only the pins?" another soldier complained loudly. "Let's see the bloody lot."

The suggestion elicited loud cheers. Some of the men in the procession turned their heads and glared at the soldiers.

But Sergeant Sanchez' platoon felt safe. Their rifles were propped against the wall behind them.

"Come, come, come on!" Sergeant Sanchez bellowed as the girl went by. "With such a broad ass it won't hurt."

Cheers rewarded this coarse quip and Private Alvarez, eager to corner some of the attention, made as if to climb out of the window to grab the tantalizing buttocks.

Behind the soldiers three Red Devils had quietly slipped into the room. One of them ripped the mask from his face with a gesture that showed he was glad to be rid of it. He opened his sack and pulled out a rifle, then tip-toed, holding it like a lance, towards the unsuspecting troops at the window. The muzzle prodded Lance Corporal Guzman's back just as he was about to launch into a vivid description of a comely matron.

On the balcony Lieutenant Garcia glanced regretfully at the last pilgrims. He was sorry the procession had ended so soon. To extend the pleasant baptism of his power a little longer he invited the guests to the mess hall. "We'll drink to the health of the Armed Forces," he announced. The guests, stiff and formal, followed dutifully.

Bowing from the hip the Lieutenant turned to Anna Maria. "Señorita, may I have the honor of your arm?" Anna Maria stared at him puzzled, then at her arm, then blushed. The Lieutenant, very much in charge, smartly hooked one arm under hers the other he slung around Feliciano's shoulders. Linked that way he faced the M14 which El Tiburon pointed at his chest from the door.

"Mierda!" Lieutenant Garcia hissed before the blood shot to his face and his lower lip began to quiver wildly.

That night El Tiburon spoke to the people from an upturned fruit box in the Market. He had declined the use of the Garrison balcony since it carried the stigma of the old regime.

Lieutenant Garcia and his unit were safely locked into the fruit cellar of Juan Diego's house and the town was in the kind of festive mood that lingers in the wake of a pilgrimage that cleanses one's sins. It was the only night of the year when people from all over the region assembled at Utla.

El Tiburon spoke of freedom and justice and how the land belonged to the man who worked it, how the machines belonged to the workers who used them and how each man had the right to sell his crop to whoever he wanted and not only to the United Fruit Company which, so everyone knew, was owned by the thieving gringos. He spoke of a Council on which everyone would be represented and which would recommend what action should be taken. But this action would only be taken if a majority voted in favor at a general assembly. Everyone, everyone over the age of sixteen, would have the right to vote on any action recommended by this advisory Council. He promised them freedom from the gluttony of Government agents and told them to hold their heads high and look any man straight in the eye. But he said it might become necessary to defend their new freedom with guns and maybe with their lives and if they were not prepared to do that they should say so now.

And they all yelled they were ready.

At the end of his speech the people hugged and kissed each other; two men hoisted El Tiburon on their shoulders and carried him around the Square. Men slapped his back, women snatched at his hand and kissed it and children were lifted on their father's shoulders to catch a glimpse of 'El Hombre'—the man who led the Revolution.

Someone strummed a guitar and the crowd joined in the old revolutionary peasant song:

"With our carbines we went to the war.
And our sweethearts they came to the war.
And our great leader he fired the first shot."

During the noisy celebrations nobody heard the crackle of static in the basement of the Garrison or the exasperated voice of a distant radio operator who insisted: "HQAF to Unit Six: come in, come in Six. Can you read me? Come in."

He became aware of a transcendental silence, suspended outside the luminous purple web, among iridescent jewels floating weightless above his consciousness, a crystalline consciousness drenching his invisible being. From above, floating, gazing down, he saw, the way a spirit must see, his own corpse, crumpled on its side, one foot drawn up, a shriveled shrunken corpse with an old wrinkled face, an open mouth, no teeth, broken eyes.

So he was dead?

From his detached being without form, some distance above his own corpse the conscious Leftover watched the body below decay, watched the flesh waste until bare bones remained coupled to a skull and sightless sockets crawling with maggots. And then, enlightened by a strange source of sagacity the Leftover marveled at the ease with which it had conceived the secret of eternity. A perfect circle where the true beginning is any point of departure, an existence purified of millennia of genetically transmitted instincts, prejudices, viruses, passions, desires, all of them humanity's accumulated inheritance. How ridiculous this existence had been, anchored to these scourges of the species. How liberated he felt now of the collective defects of his forefathers and his own constant striving for fame, fortune and the admiration and subjugation of the other gender. Now he was a being without needs, without wants or a sense of time, body-less, a spirit understanding the futility of existence, unchained, floating free.

So this was eternity.

All this made perfect sense to the Leftover. Thoughts flowed smoothly on a broad stream of awareness. Life was a pyramid; the cabin symbolized the last rung to the summit. At the base was Teotitlan, mean, ravenous, caught in its own vicissitudes, a place where evil was justice, power law and people offered their excesses to a God-sponge who absorbed their guilt, an idol with a vast capacity for forgiveness, a capacity devised by his servants to justify and expunge the evil he had seeded in them. Teotitlan was a walk through the muck, inhaling the putrid stench of rotting humanity. The Sierra was the intermediary stage: The lone plain on which the searching spirit wanders towards an unknown goal on a hike plagued by traps, a maze of cul-de-sacs, torturous detours, all returning to the beginning. Here, having escaped the debauchery below, the spirit groped for truth. Yet here too the majority was devoured by fear, conformity and a subtle debauchery, like the one practiced in the cave. Few dared or desired to continue their search. Proud at having escaped the lowest level they happily settled for second best. Only the adventurous few, those seeking true illumination clawed to the top of the pyramid to confront themselves in the mirror of their own Psyche.

Was this the secret of eternity, Serge the Leftover mused high above his rotting corpse? He had no doubt. This was it, a miraculous awareness, a lofty logic stripped of all emotions, the striving, the passions, the ambitions all now left behind below. Up here in this universe with no borders and no tasks the Leftover marveled at the ease of floating unencumbered.

Magnificent. Liberated. Floating and knowing for Eternity.

No shackles. Only understanding. No purpose only knowledge. No targets. No struggles. No desires ... So what then? What then was the purpose of existence as a Leftover? To gloat? To understand without passion, ambition, with knowledge exhausted by knowing all? Did he really want to give it all up? Did he really want to exist in this void forever, with no desires, with full understanding? Of what? The futility down there? And what of the futility up here?

"No" he suddenly yelled into the void. And then even louder: "I want to live." Hardly spoken he slipped back into the magic circle, back into his body. He was alive. Again.

But once alive he panicked. Instantly he wanted to escape the cabin. The way was through the door. The barred and bolted door! Through it he would return into the world and mend his egocentric ways. Another chance! Oh how he craved another chance, offering his promises to an unknown force, pledging a better self.

Life. Instinctively he realized he must do something to make his survival come true. As always it was and would be up to him.

Unsteady he rose and staggered through the cabin towards the door, pursued by Maria Sabina's rising chant. He passed Thad, sitting at her feet, spindly legs crossed, back arched, hands resting on both knees, palms turned up. And Thad smiled a knowing eerie smile from a face of alabaster. It struck him like the blunt side of an axe: Thad was not real. Thad was only the guide. He, Serge, was the victim. Thad had only accompanied him, implanted the idea and had nurtured it. He had followed sheepishly all the way to the cabin. Thad was only the guide.

Xochitl blocked his way, one hand beseeching him to stay, the other clutching the baby to her breast. She was temptation. She was the Siren to chain him to the cabin for eternity. He brushed her aside. A hand snatched at his ankle. The little boy! A gargoyle! With claws to fetter him. He pushed the child aside and bulldozed on. A grunt. The sow. He stumbled across the beast and crashed into the door.

Her chant now caught him like tentacles, soft and alluring, drawing him back into the circle, into her power, promising eternal suspension in the full awareness of life's futility. No, no, he did not want it. He wanted to savor it all, the life, the real life, the mortal life, the life without old hang-ups she had cured, a life without the pain in his liver, a mortal life, but useful, healthy and unencumbered by the complexes accumulated in his youth. She had cured him of so much. He now felt strong, physically and mentally and ready to face the future. But he must get out.

He hoisted the pole from its tiepins and dropped it on the floor. He was grappling with the latch when a tidal wave of fear swept over him like a freak breaker on the beach. What waited for him outside? What would he find? A yawning abyss? A flaming inferno? A nothing-go-nowhere space? Would he be condemned, like some figure in Greek mythology, to perform a useless task—forever?

Fool! He cried, you are safe inside, why tamper with the unknown? Stay safe. Stay inside. Return, relax, let timelessness take care of you.

But the outside was his chance, his only chance, his chance to redress his self. Fear choked him, her chant lured him, Xochitl's outstretched arms promised him. Everything swaddled his will power. Indecision! His greatest defect and again it would stifle him at the very door of freedom. But what was beyond that door? Anguished, he pressed his eyes to the planks and squinted. The wood was solid, without cracks. Energy leaked from him like a sieve and he knew soon he would be adrift again in oblivion, soon.

He punched the latch upward and yanked the door open.

The cold night slapped his cheeks the way his father slapped him in front of the girls when he found him walking home from the beach, one girl on each arm. He was sixteen years old. The shame.

He stumbled over the threshold and out into the night, leaving the heavy door ajar. The fresh air, gulped greedily, made his head swim. Above a pale moon was as intrusive as a spotlight. White cushions drifted in a velvety sky, their hems aglow by moonbeams. Below, dots in the distance, the lights of Utla blinked.

Encouraged he took a step forward and walked into her net. His arms shot out mechanically to protect himself but met no resistance. The net had gone. He turned. The net was outlined against the sky above the cabin, its extremities braided with pearl strings in colors he had never seen. From the roof of the cabin, glittering purplish, the net cascaded to his feet and he stepped back mechanically to escape its snare.

And then Thad suddenly was by his side, pale, unreal, ponderous, stroking his chin while gazing down into the valley.

"Which way do we go, Thad?"

Thad massaged his chin and squinted. "You really want to go down?" he asked, gravely.

"Of course! You remember the way?"

Thad smiled: "I'd say it's to the left," he muttered.

Serge hesitated. Left? It meant heading away from the town lights. The wind bit through his denim jacket and he saw Maria Sabina's net casting for him.

"Let's go," he said, urgently.

A hundred paces down the track a ghostly structure loomed out of the night. Serge stopped. The structure was faintly familiar. Of course, it was the poultry shed they had passed on the way up. Thank Heaven they were on the right track.

"Good old Thad" he cried. "You're the guide. I knew it."

And suddenly he bounded down the mountain in giant leaps, possessed by an astonishing confidence, acting as if the earth had lost its gravity. "I'm the pilot," he shouted. "Thad's the guide and the past-in-the-net is our burden. You see, it's the trinity of human life: A guide, a captain and a burden. Oh, Thad, I can fly, just look at me!"

He bounced ahead, the track his trampoline, turning bends, clipping corners, racing down the mountain, feeling buoyant on a deluge of wondrous elation.

All of a sudden the track ran into a wall of darkness. Fear and doubt, banished in the heady flight, returned as quickly as the two had vanished. He realized then fear had followed him down and behind it, latticed, wafting gently, beckoning in psychedelic colors, came Maria Sabina's net and from inside its jeweled webbing the hideously grinning visage of the

Curandera.

"Where do we go Thad?" he blurted.

Thad stroked his chin, head cocked to one side, his gentle eyes fastened on the darkness.

"Come on, Thad, you're the guide."

"I'd say it's straight ahead."

Without hesitation, blindly, Serge barged into the wall, bracing himself for the collision. But the wall lifted, the mask vanished, so did the net. He was back on the track. A breeze fanned his flushed face. His chest expanded.

"You know," he bellowed over his shoulder. "That wicked old lady is still trying to trap me, still placing obstacles on my road. But she can't get me back."

He ran, feet hardly touching ground, a spring in his ankles, a power in his muscles, a freshness in his lungs, jaw set, eyes aglow. And so he rounded the bend and faced a cluster of huts sprinkled along the track.

From below stilted floors a pack of dogs darted, yapping, fangs bared, hair bristling, tails out like rudders. The half-moon enlarged their taut bodies and snapping fangs. Serge chuckled and without checking his stride he threw out one arm in an imperial gesture signaling: Halt.

The pack stopped, one dog gave a final half defiant yawl, then all the dogs wheeled and tails tucked between their hind legs slunk away, heads half-turned to keep one eye on this madman. From below the huts the dogs whined softly once or twice, as if in a nightmare then kept quiet.

Serge flung out his arms and shouted: "Nothing can stop us!"

He was running ahead again when a jagged crack across the track gaped at him like an old and toothless mouth. He knelt down to examine its edges and peer down into the dark but saw only darkness, a gaping bottomless darkness. Nervous, he walked along the crack which severed the track like the cut made by a serrated machete. No way into Utla. Leaden numbness permeated his body, his respiration slowed, became painful. Already her jeweled net was catching up. Perhaps his escape had only been an illusion? This flashed through his mind and with it came the bitter thought he might be the jackass of her game.

"Which way, Thad?"

Thad smiled.

Serge gazed at the crack to which Thad had pointed "But man, it's …" he began but checked himself. Faith, he thought, faith.

"Thad! Perseverance is the essence of a successful existence, don't you think? Alright, smile, but what is the good of talent if you don't persevere with it? It's like having a gold mine and not exploiting it. It's like getting down this bloody mountain in the middle of the night. If you set your mind to it nothing is impossible. It doesn't matter which way you do it, as long as you do it."

He thought for a moment. Could it be possible they had been condemned to walk around in circles, forever? With the lights of Utla blinking below them, forever? He and Thad would stumble around the mountains forever, stuck between life and death because he had left the net, had escaped his predestined fate. He was a living dead. What was dead anyway? Wasn't it the name the living gave to the incomprehensive phase ending their earthly existence? But couldn't death be a permanent rerun of life, a film being reeled off again and again, a thousand, a million, a billion million times. He was walking through a world of make-believe, a stage created for his own drama with the same props, a stage on which he moved back and forth, leaping obstacles, confronting doubts, plunging into despair only to be raised to dizzy heights of euphoria.

"Thad, we are going around in circles. Did you know?"

Thad smiled.

Of course Thad knew, Thad knew everything, Thad had set the automat that revolved the stage. Thad was the guide.

He stared down at the lights of Utla. "Which way, Thad old man?" he asked listlessly, already knowing there would be no answer this time: "Which way?"

Thad was silent. He could expect no solution from Thad this time. This was part of her game. Humans had assistance all their life; they depended on others, obtained, evaluated or discarded the advice of others. It was the easiest way to move through life, allowing others to do your thinking, allowing others to propel you into action, to show you the way, to point you in this or that direction. Then comes the time when an individual must think for himself, when he comes to a crossroad where he must make his own decision, when no one, not even his best friend can make it for him.

Standing there on the edge of the track, darkness below, the psychedelic lights of the net beckoning above and Thad silent Serge suddenly knew what he must do. A feeling of elation again swept over him. It would be momentous but he had managed it before when he tore open the gate. He would do it again. It required determination and a zest for life. And it required courage. He now possessed them all. He glanced down, just wondering for a moment what lay at the bottom of this dark pit that gaped between him and the life-giving lights of Utla. He must reach the lights. The shortest way between two points is a straight line—basic geometry.

"Let's go!" Serge yelled and leapt over the edge into the abyss.

The air was chilly.

El Tiburon pointed at the pile of papers on Feliciano's desk: "We won't need those anymore, Mayor," he announced.

"Documents always impress people," Feliciano protested.

"Pah! We'll impress the people with deeds not with pieces of paper," the peasant cried, turning to the Axeman and Tonino who both nodded vigorously, sharing the illiterate's scorn for the written word.

Feliciano fidgeted with the papers unhappily. "Shouldn't we at least keep some record?" he pleaded. "Something to remind us? It's useful, a kind of proof, you see."

"A man's word is more important than a piece of paper," El Tiburon said. "A man's word comes straight from his mouth. It can be heard by everyone. But you can write anything on a piece of paper and no one will ever know if it's true."

Feliciano sighed. "As you wish," he said.

The conversation was interrupted by a booming noise outside which gradually grew to a deafening crescendo. The men jumped up. "What's that?" Ubaldo cried. Everyone ran from Feliciano's office into the street where a market woman screeched: "An earthquake!"

The cry was picked up and repeated like an echo across town. "An earthquake, an earthquake … Santisima Virgencita, an earthquake!"

The metal bird swooped down on them quite suddenly, flying just above rooftop level, leaving in its slipstream a cloud of dust and leaves.

"An aeroplane! An aeroplane!" Ubaldo shouted, pointing, while the rest of the people ducked or guffawed at the sky where the plane was vanishing towards the south, over the ridge of the mountain comb, followed by its trail of dust along the ground.

"So that's an airplane," Feliciano mumbled, reverently, gazing after the cumbersome flying object which now banked sharply, described a wide arc and accelerated back along its original route, single engine howling as it approached, its double-decker wings rapidly spreading in size, the whirring propeller sketching a transparent oval wheel into the morning air.

"It's coming back" Ubaldo screeched, leaping up and down with glee. El Tiburon stood in the middle of the road, legs apart. "Just like a dragonfly," he observed, then ducked with the rest of the people as the plane roared overhead. Printed on the bottom of both wings was the code XJ002" and twin circles in red and blue on the tail tip. Several people later remembered seeing a man in the cockpit point a metal pipe at them. How could they know that from the blown-up photos the photographer took, Diego the Jailer later positively identified El Tiburon and Tonino as two of his former inmates while Horacio recognized Feliciano as the Mayor of Utla standing beside them.

These identifications would suffice for the military to launch 'Operation Hunchback.'

"I wonder why it flew so low?" Feliciano mused later.

"Maybe it spied on us," an old man offered.

"Pah! Why worry," El Tiburon snorted. "What can they do from the air? Let them have a good look. If they bother us we'll shoot them down. In the great peasant revolution our fathers shot down such planes like ducks—bang, bang—just like that." He squinted along an imaginary rifle barrel and everyone laughed.

Back in Feliciano's office however the peasant paced up and down restlessly, pulling at his nose the way he always did when something puzzled him.

"What are we going to do about money?" Feliciano interrupted El

Tiburon's pacing. "We have very little and we need more for the Market. People want money for their goods."

The question jolted El Tiburon from his thoughts: "Let them give goods in exchange for goods," he grumbled. "The way our fathers did. It was always a good system, better than paper money."

Feliciano looked down on his table top. "It's complicated," he said.

"Maybe we need our own store system," El Tiburon went on. "But not like the Haciendas, chalking up goods against a man's harvest. It's a thieves' system. The Haciendaros make their own prices and our debt is always larger than our income from the harvest. What we buy from the Haciendaros is three, four times more expensive than the price the Haciendero paid in the city shop. No, my friends, we will run a fair system with one central store and honest prices. It can be run by the municipality, with fair prices for everybody. That way we will never need money."

He slammed his fist on Feliciano's desk. "I hate money, it's dirty, it's useless and it stinks."

"But then we need someone to do the paperwork," Feliciano added hastily: "To keep the credit and debit in order."

"Bueno! You're so keen on paperwork. You do it."

"But I still think we need some kind of money," Feliciano insisted.

"Oh let's not worry about that now, if we really need some we can make our own. The government does it, why can't we? You get a piece of paper and scribble on it and then you put someone's picture over it, maybe Teodimo's picture. Ola, and there you have your money."

"Great idea, Jefe," Ubaldo cried enthusiastically and Feliciano whose orderly mind could not quite cope with such a momentous task was about to protest when he was cut short by the entry of a man who, trotting uneasily from one leg to the other, sombrero in hand, tried to catch El Tiburon's eye.

"Jefe!" he said at last with a note of subservience peasants' reserve for the Patron. "Can I bother you for a moment?"

El Tiburon, embarrassed, patted the man amiably on the back: "Listen hombre," he said. "The days of the Patron are over. You don't have to take your hat off for me. I'm one of you, understand?"

The man glanced around the room and when he saw that everyone smiled and wore their hats he slowly set his own hat back on his head and stuck his hands in his pocket. "We've found a man in the haystack," he blabbered. "A strange type who keeps calling me 'brother'."

"What was he doing in the haystack?"

The campesino shrugged his shoulders and made a face. "Search me, Jefe, wouldn't have seen him but for Eduardo, my boy, who saw his legs dangling out. Either dead or asleep I thought, only one way to find out. So I gets the pitchfork, Jefe, and pokes him in the leg. Oh he was alive alright. Young fellow, tall and a bit mad looking. If you ask me one of them hongeros, a little bit too much Si-tho, you know."

The man winked and tapped his forehead. "But we brought him along anyway, thinking maybe he is one of them, you know, the ones you told us to keep an eye out for. He's outside if you want to look at him."

"Good, bring the bird in," El Tiburon shouted, winking to the others.

"Sure Jefe. Eduardo, bring him in."

Outside, Eduardo, convinced he had caught an enemy of the Revolution, gave Serge a violent push that sent him stumbling into the office of the Mayor of Utla.

"Amigo!" El Tiburon exclaimed. "Where have you been?"

"José! Bloody hell! I must be back among the living."

El Tiburon slapped his thigh. "Haha, don't tell me you've been with the dead?"

Everyone laughed, even the peasant and his son who really didn't know what it was all about. El Tiburon wrapped Serge in a bear hug, then turned to Feliciano. "That's my good amigo, Serge, a true friend of the Revolution, even though he is only a gringo."

Feliciano wrinkled his brows. The true friend's face was not unfamiliar.

"So where've you been, gringo?" El Tiburon demanded.

Serge looked at him for a moment. He didn't seem the same José he knew not so long ago but then was he the same Serge Dunlov? He sighed and heard El Tiburon repeat the question.

"To see the truth, José, to see the truth," he said softly, quite unaware how the men exchanged glances and winked at each other.

"Sit down, hombre," El Tiburon said, guiding him to a sofa. "Your head will soon be your own again. Ubaldo fetch our amigo a cup of hot coffee and some tamales."

Just then everyone's attention was caught by the Axeman who dragged into the room, by the scruff of his neck, a spidery young man with a tapered skull and a narrow slit of a mouth.

"Move you little worm," the Axeman demanded, propelling his victim towards El Tiburon who frowned. "I've told you before," the peasant snapped. "I don't want anyone manhandled. We are not the police and we are not the army. Now what's the trouble?"

"Caught him red-handed on the northern road," the Axeman cried triumphantly, ignoring the rebuke: "And when I asks him 'where you going my good lad ' he has the cheek to tell me, 'Down to Wednesday Market in Teotitlan'. By the cloak of Huetzin says I, our first rat."

"Take it easy," El Tiburon said, giving the Axeman a withering look. The captured young man licked his lips and looked down at his huaraches.

"We always go to the market," he muttered: "My father went before he died. I've gone since I remember. It just didn't feel the same, not going I mean."

"Hombre!" El Tiburon cried, and they could tell he was trying to stay calm. "Thank Chicun Nanda this man stopped you because I tell you, as one that knows, if you go down there now you'd be in jail in a tiff and maybe for years. Don't you understand we are at war with those down there?"

"I've done nothing," the man moaned.

"You don't need to do anything!" El Tiburon's voice now rose to a bellow. "They'll just put you behind bars because they don't like your face or because they don't like where you came from, or because they want to bleed your family for money, understand, hombre? They put me in jail because I told my village to vote for the man with the Long Nose."

"They didn't mind my face before," the man insisted stubbornly. "And I've been down to Teotitlan since I could reach my Mamma's skirts."

Everyone looked down, bracing themselves for the thunder, but El Tiburon only nibbled at his lips. "You really want to go down?"

"I do," the young man breathed, averting his gaze.

"Then go."

The young man looked up, astonished.

"No!" the Axeman protested. "He'll talk."

"I can't stop him doing what he wants. We are free now. It's his choice."

"No, I'll beat his stupid head to a pulp if he leaves," the Axeman yelled. "I'll skin the little ..."

"You'll do nothing of the sort, Antonio," El Tiburon thundered, facing his old jail mate squarely. "Because I did not start this to become another big-headed Don-Something ordering people to do what I want. We can convince them about right and wrong but if they refuse to do what we want then we must let them have their way. And I want no more arguments. Understood?"

"I'll convince him," the Axeman muttered under his breath as the young man made a cautious detour to reach the door. Then, more loudly, he added: "You'll get us all killed, José, with your easy ways."

"Better to die for what you believe than to live as a bully to others," the peasant replied.

"Power has made you soft," the Axeman spat just before he slammed the door shut. Outside they could hear him savagely kick a crate.

After a few moments Ubaldo tried to ease the tension. "Oh, I forgot," he said cheerfully. "The tractor on the Rancho de los Rios has broken down."

"Well get the mechanic to fix it," El Tiburon snapped.

"He lives in Teotitlan."

"Great!" El Tiburon said.

For a while there was only the sound of Feliciano shoveling paper from one side of his desk to the other. Serge sat, his head tilted to one side, in a state of stupor.

El Tiburon paced up and down, pressing his hands together till the knuckles cracked. "Why do we need tractors anyway," he said, barely audible. "We can go back to mules and oxen, like our fathers. We produce too much already. We can easily do with less. We don't need to sell, we grow enough for ourselves." He raised his voice. "Why do we always want more, I ask you?"

No one answered.

A hesitant rap came from the door.

"Come in," Feliciano shouted eagerly, relieved by the interruption.

Two bulging eyes and a fluffy moustache peered into the room: "We are not disturbing, Señor?"

Feliciano rose from behind his desk, straightened his vest and held out his hand to greet the new arrival, a gangly youth with a virgin growth of a beard that failed to hide the scars left by chicken pox. He was dressed in his best pantalones and shirt, hair plastered down on both sides. Timidly behind him followed a plump maiden with plaits thick as ropes.

"Ah, yes," Feliciano said turning to the men in the room: "This is Jesus Gomez from the Rancho de las Joyas. And his fiancé, Señorita, ah, I've forgotten your name."

"Juanita," the girl said, giggling bashfully and hiding behind her fiancé. "Juanita Maria Perez de Sanchez at your service, Señor."

"Right, Juanita Maria Perez," Feliciano repeated. "You two want to get married, am I right?"

The couple nodded eagerly. The girl blushed and lowered her head coyly. Yet her lively eyes flashed from left to right like two marbles rolling in a cup.

"Caramba!" El Tiburon shouted. "The first marriage of the Revolution. Let me be the first to congratulate you."

He held out his hand and the surprised youth took it, rather limply. The girl snuggled deeper against her fiancé's back and stared at the floor.

"Bueno!" Feliciano said, rubbing his palms together briskly as if he was trying to kindle a fire. "We're all set then. Plenty of witnesses, we'll do it right now, alright?"

The young man fidgeted. It seemed he wanted to say something but could not formulate the words. Everyone waited patiently, their smiles oozing benevolence and encouragement. This only seemed to make him more nervous. Finally the girl gave him a nudge, hard enough to make him stumble forward.

"She's only sixteen," he blurted, then using the momentum of his own courage. "Her father won't agree." He dabbed his forehead with a sleeve. The girl had almost disappeared behind his back.

"I see," Feliciano said, rubbing his palms together again, slowly this time. "The law specifies that she has to be eighteen before she can marry without her parents' consent, you know that?"

The couple nodded, heads lowered.

"What law?" El Tiburon asked.

"The law of the Republic, of course," Feliciano said.

"Pah! The Revolution does not recognize the laws of the Republic. They stink. They have always stunk. We make our own laws."

El Tiburon pivoted to face the men in the room: "You agree?"

Everyone nodded.

"Good," he went on. "Then the new law allows anyone to marry at the age of sixteen. If you agree say 'yes' and it is the law."

"Yes!" Everyone chorused but the one that said it loudest was Jesus.

"Go ahead," El Tiburon said, beckoning Feliciano to carry on with the ceremony.

"Well, come up to the desk then. That's it. Hold each other by the hand. Now we can start."

"Señor!" The girl's voice was very small and everyone held their breath, surprised she had interrupted—except Jesus who looked straight ahead as if he had expected it.

"What is it, Señorita?" Feliciano asked in his best avuncular manner.

"Do we still get the document?"

Feliciano looked at El Tiburon.

"What document?" El Tiburon asked.

"Well, it's the document that comes with the marriage," Feliciano explained. "The document on which their names are written, with the seal of the Republic. It makes it legal, see."

"Pah! Who needs a document?" El Tiburon said with disdain. "It is not going to make you any happier having a document. It is not going to make you love each other more, is it? And your children won't be healthier or happier because you have a document, will they?"

Jesus wriggled his neck uncomfortably. "But, but, everyone gets a document," he piped and his fiancé nodded fervently.

"Because it is a silly habit, it only gives more power to the Republic. Tell me what does the Republic have to do with people loving each other? Tell me. Nothing! If two people want to marry when they feel like it why do they have to get a document from the Republic? Damn the Republic, it only wants to interfere in everything we do or want to do, even people's feelings for each other. Go ahead, Feliciano!"

The Mayor foraged in his desk drawers. He emerged with a tattered brown card on which he had written the text of the wedding vow. "Do you …" he began.

"Señor!" Jesus interrupted. "Everybody gets the document. My father received it and his father before him—and it hangs over the mantelpiece so everyone can see it."

He fidgeted with his sleeve. "I'd rather have one, if you don't mind."

"Rubbish!" El Tiburon barked. "We are living in new times. We do not need those useless papers."

Jesus kept stepping from one foot to the other. He tucked at his virgin moustache. "Her father won't accept the marriage unless I can show him the document," he complained. The girl nodded vigorously. Her finger drew strange patterns on her fiancé's back.

"Pah!" El Tiburon exclaimed, but it was obvious he was not so sure any more.

"If I may suggest," Serge interrupted, having almost recovered from his psychedelic stupor. "Couldn't you design your own certificate, issued by the Revolutionary Forces? It would be just as valid."

"Brilliant! Always the bright boy," El Tiburon applauded. "Let's draw one up."

Everyone in the room, except the couple, was instantly inflamed by the idea and Feliciano rummaged through his drawers in search of a piece of paper.

"Señor," the girl said, but she had to repeat herself before anyone took notice.

"What is it, Señorita?" Feliciano asked, his hands still inside the drawer.

She was sketching imaginary figures on the back of her fiancé's shirt again. "It must have the red mark on the top right-hand corner my father says, or it's no good." She lowered her head when everyone gaped at her.

"Oh, no!" Ubaldo cried.

"It's the only way for us to tell whether it's good," Jesus whined. "We can't read."

"What's this damn red mark then," El Tiburon demanded roughly.

"It's the stamp of the Republic," Feliciano replied nervously shoveling papers on his desk.

"Can we copy it?" Tonino asked hopefully.

"It's got to be the real one," the girl answered quickly before anyone had a chance to give an opinion.

"Well, that's it," Feliciano said in his most officious manner. "No wedding, sorry."

The young couple glanced at each other quickly and then the girl, her eyes demurely downcast, nudged her fiancé once, twice, until he pulled at his moustache quite frantically. Everyone waited. A last rude nudge loosened the young man's tongue. "We … we …" he stammered: "We have to get married."

After the embarrassing silence that followed El Tiburon kicked the desk with the tip of his boot. He chewed his lips, gave the desk another kick, then snapped: "Give it to them."

The couple looked at each other quickly, then at the floor.

Later that day during the Siesta hour El Tiburon and Serge strolled through the empty streets of Utla. The coffee had miraculously restored much of Serge's mental equilibrium, tearing apart the cobwebs and destroying the rainbow flashbacks. From the moment he woke up on the haystack, prodded by the pitchfork, one part of him had returned to reality the other had remained trapped inside the purple net which still appeared and vanished sporadically.

At times he would see the world around him through a frosty window, at times through an immaculate crystal. He had lingered in this twilight zone until the coffee tipped the balance in favor of reality. Now he found his mind amazingly agile, the thoughts clear and sharp, his body as if cleansed, his blood pumping as it had not for a long time; his liver no longer throbbing as it did periodically since the soldier rifle-butted him on the Square of Tlatelolco, blows that caused a bout of hepatitis. He was even urinating clearer and having been confronted with his hang-ups under the spell of the mushroom he knew his complexes would no longer bother him.

More amazing still, he no longer had the desire to chase Haberstone who apparently roamed the mountains determined to remain lost. The man had obviously dropped out. He deserved to be left alone. Maybe he felt ashamed, just like the Orlando brothers in Brazil, the great explorers of the Amazon, who contacted new tribes only to see them die of the common cold, chicken pox and venereal diseases carried to them by white settlers. Haberstone too must have realized by publicizing the mushroom cult he had brought disaster to the Mazatec Indians and had doomed their culture.

He must leave Haberstone alone. This was a small price to pay for what she had done to cure him. Sure, Santomoro would yell blue murder and would make sarcastic remarks about Dunlov being a flop. But Serge didn't care. Not now.

More surprising even was the message from Thad, sent to him via a young Indio. Thad wrote he was fine and would be staying on in the Sierra. He had never been happier in his life. Serge understood. Thad, a veteran of the Vietnam War, had wandered the world in search of a hideaway. He had obviously found it. He wondered if Thad had jumped when he jumped. He doubted it. Thad would have gone back to the cabin or sat down. He would have come down the mountain in daylight. Whatever, he was convinced Thad had found a place to live.

And then there was El Tiburon and his Revolution. What a surprise. José had really done it, with one rifle and a couple of illiterate peasants he had taken over an entire mountain region. What a man. But now his revolution was facing its first test.

"It will take some time, José, before people forget their old habits," he said, almost mechanically as if his mind, working independently, had already formulated the phrase before he was conscious of it. Somehow the two, mind and consciousness, were still not properly synchronized.

"Pah!" El Tiburon snorted. "By the way they behave you think nothing has happened. I bring them freedom and all they worry about are foolish documents, glass windows, the supply of nails and how to mend their ploughshares and machines. Our fathers managed without all this muck. We had our own smithies, we had oxen to draw carts and nobody complained about machines. Everyone has become soft. This modern life of buying more and more has corrupted them. They are the slaves of the buy-buy-buy madness. I am beginning to wonder if they want to be free."

"José it's difficult to turn back the wheel of time, in fact it's impossible.

You have to live with the changes. Once people have been used to comforts they hate to do without them. Everyone expects an easier existence from a revolution not a more difficult one. You are not the first to face those problems and you won't be the last. This is a tough road, amigo. People's enthusiasm for a cause can fade terribly fast if life becomes too harsh. When that happens they are prepared to call on the very devil to save them or the leaders of the revolution have to use force to make people accept their ideas. Are you prepared to use force against your own people?"

"Pah! My people are different. We've suffered too long. We'll find a way. We'll use wood instead of iron and cloth instead of glass, our muscles instead of machines. What's wrong with that?"

Serge grinned: "Nothing, if you can educate people to accept your way. But I personally believe at least one generation has to be sacrificed to bring about fundamental changes in any society. Even then you have to isolate your new society from the rest of the world to stop them from being corrupted. But this isolation is more and more difficult in our modern world."

"I don't know what you are talking about," El Tiburon replied impatiently. "All I know is this: We have to make a start."

"José, making a start is not difficult it's like walking from Utla to the Capital. You say you do it and off you go. The interesting part is how far you get—to Tehuacan? To Oxaca? All the way? It's a long hard road."

El Tiburon smacked his thigh. "Hombre, your problem is that you know the road too well, so you never walk because you know about the distance and the hardships and that makes you tired from the start. But we don't know the road, so we start off in ignorance. We are like children who don't know what awaits them. Do you see the difference?"

Laughing, Serge slung an arm around the peasant's shoulders. "I wish I had your logic sometimes, José," he cried.

"What is this word 'logic?' If you're saying we are all different I agree because we are made by the life around us and that's why you and I think in different ways. Anyway, are you staying or are you leaving?"

"José, my friend, I have to get back to work or I'll be out of work. I am leaving this afternoon. I'll walk back to Teotitlan and then hopefully hitch a ride. My friend Thad is staying on. He has found some like-minded people up in the mountains and wants to move in with them. I think he has become converted to the mushroom cult. But you and I will see each other again. I want to come back. I want to keep an eye on your revolution. I feel like a member of the family now. One last advise, amigo: Try to keep it peaceful if you can."

"You must come back soon," El Tiburon said. "I'll miss chatting with you. There is so much I have to learn. And time is running short."

Three days later the air-raid was launched at 00.03 EST, precisely three minutes behind schedule. The wallop and the shock waves from Big Bertha shattered every window around the Square and folded the Market stands like a deck of cards. A sheet of flame shot up at the back of the Municipal Hall and licked across the facade of the old church. The bomb, aimed at the Hall, had dropped into the alley behind, only half a block short of the Square where Utla had celebrated the Coming of the Revolution. Huetzin Oliveira and Sarita Gonzalez, kissing furtively in the alley, were caught in the epicenter of the explosion. All they found of the couple later was Huetzin's left shoe and Sarita's turquoise ring, a present from Huetzin on her 15th birthday. Sarita's little sister, Alma, sent as chaperon, had been determined to carry out her mother's orders to stay close to the couple. She had both her legs torn off above the knees and mercifully fainted before the flames carbonized her.

The town had been asleep and nobody heard the approach of XJ002 until it was too late. The biplane came in at a higher altitude than during the reconnaissance mission a few days earlier. It headed for the target at minimum speed. The hatch above the fuselage was open and two men, each secured by a safety harness, laboriously rolled the bomb towards the exit. It was a fairly haphazard way of aiming a bomb even though the target was close. Once the bomb had been pushed out of the hatch XJ002 continued south and then banked gently to port.

By that time people had rushed out of their homes and someone shrilly shouted: "It's coming back ... it's coming back!" In the panic everyone ran towards the nearest wall, a useless shelter. El Tiburon had rushed onto the balcony of the municipal hall where he raised his arms and yelled: "Be calm! Be calm!" But no one paid him heed and he soon had to evacuate the balcony when flames began to engulf it. A few mothers, squawking, chased their children and some of the men impotently waved their fists as the plane picked up speed on its second run at the target. In the wild rush for safety four people were left injured in the Square and Manito Suarez, an old man with an arthritic leg, fell and people trampled him senseless. A little boy and his sister, holding each other by the hands, ran weeping towards the burning Municipal Hall which seemed to them the only open space. Behind them, long skirts flying, their mother ran wailing their names. Just then there was a loud crash and the back wall of the Hall collapsed. The two children, scared, stopped in their tracks. Their mother pounced on them covering them with her body, throwing herself onto the ground in the Square as the biplane zeroed in on its target.

On the balcony of the Garrison the Axeman raised the barrel of the M14 and squinted along the sites until the fuselage of the plane appeared. He could see the two men in harnesses pushing a metal cylinder towards the open hatch, their heads turned towards the cockpit awaiting the order 'drop.' The Axeman clicked the firing mechanism to 'automatic' and squeezed the trigger. The gun jumped in his hand and the first round went wild. He released the trigger and steadied the barrel on the railing. He aimed at the two men holding the cylinder at the edge of the hatch and fired as one of them bend down to give the bomb its final shove. One of the Axeman's bullets knocked the man back into the cabin. His companion turned and hesitated. It proved fatal. He was hit below the knee, lost his balance, grasped at the hatch handle, missed it and tumbled, arms rowing, into the open where he dangled, suspended by his harness, below the belly of the plane. XJ002 wobbled for an instance and then the cylinder slowly rolled back into the cabin.

The Axeman kept firing, aware he was scoring hits. Suddenly the biplane's engine missed a beat, regained its hum, coughed, spluttered, hung motionless in the air for a moment, dipped to port and plunged to earth just beyond Utla on a maize field. A dull explosion and a billowing orange column of smoke marked the impact. Black smoke belched and a flame speared into the sky.

"Ole! Got the bitch! Got her good and proper!" The Axeman cried from the Garrison balcony, waving his gun above his head. But nobody listened. Everyone was running towards the crash site.

At the far end of the clearing, where the mule track emerges from a cluster of trees, the lower branches of a silver fir had quivered long enough for the keen eyes of Ubaldo to perceive the movement.

"Look!"

"Psht!"

A multiped advanced with grim determination over a bare ankle and a hand slapped at it, drawing a track of chlorophyll ink.

"Psht! Idiot!"

The man below the silver fir at the end of the clearing wore a helmet, camouflaged battle fatigues and ankle boots. A sapper's green knapsack rode on his back. In his hand he held a rifle and his neck craned forward like that of a fox before he leaves the lair. He scanned the clearing with meticulous care. His gaze traveled along the thorn-bushes at the fringe, the two oaks at the northern end, the scattered boulders and tufts of high grass and the lone bull-reeds in the center. He took his time like a man who takes care in his job.

"Only one?"

"Psht"

The Scout stepped two paces forward and dropped to one knee. The gun in his arms rotated with the tip of his nose; the muzzle rested on a small cone-shaped boulder near the edge of the clearing. The Scout dropped the gun and raised the pair of binoculars dangling from his neck by a leather lace. The eerie silence in the clearing obviously made him uneasy. Even the birds had ceased chatting. He re-examined the large boulder at the far end then beckoned over his shoulder. A second soldier burst from the trees, ran a few steps, dropped to one knee and aimed his weapon across the clearing at the large boulder.

Behind the boulder Ubaldo whispered. "Suspicious, aren't they?" He was kneeling on a patch of wet moss still glistening with morning dew.

"Quiet!" El Tiburon warned, watching the reconnaissance Squad form an inverted wedge with practiced precision, each man dashing from the trees to his predestined position. The last to emerge, jaunty and unharmed, was the youth with the tapered skull who had been so eager to reach Teotitlan for the Wednesday Market.

"Santo Dios!" the Axeman exclaimed: "It's Norberto, the little rat."

An excited murmur rippled along the row of men stretched on their bellies behind the boulder. The Axeman spat a load of spittle towards the indicated villain: "Bloody traitor," he hissed and raised his rifle until Norberto's chest appeared in its sights. "Son of a puta," he murmured, tightening his trigger finger. "Now let's see how tight your bowels are."

"No!" El Tiburon slapped the barrel down. Its clang, as it struck rock, caught the attention of the Scout standing with his back to them about 40 paces away. The man wheeled, gun at the ready.

"Did you hear that, Picho?" he called to the nearest soldier.

"Didn't hear a thing," the man replied nervously.

"Chinga la madre!" the Scout cursed: "Go and have a look, Picho. We'll cover you."

He dropped to one knee and aimed his gun at the boulder. The rest of the Squad did the same.

El Tiburon and his fifteen men hugged their guns to their bellies and waited as the scout approached. Some of the men began to perspire, others trembled, some with fear, others with anticipation.

The soldier advanced stealthily, step by step, the leather boots squeaking a little on the grass. His breath came in short agitated gasps and they could hear him mumbling: "Virgincita, five big ones if you protect me. Santa Maria who art in Heaven …"

The Axeman, squinting through a crevasse, thought it best to plug the soldier before he walked right on top of them. Without undue haste he inched the M14 into position, making sure the barrel would not protrude on the other side.

Just then the soldier halted. "It's alright!" he said, almost to himself, then louder. "It's alright!" Then yelling with full voice across the clearing. "There's nobody here, nobody at all."

The Scout lowered his gun and sat down. He pulled a packet of

Raleighs from his breast-pocket and struck a match on the heel of his boot. He sucked the smoke greedily, watching the rest of the regiment from the Olympic Battalion spill from the woods, one man behind the other, Indian file, at the regulation distance of two arm lengths, the guns cradled crossways. Meandering along the track the troops resembled a bristling caterpillar. They were the best in the Republic and the scout was proud to be one of them. He dragged on his cigarette and whistled softly.

Behind the boulder Ubaldo's eyeballs turned up. "Santo Isidoro!" he moaned: "At least one hundred, like ants on the march, Santo Isidoro."

"Told you, didn't I?" Ernesto whispered from his right flank, unable to hide a note of triumph. "I was right, wasn't I?" Now they could see he had not exaggerated when he brought the news that a large contingent of troops was moving up from Teotitlan. Now they would have to give him credit for the tip-off.

"We'll soon reduce them to a more handy size," the Axeman promised, patting his gun. "And then we quickly show them our tails. We can hit them again at One Hundred Trees, even at Tortilla Point and if we want at …"

"No!"

The men turned towards El Tiburon.

"What do you mean, no?" the Axeman protested.

"It's not necessary," El Tiburon explained. "All they need is to be scared a bit then they'll go away. All they need is a warning that we are serious and intend to defend our new freedom."

The men's eyes lit up, just as they had done when El Tiburon promised them the miracle of their own land. Only the Axeman scowled. "I doubt it," he said bluntly: "They're not carrying all those rifles for the fun of it. Sure they'll run, but just as far as the nearest tree. Then you'll see some fireworks."

The men gazed at El Tiburon in alarm. "Nonsense!" he said. "They are just men like you and me, men who scare, men who don't want to die, men who have families, men who would rather be at home with their wives and children. We'll shoot over their heads. That will scare them away."

"Over their heads!" The Axeman winced, shaking his head. "No, no, José, you're dreaming. We must kill as many as we can and then whoosh—away. Look!" He crawled a bit closer towards El Tiburon and whispered urgently, his usually hooded eyes now wide open. "Look at us, we're just a few. Look at them. And how many bullets do we have? How many do you think they have? Chinga madre, hombre, we have something they don't have: All of us know the country, know every valley, every crag, every hole—and we can move fast and we can hit them when they least expect it, anytime, anywhere—and that's how we'll really frighten them. José, don't you see, we hit and run, like the mosquito, sting, draw blood and run."

"No!" El Tiburon protested shrilly—and the men quickly peered into the clearing to see if he had been heard. But the column below moved on relentlessly. "No! I don't want a war. I don't want more blood, more dying, more running. Caramba! Haven't you learned yet that violence brings more violence? I want to live in peace and work in peace and I want our people to have peace. Killing any of them will only cause more trouble, bring more bombs, bring more troops and cost more blood until the Sierra is afloat in blood. No, enough …"

"But José …"

"No! Shoot over their heads, all of you, understand?"

The men nodded.

"Shit!" the Axeman muttered between gritted teeth. Then he peered through the crevasse at the distant figure of Norberto standing beside the Scout and explaining, with expansive gestures, the terrain ahead of them.

"You lousy little runt," the Axeman muttered and balled his fists.

"Now!" El Tiburon barked and the men fired their weapons, most of them for the first time. El Tiburon fired with eyes closed, the muzzle pointed into the sky. Near him, Eduardo, mouth open, watched in awe as his rifle jerked wildly. Ubaldo propped his rifle against the boulder, buried his face in the soft moss and kept his finger on the trigger until the magazine was empty. Tonino even more cautious, propped the stock between his legs and pointed the muzzle into the sky. The rest fired blindly in all directions, but not into the clearing.

Only the Axeman, eyes wide open fired with cold deliberation. His first volley balled over Norberto and the Scout. The 'traitor', clutching his chest, managed to crawl a few yards, clawing at the ground, then died.

The Scout, mortally wounded, keeled over with the burning cigarette still drooping from his mouth.

The marching column had disintegrated at the first shots. The soldiers sprinted, ducking and weaving, for the closest cover. In a few seconds the clearing was empty, except for a short bow-legged man, surely a son of the North where bowlegs are the heritage of generations of horsemen. He limped towards the woods, hand pressed over a wound in his thigh from one of the Axeman's bullets. He had dropped his rifle, his pack and his helmet and kept glancing over his shoulder. Two of his companions waved from the edge of the wood, shouting encouragement, holding out their hands to pull him to safety. The injured man paused, but seeing the offered hands and hearing the shouts of encouragement he staggered on in great agony. A single shot crackled across the clearing. The wounded soldier fell, one hand still groping for his companions as he died.

The Axeman lowered his rifle behind the boulder. "Paid killers," he said. "The lot of them."

The men stared at him both in awe and fear while he discarded his empty magazine and replaced it with a full one. He ignored El Tiburon who approached with clenched fists. "I ought to kill you," the peasant croaked. The Axeman looked up in surprise.

"Why?" he asked nonchalantly before El Tiburon's fist crashed into his mouth and sent him reeling against the rock. He looked up with the same expression of surprise, the back of his hand wiping the first blood from split lips.'

"You stupid fool," El Tiburon screamed: "You've ruined us all. You just had to know better."

The Axeman, up on one knee, still wiped blood from his mouth. "You're an old woman, José," he said calmly and without rancor.

"Blood-thirsty leech!" El Tiburon ranted and lashed out again. But this time the Axeman saw the punch and threw his head back, so El Tiburon's knuckles only grazed his jaw. "Get out, get out, and don't let me see you again. You are finished, we don't need killers, we don't need you. It's your kind who are the enemies of the people, you and your bloodlust and your machismo which we have carried like a weight on our backs for all times. Go, before I forget myself and put a bullet through your skull."

Without hurry the Axeman raised himself to a crouched position. "It would be best if we all went," he said calmly.

"Go!"

The Axeman shrugged his shoulders. He rubbed his jaw with one hand, turned and quickly crawled off into the bushes. For a while the men listened to the snapping twigs and rustling leaves that marked his retreat.

After he had gone El Tiburon took a deep breath.

"We might have to make a fight of it now," he said.

"But I'm not going to run away, I'll make my stand here. If any of you wish to leave you can do so. I won't blame you."

The men looked at each other and shook their heads. "They've all run away," Tonino said. "So what are we worried about?"

The men visibly perked up. "Sure, they've gone," they cried. "None of them would dare to come back, would they?" Everyone agreed emphatically. Their spirits were on the mend.

"Teodimo!" El Tiburon called to the dwarf who sat quietly with a machete between his legs. "Go back to Utla and find more ammunition at the Garrison. Cases like this, see?" El Tiburon held up his empty magazine. "Go!"

For a moment Teodimo's watery eyes stared miserably at his master. Then obediently he left, crawling through the same bushes the Axeman had used for cover.

The men stood up and peered through the crevasses. The clearing was empty but for the two bodies. To obtain a better view of the woods Tonino scaled the boulder: "I think they are still running back home," he shouted merrily from his lofty lookout before the dum-dum bullet ripped half his head off. He was dead before his body fell across Ubaldo.

At the far end of the clearing, the sharpshooter, astride a fallen fir, patted the telescopic sight on the rump of his rifle: "Got him!" he said and stuck up his thumb. The men nearby gave the thumb-up sign to the First Lieutenant who passed it on to the Major. He barked: "Fire!"

The concentrated bombardment of the boulder lasted ten minutes according to Army records. During that time the 115 men of the Olympic Battalion emptied their magazines four times at the boulder and dispatched twenty-eight mortars at a target which became gradually reduced from its original size of a train carriage to that of a wheel barrow. A cloud of smoke soon enveloped the boulder after the mortar men had zeroed in on the target and fixed their elevations. When the order came, 'Cease Fire!' the boulder's immediate surroundings had been flattened like a pancake. Once the firing ceased a platoon under Sergeant Herrera was ordered to ascertain if there were any survivors

Herrera and his men approached the rear of the boulder taking all the precautions specified in the Army manual. At the sight of the mangled bodies two of the soldiers puked. The majority of the victims had been torn apart many times. "A maniac gone wild with a cleaver" one of the men described the scene later. The remains were afloat in a bloody lake which had turned the green moss red." Some of the soldiers discovered human parts splattered against trees fifteen yards from the boulder. Severed limbs still wrapped in bloodied rags were strewn in a wide arc around the shaved rock. Inside one torso, split open like a melon, an exposed lung still contracted. A disemboweled trunk quivered on a tuft of grass. A pair of reddened hands covered a gaping hole into which the man had tried to stuff his entrails in a last futile attempt to cheat death.

Two men still breathed. One, legless, was dying, the other the Sergeant prodded with his rifle. The survivor had been buried below a heap of bodies hurled across him by the shock waves of the mortar explosions. His face was streaked with blood, his chest peppered with splinters and one leg, askew, was obviously broken. He looked up at the soldier with drowsy eyes. The Sergeant beckoned his men to move some of the bodies under which the survivor had been buried. The soldiers did so reluctantly and with averted faces.

"You've been very lucky," the Sergeant said, poking a finger at the man's chest: "The rest have all been cut to pieces, except one. But he won't last too long."

El Tiburon blinked. His eyes brimmed. The cracked lips moved and the Sergeant bent down to catch the words.

"I was wrong," El Tiburon breathed.

Sergeant Herrera nodded. "Sure you were. Silly thing to do," he said, unaware he had utterly misinterpreted the meaning of the peasant's words.

◆   ◆   ◆

Sometimes, as a small child, José Cabezavaca stuck his nose out of the adobe hut, closed his eyes and inhaled the sweet scent of the lavender. On those rare occasions, when the earth was pregnant with young crops and the air clear of dust, he forgot his miserable life and pretended he stood in one of those magnificent houses, decorated with paintings and murmuring fountains, a house tiled and colonnaded, strung with begonias, bougainvillea and green creepers the way Tata had seen them during his days as a soldier of the Revolution. But when he opened his eyes, after indulging in such pleasant fantasies, he always saw the barren patch of land that ran from his father's hut down the track, and on it, the one lavender bush. And then he would always stamp his foot and close his eyes again. But the vision would not return, hard as he tried to conjure it back.

He opened his eyes now and looked across the Square of Utla. He saw the red banner which announced in bold print: "La Patria Vive." Next to it, one in green, proclaimed: "Progress, Unity and Justice." His tired eyes caught sight of a few market stalls where vendors sold pocket-sized paper flags of the Republic for one peso apiece. Above the vendors' heads fluttered a huge banner with the portrait of the President of the Republic.

"Viva El Presidente," the print underneath said.

Two soldiers, propped against a lamp post, supervised a group of campesinos rebuilding the collapsed back wall of the Municipal Hall. The campesinos had stopped working and stared at El Tiburon.

He had closed his eyes again and tried to recapture the scent of his youth. He saw his father leaning against the heavy hoe, wiping beads of sweat from a face on which the skin stretched tight over the cheekbones. His father glanced across the field and his brows furrowed. "Get on with it," he growled and young José dug on in search of the tiny spuds which might have escaped his father's hoe and his mother's eyes. The sun was hot and he was thirsty. From the track came a peal of laughter. Raising his head he saw young Don Alfonso astride the piebald mare, in white satin breeches and silk shirt, holding the reins loosely in one hand while the other, with the crop, described something to a Señorita mounted sidesaddle on a white stallion. The girl's embroidered white dress fell cape-like over the stirrup, a jet of black hair, caught by a brooch, plunged from beneath a yellow sun-bonnet. Both riders were about his age. He gaped, the trowel in his hand dropped. Never in his life had he seen such a beautiful girl.

"Hoi you, chamuli! What are you gawking at?" Young Don Alfonso called, spurring his horse across the field, followed by the girl. Shocked out of his reverie, young José fell on his knees picked up the trowel and busily dug at the hard earth. The shadow of horse and rider brought a touch of coolness to his furrow.

"What? Not finished yet?" the haughty voice of the landowner's son inquired, imitating the way his father addressed the peasants. "Should have been done last week," he added, turning in the saddle to face the girl. "These chamulis get lazier every day."

José knew his face was flushed by the unjust rebuke and so he dug furiously at the soil.

"Get up when I'm talking to you," young Don Alfonso snapped and José clambered to his feet and whipped off the tattered straw sombrero just as he had seen his father do in front of Don Miguel.

"Well?" the rider asked.

José said nothing just as his father said nothing when Don Miguel confronted him with a similar vague question.

"Lost your voice? Have you, chamuli?" Young Don Alfonso teased. "They don't work, they don't talk, what can you do with people like that?"

The girl urged her mount closer. "What's your name?" She asked gently and to José her voice sounded like the tiny bell Tata had brought back from the Revolution and which, when no one was about, he sometimes rang.

"Well, answer the Señorita, chamuli," Young Don Alfonso prompted, swishing his crop at the peasant boy.

"Leave him be, he's just shy," the girl said and José gratefully looked up into two dark eyes set in a face as white as Mama's tortilla flour. A tiny rouged mouth smiled down at him.

"My name is José—José Cabezavaca," he said, forgetting to lower his gaze.

The girl smiled. "Do you like sweets?" she asked, foraging in a little suede bag suspended from the saddle knob.

"Don't waste your sweets on Peones," Young Don Alfonso said gruffly, visibly irritated by her attention to the boy. "He's so stupid he'd probably seed it."

He cackled at his own joke.

The girl ignored him and leaning down from the horse offered José a caramel wrapped in glistening silver paper. "Take it", she murmured: "It tastes very good."

He hesitated, thinking her sweet face was just like the Madonna over Father Felipe's altar. Then he stepped forward and took the caramel. Their fingers met for a second and his skin prickled at the touch. What soft cool hands she had. "Thank you!" he cried and feeling suddenly gay and reckless he ran to his sisal-bag and extracted a little round spud, still crusted with cloys of soil. He rubbed it clean against his pantalones and offered it. "That's for you," he said and the same sensuous prickling passed through his limbs when their fingers met again.

"Don't take it, you'll only dirty yourself," Don Alfonso warned, but the girl was already stashing the gift into her suede bag, unconcerned it had left dirt stains on her fingers.

"Thank you, that was very kind," she said and smiled. Oh, she smiled so sweetly. José thought Father Felipe's Madonna was rather an old tart compared to this beautiful creature. Annoyed, Young Don Alfonso roughly pulled his horse around. "Get back to work," he ordered. But José, mesmerized, ignored the order.

"Adios, José," the girl called out as she galloped off behind Young Don Alfonso. He waved with his trowel. He kept waving long after she had vanished along the track which leads down to the river.

For years he kept the caramel under his petate, pulling it quietly out at night to sniff the silver paper which she had touched. And each time his skin prickled at the memory of that wonderful moment when he touched the fingers of that young Madonna. Whatever had happened to that caramel? He concentrated but could not remember—and in the effort the vision faded.

El Tiburon opened his eyes and saw their helmets. Across the Square, a priest in black cassock tried to break down the old church door with a hammer and screwdriver. How strange, he thought, that soldiers and priests always arrived together in the Sierra. It had always been that way, since the days of the Spaniards. Next to the Church a green truck from the United Fruit Company was parked. "The vultures are here already," he suddenly shouted and the soldiers looked at each other uneasily.

A bald man in a blue uniform finished hammering a plaque against a door and stood back to survey his handiwork. 'Policia Federale' the plaque read.

El Tiburon sighed. He seemed to have been standing in the Square for a whole lifetime. The splinter wounds in his chest ached. So did his broken leg. The sun was hot and he felt thirsty. Behind the helmets he saw the people. The whole town was present it seemed, heads bowed and silent like schoolboys waiting for the cane. Everyone dutifully held a paper flag of the Republic. A feverish shudder raked his body and he changed the weight from his broken leg. The Square began to rotate slowly and he gritted his teeth. He must not collapse, no, he must not give them that satisfaction.

He closed his eyes and found himself by the river, beside Tata who dangled a short cane in the water and talked in the low monotone the old man used when flipping through the pages of his memories. It was cool under the willow. The water, stagnant in the summer heat, exuded the musty but pleasant smell of wetness. He reclined drowsily against the trunk of the tree, listening to Tata's story. But hard as he tried now he could not hear what the old man was saying. He only knew it was important and he strained to hear, but in vain. Though the old man's lips moved he could not understand a single word.

"Atten … tion!"

El Tiburon opened his eyes and stared across the Square. How long had he been propped up against this wall? The line of soldiers had turned their heads to the right. So he too turned his head in that direction, with some effort, stabbed by pain in his chest. The double doors to the balcony of the Garrison were open and General Plinio Plutarcho Pereira y Sallende stood on the balustrade hitching up his trousers with a quick heave. A short fat man with a swarthy face, the General gazed imperiously down into the Square. Anna Maria stood behind him, bearing the same aloof and vague expression she had worn on that same balcony on the occasion of Lieutenant Garcia's induction.

On the other side of the General stood the man who had given El

Tiburon the rifles in return for the right to build schools and run them. He had probably made a similar deal with the General, El Tiburon figured, only this time he would pay in money not rifles. The peasant bit his lip, what kind of schools would educate the children of the Sierra? Surely they would not teach them about their ancient culture or the ways of the Sierra but it would be the ways of the gringos. He had been a fool and it was only right he should pay for being so stupid, so ignorant, so trusting.

The General's pudgy hands gripped the rail, his paunch pressed through the slats. A hum ran through the crowd and some of the soldiers on the fringes turned nervously and leveled their guns at the nearest citizen. It brought instant silence.

Lieutenant Garcia, resplendent in his tight uniform, marched towards the wall, lifting his knees the way he had learned on the Parade Ground. He had a lot to redeem. He had not only lost the town but had to relinquish Anna Maria to the general. He had volunteered for this current task. It would be his revenge. In his right hand he clutched a red blindfold. In front of El Tiburon he blinked and twisted his neck as if the collar of his jacket was suddenly too tight.

"You want it?" he croaked, licking his lips.

The peasant shook his head.

Turning neatly on his heels the Lieutenant marched back to the wing of the platoon. He drew his saber from its scabbard and held it out at arm's length.

"Squ ... ad Ready!" he yelled then glanced expectantly at the balcony where General Plinio Plutarcho Pereira y Sallende brushed his bushy moustache with one finger, then leisurely held up one arm. The Lieutenant lowered his saber. An excited murmur rippled through the crowd.

A reprieve!

"People of Utla," the General began in a crackling voice that rang across the Square like gravel turning in a metal drum. "La Patria is patient but it is also just." He waited for the applause but none came. "But when it is betrayed it can show no mercy. We are all part of one big family, a family that needs to be united in order to be strong and when members of this great and powerful family resort to murder, rape and pillage and connive with foreign Governments to harm the rest of our great family then it becomes our duty and our right to make an example of them."

He drew himself up to his full height, pushed out his chest and tried to pull in his paunch. One arm pointed dramatically at the figure of El Tiburon against the wall. "People of Utla", he thundered: "So dies a traitor. Proceed Lieutenant!"

"Squ … ad, aim!"

As the soldiers raised their rifles, El Tiburon's brows contracted in a desperate effort to remember. And then, all of a sudden, he could hear his Tata's words very clearly.

"He was the bravest man I ever did see. Ramrod straight he stood there, my boy, chest out, knees and heels pressed together so nobody could say he was trembling. The proud head was up and he looked straight into the faces of the gringos. And just as the bullets were about to fly he roared: "Viva la Revolución!"

El Tiburon's last cry mingled with Lieutenant Garcia's order: "Fiiirrre!"

Once the rolling echo of the volley had faded, Lieutenant Garcia sheathed his saber and walked briskly towards the fallen man who had come to rest on his side, hands tied behind his back, legs drawn up, knees and heels still firmly pressed together. Blood trickled from his mouth and chest but the big soulful eyes were wide open and the cracked lips moved. The Lieutenant pulled his service revolver from its brown holster and pointed the muzzle at the back of the heavy neck. He steadied his right wrist with his left hand and pulled the trigger. After the shot, the body twitched just once.

From the balcony General Plinio Plutarcho Pereira y Sallende waved to the crowd which stood motionless, awkward, heads down. Then the General walked into the committee room, squeezing Anna Maria's backside.

The slopes of Nindo Tokosho were gilded by the sinking autumn sun. On a horizon awash in shades of blue and purple two buzzards circled, gliding on a thermal off the valley. The birds either hunted for a last catch before nightfall or playfully gamboled on a balmy southerly breeze which rustled the leaves of the lemon tree through which the Axeman peered into the

Square.

Four soldiers rolled the body into a grey plastic wrapper.

"I'll make them pay for this, José," the Axeman sobbed, brushing his cheeks clumsily with the back of a heavy paw. "You damn fool!" he suddenly burst out. "You silly bloody ox with your dream and your silly belief they'd let you do it. Now see where it's got you. Just look at yourself!"

He sniveled a bit, all the time watching the body disappear into its wrapper. Then he clasped the M14 so hard, the sinews popped on his neck and arms: "That's the way," he cried, shaking the gun towards the valley. "That's the only way. You had it right in the beginning but then you weakened, didn't you?"

He lowered the rifle slowly and watched the soldiers in the Square carry away the wrapper, one man on each end.

"You were too good for them, José," he muttered, nodding his head. "But I'll give them hell, you'll see."

The soldiers carried the corpse into a shed across the Square, the one the market vendors used to store vegetables and fruit overnight. The Axeman wiped his face with his scarf, then turned abruptly and walked uphill into the mountains. He did not look back once.

Just before dawn, when the soldiers came to bury the body, they found it had been taken from its plastic sheet and laid out in the center of the shed. A posy of white lilies of the vale had been clumsily arranged near the head and a large sombrero, tattered and moldy, was laid at the feet of the dead peasant. Draped across the bloody chest, hugging the body in the way a child hugs its mother, rested the head and arms of a bald dwarf.

The soldiers, by nature superstitious, crossed themselves and hastily buried both corpses in the same hole.

They left no sign to mark the grave.

From his skyscraper office, Serge Dunlov squinted through the haze of pollution under which the monstrous city choked in its mountain-ringed cauldron. On the Avenida Reforma below, a ragged beggar woman cuffed a little girl while a portly tourist pointed a camera at them. Near the Hotel

Reforma, a group of campesinos huddled on the sidewalk. The knotted sheets slung over their shoulders held their few possessions and identified them as rural refugees routed from the land by tractors and machines and destined now for slum life on the periphery of the capital.

Serge loosened his collar and recalled his meeting with the minister a few hours earlier, a meeting he had intended to be an indictment but which turned out to be a graphic example of how easily injustice and brutality can be officially reclassified.

"My dear, dear friend," the Minister had shouted from behind his vast desk. "How glad we are to have you back safe and sound ..."

Before Serge had time to launch his prepared speech, the Minister continued: "I can assure you the situation in Teotitlan will be fully investigated and ..." He had leaned across the desk and winked ... "we did not believe a word of their charge that you and your friend carried marijuana."

The Minister had folded his hands piously and rested his elbows on the mahogany desk. "The Republic is so vast and we are—let's admit it—we are still an underdeveloped nation in many ways, a country that needs time and comprehension and certainly help. And that is why we look to your great nation as a friend and an example."

At one stage the Minister had paused to draw air and Serge had rushed into his little speech, at least a part of it. "Perhaps a fairer treatment of the peasants and a better justice system ... ," he started but the Minister held up his hands. "Come, come now," he said impatiently. "Surely you would not defend anarchy and the kind of violence you have witnessed, with the massacre of Government officials and innocent citizens?"

"There was no massacre!" Serge protested.

"Really?" the Minister asked cynically. "And how would you know? You were not present. Or were you?"

Contemptuously he tossed some photos on the desk. "Take a look!"

The first photo showed the dismembered body of El Agente.

Serge instinctively turned his head away. "If there was more justice such reactions would not happen," he said. But the Minister smiled and with that air of indulgence, a standard expression among politicians, he said: "But let us no longer dwell on these atrocities. You've had a rough time. But in the end good often comes from evil. We have rounded up a score of hippies who will be expelled from the Republic as undesirable aliens. Our army posts are being reinforced and the area is now closed to unauthorized persons. We have caught and punished the rebels. And you, my friend, have had a valuable opportunity to see for yourself the real problems created by drugs. You can write with authority about their detrimental effect not just on the health and minds of young Americans but also on the minds of those simple Indios whose moral backbone is not yet strong enough to resist temptation. As you must have seen for yourself, these people are like children and for the time being we must treat them as such, taking away any toys, so to speak, that could harm them."

When Serge protested that he did not consider the Indios children or their culture toys, the Minister smiled indulgently and glanced at his wrist watch. The heavy wooden door had smoothly clicked shut and Serge was out in the corridor, left with the frustration of one expertly steamrolled without a chance to have his say.

Down in the Avenida dusk approached.

The campesinos looked lost. The haversacks, empty, drooped from their shoulders like flags of distress. He ought to go down and buy them a meal, tell them something about the city, tell them about El Tiburon's rebellion, see if he could help. Yes, he ought to do it, for the sake of the dead, and the living.

Serge sighed. He turned his attention again to the telex message in his hand:

```
Produnlov exsantomoro,
shocked your long absence office and blank
haberstone saga STOP want explanation soonest
STOP fyi opposition agencies quoting government for
successful army shootout with escaped prisoners while
you claiming massacre STOP we prefer adhere official
version STOP both tourist and finance ministry signed
contracts for agency service STOP suggest you file
1000 words speediest for weekender on joint
republic-american anti-narcotics campaign view
republics recent anti-drug successes. Rgds.
```

Serge crumpled the message in his fist and hurled it across the room. No doubt the authorities had already complained and threatened to cancel subscriptions to the agency's service. His story would be judged 'not objective.' In the end it was his version against theirs, the outcome a foregone conclusion.

"Bastards!" he hissed. His eyes checked again the answer he had prepared. He had marked it with codes that made sure it would not go only to Santomoro but around the world.

The message was succinct and a masterpiece of cabelese. It read:

`Prosantomoro exdunlov upstick job uparse. Rgds.`

—

"IN THIS WORLD OF GOOD AND BAD
THE BAD ALWAYS WIN, SOONER OR LATER.
AMIGO, GOOD IS ONLY AN ILLUSION
THAT BAD PEOPLE INVENTED TO HIDE
THEIR BADNESS"

THE AXEMAN

THREE

Farewell Si-tho

FORTY YEARS LATER

The night is still yielding to the dawn. The dew still clings to the cactus leafs in pin-prick pearls the sun will soon gobble up. The other bus passengers are still wrapped in serapes and rebozos. Only their faces peer out, like rabbit heads from warrens. The driver, draped into a dark poncho still yawns, now and then. He might have climbed out of bed a few moments ago and is not quite sure yet if he is driving or dreaming. Most passengers cross themselves after he ignites the engine on the third attempt, mutters something under his breath and crunches the ancient bus into gear.

The chill seeps through my lumber jacket and leaves goose pimples on my skin. And yet within three hours, so I recall from the old days, I will walk about in shirtsleeves. The weather here is still predictable.

The road is still empty, still pockmarked with potholes judging by the bumps we hit, each jolting us out of our seats. Potholes were also everywhere on that morning forty-four years ago when Thad and I headed to Teotitlan, the last part on foot after Thad's superannuated VW camper broke down. This time I will arrive on wheels, not the tired soles of my feet.

I intend to rekindle my memory of that long gone past and find out how it all turned out. This I owe to him—and to my conscience.

Oh yes, before I forget, the cactus desert is still the same, a carpet of pale green plants, three-pronged or single 'up-you' fingers pointing skywards letting everyone know 'we are here forever and you can all get.' No animal large enough to perceive with the naked eye lives here, no poor-man's hovel breaks the spiky monotony; no tree has sunk roots. Alien seeds are swiftly suffocated. The cactus tolerates no immigrants. The hills still roller-coast as far as the eye can see and once the light has chased away the dark the hills vanish into the haze that always hovers over the cactus desert until the sun reaches ten o'clock high.

I sit back in my plastic bus seat, hard as wood and with so little leg room my knees are raised belly high. There is not much to see in this monotonous cactus desert so I have time to contemplate why Latin America has become once again a test tube for the same breed of charlatans I knew back in my young days still barking their timeless promises into receptive ears, spouting populist slogans gift-wrapped in shreds of ideologies borrowed from left and right, stir-fried in the cauldron of materialism and cooled down with fake socialism. After the horror, the persecutions, the mass graves, the bodies tossed into the sea and the institutionalized torture of the Dirty Wars the populists now promote themselves as liberators. All of them claim to be the enemies of globalization, that cunning device by trans-national corporations and financial institutions to gain access to national resources and know-how by pressuring and bribing governments to privatize public property which the corporations can then acquire. While campaigning for votes the populist rabble rousers insist globalization was peddled by the 'capitalists' to a gullible public under the label 'New Deal' when in reality it made the rich richer and the poor poorer. But from experience I know what will happen next: As soon as these liberators with their seductive formulas for social equality are elected they will embrace globalization and privatization whole-heartedly because it will make them also rich. And so, you can be sure, once again peoples' bowls will remain empty.

But sometimes I also wonder if one of those noisy 'populists' might be the real McCoy, the real Savior, the one who will not cheat, the one with the pure heart, a heart like my naive friend El Tiburon.

My journey into the cactus desert and beyond began a few days ago. Sitting again on my beach watching the clouds drift by, a sudden rush of energy gushed through my veins, the kind that bursts through layers of an elderly man's complacency and makes him stow away the golf clubs, fold the fishing rods, cellophane-pack the beach gear and retrieve the backpack from the attic. Invigorated by this sudden rejuvenation (which can whittle away as quickly as it surfaces) I decided to revisit Utla, a place I had not seen in over four decades but had never forgotten though I had traveled all over the planet on assignment covering wars and mayhem. But never had I been as close to a protagonist as I was to El Tiburon. Had anything changed for the better since they executed my friend and dismantled his brave new world? Where the same kind of brutal town officials still in charge of Teotitlan? That nagging question had bothered me for years, the way a sensitive tooth makes itself felt now and then. Only it wasn't my tooth that bothered me, it was my conscience.

On a day when the sea was smooth, the sky a transparent blue I picked up the airplane ticket to Mexico City and then another ticket to Oaxaca City. Four days after walking off the beach still clutching the newspaper page referring to Maria Sabina's passing away I sit in this torture seat aboard the pre-dawn bus to Teotitlan.

The first sight is still the tower of the church of St Michael the Archangel. This time I discover it was a 17th century Franciscan church. I had to laugh because the church façade and the tower wore a brand new coat of gold. Now the gold looks almost real, superior to the mustard color pretending to be gold decades ago.

I squint up at the belfry. No Bartolomo is spying across its railing. Father Ignacio has died years ago. In his will he made it clear he wished to be buried elsewhere. Even in death the parched old priest made sure he would not be part of the cactus desert. His successor informs me of Father Ignacio's 'passing away.' This successor has quick fiery eyes and walks with purpose. He holds his knuckles out regally to be kissed by the peasants. He bows from the waist when he meets the lords of the land.

As a foreigner the new priest deigns to talk to me but not before he mentions the church of St Michael is destitute and donations are welcome.

We stand below the church ceiling painted a pristine Raphael blue. The bright oil paintings of St John, St Mathew, St Luke and St Mark gaze benignly down from the walls. I crumple a piece of paper in my pocket and squeeze it through the slot on the box marked 'oferta.' The priest thinks it's a big bank note and thanks me profusely. He insists, as a way of introduction, that Teotitlan is still in charge of the region beyond the cliffs. But now the road to Utla is paved, all the way. He says this with pride, as if he paved it himself.

Perhaps he figures I might hand over more donations because he becomes loquacious. The crime rate, he says, is high due to the high unemployment rate. Most of the young locals try their fortune as 'wetbacks' crossing the Rio Grande into the USA or as 'rats' crossing the Arizona desert. A few have crossed successfully and found work in California. Their remittances, the priest says with a contrived sigh, keep the town and his church from being overgrown by the cactus desert.

He sighs again when he talks about the Indios. The ignorant unfortunates, so he complains, refuse to take out permits to sell their goods in the market the old El Presidente built in concrete to make it more durable. But then he adds, crossing himself, the Indios are beginning to forsake their old deities and are embracing the one and only true God, his son Jesu Cristo and La Virgine Maria de Guadalupe. This development, the priest explains, crossing himself once more, was something to be grateful for. As for the town it has its Attorney General, its Sheriff and an Agente. A circuit judge still visits periodically to impose fines and pass judgment though serious crimes are moved to the state capital. No, he cannot remember the name Angel or those of the others I offer him from memory. Officials are often transferred to other towns, so he says. No, thank God, the town has never had a scandal about corruption or miscarriage of justice. It's a good town. Yes, yes, those poor wretches in jail are being looked after; no, no, not only by their families but sometimes, when it is possible, when the Lord has sent his spirit and the citizen are generous, the parish sends them food, some clothing and of course his priestly blessings. No, he has no time to hold mess for those poor unfortunate wretches in jail; he has too many souls requiring his attention at St Michael's.

The air is liberating outside. The priest hurries away, cassock swishing, but not before he stresses the trials are fair, the circuit judge a man of honor, the fines just and order must be order 'or where would we all end up?'

No reincarnated Bartolomo slouches on the Zocalo bench. Now there are several benches, all occupied by the unemployed and the unemployable, all busy killing time while waiting for someone to come by and offer them a day's work. The time-killers watch me with calculating eyes as the unemployed are prone to watch a newcomer, a look filled both with hope he might offer them work and apprehension he might be another body competing for a job.

I sit down beside one. He is a youth in his late teens. His name is Jorge, just as my late friend the deer dancer. I coax him into a conversation. His brother is in jail in Tehuacan accused of murdering the son of a Don Pepe. He is serving twenty years for a crime Jorge says he did not commit. Jorge says it is common knowledge Don Peppe's son was killed by a rich rival for the attention of a pretty Señorita. But the police had to find a culprit, so the crime was pinned on his brother, Arnolfo.

"The 'pinche' policeman came to the house and said Arnolfo could be free if we paid ten thousand 'pinche' pesos. We didn't have the 'pinche' money, ah, hombre, so my older brother goes to America. He sends money for a while then he is pinche killed. A pinche accident they said. Bullshit I say. So I goes to pinche America. Crossed the Arizona desert for three days, hombre. Without food or water. Then our pinche guide sells us out to the gringos. That way he gets money from us and he gets money from the pinche gringo cops. So I am sent back here. Had no money to pay another guide so I pinche look for work so I can pay another pinche guide to take me across the desert. So there is no pinche work for me here so my parents are selling the land so we can get Arnolfo out of pinche jail. Then we can both go to America."

I give Jorge a hundred pesos—for his brother. He looks at me as if I am daft. I walk away quickly suddenly aware charity to the unemployed is like adding insult to injury.

On the football pitch four boys in tattered shorts and bare torsos kick up dust and dirt every time one of them connects to an old leather ball, the ones with an inflatable pig's bladder inside. Not a blade of grass, no sign of any green. The town is parched. I talk to an old man leaning on a walking stick watching the boys. How come everything is dry in Teotitlan when just a few miles up the road in the mountains water flows in cascades all year round? The old man looks me up and down as if I was some kind of interplanetary traveler dropped in by accident. "Why don't you ask El Presidente. Ask him what happened to the federal funds for the water pipes?"

The prison is no more than a stone's throw from St Michael's. I had forgotten the girl had to run uphill to reach the church; then she had to run along a dirt patio, tiled today, to reach the church portals. El Agente caught her after she threw herself in front of Father Ignacio begging him in vain to save her, right in front of the altar which today bears Pope John Paul II's slogan: 'Tutus tuus Deus.' Some of the 'u' letters are missing.

A new coat of yellow paint, to match the twin domes of the church, has been dabbed over the iron entrance gates at the jail. Nothing else has changed. The guard on duty sits on a stool picking his nose. His ancient carbine leans against the old brick wall, the same wall built by the Spanish two hundred years ago to house their garrison. The guard is a burly fellow, just like the one I remember. He looks up, curious, a right index finger stuck in his right nostril.

"Warden be here shortly," he says.

The warden comes, eventually. He could have been Diego's clone. He has obviously been asleep in the guard house off the entrance. He is grumpy.

"Who you want to see?" he asks, gruffly.

"José!" says I, sure a José always exists among more than two people in this country.

The warden frowned for a moment.

"Ah, José? You mean José Bustamante?"

That's how I knew the system was still the same. The inmates were still fed and clothed by relatives and friends. The authorities made the arrests, a judge imposed a sentence that could be suspended by paying the fine and the municipality provided the lodgings. Family members and friends, or acquaintances going to town, dropped by the jail to deliver food, wood for carving, beads for stringing and sometimes clothing.

"Yes, José Bustamante," I say.

The warden looks me up and down. Being of a certain age and a foreigner to boot he swallows the obvious question how come I wish to see this José Bustamante when I carry nothing to give him. Almost reluctantly he beckons me to accompany him to the heavy iron door leading into the courtyard where he yells: "José! José Bustamante there is a foreign gentleman to see you."

The courtyard is still the same. That's what I wanted to see.

The inmates still squat on their haunches carving idols or threading beads. The grilled iron gates of the cells stand open as they always did during the day, just as they did in my days, forty years ago. Nothing has changed. At the far end I see Four Holes, just beyond the lemon tree. The tree is still there, gnarled, older like all of us, yet still bushy with leafs that surely must still serve as toilet paper. For a moment I expect Teodimo to appear with his bucket. Instead a short-legged man in his mid-thirties trundles to the gate. He stares at me perplexed.

"Do you want me, Señor?"

"José?" I say, flashing my most ingratiating smile. "You don't know me but a friend of yours gave me this to give to you ..."

I pull out my wallet and peel off a hundred peso note, offering it through the grill. "Take it."

The man stares at me. "Who is this friend?"

"Take it," I urge. "He doesn't want his name mentioned. But take it."

José Bustamante's eyes narrow: "You can tell Don Alfonso he cannot buy me, not even in jail." And hissing, "If I live to be a hundred in this hole I will not sell him the land. You tell him that. A hundred pesos! For what? For my land? Oranges, lemons, pineapples, never! Never! Never will I sell. The land goes to my son and his son. Tell that to Don Alfonso. Adios, Señor!"

José Bustamante walks away, deaf to my entreaties, my protestations the benefactor is not Don Alfonso but someone else who wants to give him money, a real friend, please take it.

"He ain't wanting it!" the warden says, licking his lips and turning away from the gate. "I'll take it. I'll give it to him later."

"I'll be back," I mutter and walk away.

The warden looks crestfallen.

While I sit on yet another bus coughing and spluttering up the serpentine road towards the cliffs above Teotitlan I can't dismiss the fear all my writings over all those years, all my efforts to expose injustice, the horror of war, the greed and corruption of officials have made no difference at all. Did anything change in Teotitlan or in the rest of the world, despite what I wrote? Did anyone ever listen or did they, just as El Tiburon predicted, simply sit back and complain 'this is terrible, something ought to be done' and then went on with their 'precioso' life?

As always I excuse myself with the excuse far greater and far more influential men and women have also failed at the same task. In fact, like them, I shall leave behind a world even greedier then I found it in my youth, a world in a state of 'permanent war,' each day more immune to the suffering of others and more immersed in the gratification of the Self. All this while the planet is dying as we look the other way and the great multitude is elbowed into the gutter together with the garbage while the few take nearly all and the oceans run over, the rains stop in some regions but floods others and the heat becomes unbearable, hurricanes and typhoons flagellate the earth and suicidal maniacs shoot, stab or run down people. It feels as if time is running out like the sand in the hourglass. Soon the truly rich will live in oxygen bubbles while the rest of us slowly choke to death on pollution and disease or die searching for a safe place to live.

When I am in one of my dark moods and cynicism sneaks into my thoughts I do believe people did learn something from my stories. What they learned was how to imitate the crooks. Why not? The majority of scandal and mayhem the media digs up as its main dish is how people were robbed, cheated, swindled and how the smart guys broke the laws to become rich and famous and got away with it. If one of these 'crooked entrepreneurs' is caught in fraudulent practices their punishment is a fine or, in the worst of cases, a few years in privileged jails or under house arrest. After this soft punishment the same crooks usually pop up again with another scam. If you have swindled the multitude out of their pensions and life savings, if you diverted millions of a company's funds into your own pockets and milked banks and enterprises until these institutions went bankrupt, if you made hundreds or thousands of workers jobless, their families ruined, you can still live a billionaire's life abroad as an exile beyond extradition—or make a deal with the authorities to mitigate any punishment. Yet if you rob a grocery store with a fake pistol and haul away a few hundred dollars you may spend ten years in jail. Where is the balance of justice here? Who then can blame the exasperated taking the same route to fortune? Or the enraged from seeking their own type of justice?

My journey continues.

The bus crawls on the serpentine road parallel to the cliffs, higher and higher towards the bellies of clouds drifting in from the Sierra towards the precipice. On the very edge of the cliffs the clouds peer down, decide to disintegrate or drift back into the Sierra.

And so the cactus desert below remains dry.

The bus labors around hairpin bends, the driver heaving at the mighty steering wheel, outsized like a wagon wheel. Below in bright sunshine the town glistens, most of all St Michael's dome. As always Teotitlan refuses to surrender its stewardship of the Sierra, refuses to vanish, to fade, to let go.

After an hour, finally, after one more bend, suddenly and without warning the town has vanished and the bus plunges into a spider web of mist, a veil that lifts and falls like the cantankerous mood of a Spanish flamingo dancer. Thin rain drizzles, then the sun bursts through and a rainbow hovers; blinding light and next, around another bend, thick pea-soup fog. Once again the bus crawls snail-like through visibility reduced to a few feet. Finally, squeaking along the side of yet another precipice but visible below, a pristine view of green valleys, of forests and meadows dressed up in lush green fur and nestled on steep slopes.

And on one slope Utla.

The taxi driver tells me the only flower children or 'ippies left that he knows are Don Juan and his family, a people he calls 'leftovers from yesterday.' He says these 'leftovers' have lived alone, isolated on the lower folds of Nindo Tokosho, ever since the taxi driver was knee-high. He says

Don Juan and his family are the only real ones left from the boom, many years ago when hundreds trekked each year into the Sierra to trip with Maria Sabina, movie stars, famous rock bands, the Beatles and the Rolling Stones. But once the venerated Curandera died the attraction died with her; the flow of mushroom seekers turned into a trickle, until even the trickle ran dry. The driver says Don Juan and his family now cultivate and sell the magic fungus because the mushroom no longer grows in the wild. Should I desire, he tells me confidentially, Don Juan's family will sell me all kinds of products they concoct in a witches' cauldron behind the house.

He seems to consider me one of those superannuated 'ippies who trek into Utla now and then to relive a fragment of their youth. He keeps staring at my short-cropped hair. It confuses him. Old hippies usually keep their hair long or tie what's left of it into a grey pig-tail.

"Forget Maria Sabina's grandson," he advises, leaning across from the driver's seat: "The boy learned only a bit of hocus-pocus from his grand-mother. And Señor I am told his mushrooms are fakes, any old mushroom picked in the woods. They have no magic in them."

We drive.

He tells me what I already know, that Maria Sabina was accused of witchcraft and dragged before a court in Oaxaca after a gringo sailed off the cliff in the belief he could fly. The gringo had been gobbling her mushrooms. I could sympathize with the gringo. I too thought I could fly. Luckily I landed in a haystack. The gringo was not so lucky. He landed on a rock.

The taxi driver said Maria Sabina stopped curing people in veladas long before she died because she believed the mushrooms she called 'my little children' had lost their powers ever since the Longhairs had turned the mushroom 'veladas' into orgies.

"She was over two hundred years old when she died," the taxi driver said, "you don't believe it?" he protested, "ask my grandmother. She is ninety-plus and her grandmother already was cured by Maria Sabina."

Utla has spread uphill, up the slopes of the once sacred mountain and so, obviously, Nindo Tokosho's magic, just like that of the little children, faded away as the mountain gradually disappeared, its slopes buried by shanties and humpies. The driver, in his late teens, looked puzzled at the mention of the name of the mountain. He knew the slopes only as 'Slumland'.

This new town has been grafted onto slopes carved by men like terraced rice paddies with streets running in tight serpentines one above the other, partly cemented, partly muddied. Gone are the white adobe homes of my youth, replaced by concrete, by asbestos, by corrugated iron, even brick, anything that could be fitted together to conjure up a roof over people's heads.

The driver points out Maria Sabina's cabin. It is buried now in a maze of hovels, derelict, just another shanty among shanties. In my days the cabin stood like a beacon above the town and it took nearly an hour to reach Maria Sabina by foot on a mule track. This cabin' looks nothing like I remember, nothing resembling that structure of wood with its caved-in thatched roof. Now the roof is made of corrugated iron sheets.

In vain I search for a commemorative plaque to the famous daughter of Utla, the Curandera of Oaxaca the High Priestess of the magic mushroom cult. Nothing, not even a road sign, indicates this is where she lived and where she administered to hundreds, maybe thousands of mushroom seekers over the years, rock stars, actors, culture gurus, people, so it was reported, like John Lennon, Bob Dylan, Keith Richards and Mick Jagger. Everyone in those days jumped on the bandwagon of the mushroom trip. You had to have done the trip to be 'in.' Sadly celebrities who had never set foot in the Sierra also claimed to have gobbled Si-tho with Maria Sabina.

Reluctantly the taxi driver heeds my order to stop. I have to see if I remember anything about this structure or that son of Xochitl.

This cabin is larger than the one I remember. The broken thatched roof has been replaced by corrugated iron sheets. After Maria Sabina died, I guess, the terraced streets kept steadily creeping uphill until they reached her cabin. Soon the new slums enfolded the cabin. Today it is just one shack among many. This shack is marked with a small handwritten sign: 'Casa Maria Sabina.'

Her grandson is eager to show me around, eager for the tip. Is he that little boy from my night in the cabin, the one with the curved penis suckling one teat while the piglet suckled the other? Or is he a brother born later? I scrutinize his face closely. But there is no resemblance. Besides, did it really happen or was it all just another hallucination? Would Maria Sabina have allowed it, a Curandera notorious for protecting her 'little children' from being profaned by the hedonistic? During our conversation the young man points to a handwritten poster on the wall and explains it says what his grandmother once told a visitor:

"Before the Longhairs came nobody ate the little children to find the God of Madness. We treated the little children with respect and they healed our sicknesses. We swallowed only a few. But the Longhairs always wanted more."

The young man (his name is Antonio) has some resemblance to his mother Xochitl, the long black hair, the high cheekbones and the bump on the bridge of his nose. I do not tell him I knew his mother and maybe I made love to her. But I ask him about Xochitl. He says she became a shaman in her own right but Maria Sabina kicked her out because Xochitl was using Si-tho for wild dancing and what Antonio shyly called 'fooling around and taking off your clothing.' So she had used the mushroom as a sexual stimulant, a common practice in ancient times when such mushrooms were part of fertility rites, prominent in pharaonic Egypt, ancient Greece and Rome and frequently mentioned in old scriptures. Like fake priests and healers she too had swapped the beneficial use of the mushroom to self-gratification.

Maria Sabina must have been livid.

The grandson is anxious to make money from the faded fame of his grandmother but I want to leave. He reminds me how old I have become, how long I have lived. And he reminds me of Xochitl and that magic night in the cabin when I was reborn, where I was loved, where I died, where I was resurrected and healed body and mind.

Was this boy the product of that night, a night in which my aching liver was cured forever? It never gave me trouble after that night, though I remained a solid drinker. And I never suffered short breath again after I coughed out reams of tar-colored liquid that night, cleansing my lungs after years of heavy smoking. Since that night in the cabin I have never ejaculated prematurely or felt inhibited about my physique. Amazingly the hang-ups I had acquired during my teenage years simply vanished once Si-tho showed me their source during that long trip from birth through life to death and resurrection. All this happened on that one night—or was it two or three nights—in the cabin on the mountain slope.

Did it all happen or was it only a hallucination?

I give the grandson a hundred U.S. dollars, an overdue payment I should have made years ago to his grandmother who was destitute and probably needed it far more than he does today. But in those days I was in search of my own glory and rarely remunerated the help of others. The young man almost falls to his knees in gratitude. Business must be slack. He clutches my hand to kiss it but I pull away and run back to my taxi.

"You know," the taxi driver says, negotiating the hairpin bends, "that's not where Maria Sabina's old cabin stood. Her old cabin was burned down long ago ... ah here we are, the 'ippy house ...'"

Don Juan's house is where the shanty-town ends and the forest begins. Surely the town's irreversible expansion will catch up and soon swallow him too. Until then the house nestles in the forest—two-floored, porched, gardened, fenced, shaded, and guarded by tall trees. The construction is solid, the place sensibly furnished, glass-windowed, cement floored, a functional kitchen with a wood oven. Behind the house, in a shed, Don Juan and his clan have built a laboratory.

A donkey is tethered to the fence.

"I'll be with you in a minute, Bro. Got to fix up my patient," Don Juan calls in a stentorian voice from a room next to the salon into which I am being ushered by a pale young man with a French accent, a delicate porcelain skin and dark shadows under his eyes. He had fed the donkey when I arrived. Now he returns to his chore and leaves me in the salon. The women, one by one, come and hold out their hand: "Brigitte" says the tall blonde in her early forties "Anja" says the full-breasted brunette, probably mid-thirties. "Taree" says the young slinky one, Irish by her accent. All three smile before withdrawing, together, to the kitchen. The house is clean. The women look fresh and healthy. So do the children. And there are many of them.

"I am a Shaman," Don Juan calls from the other room: "Believe it or not, Bro, the Indios come from far and near to be cured by yours truly.

Ain't that ridiculous, Bro? Me, from the Bronx in New York. Me, curing Indians with their own medicine. In just a generation they've lost all their knowledge. Can you believe, now they go and see one of the quacks with a fictitious medical certificate who prescribes pills from pharmaceutical companies making fortunes by peddling sugar-coated bullshit that does more harm than good? But hey, Bro, I charge them too. I have to live. My family has to live."

His invisible patient grunts.

"I'm just finishing him off."

Eventually he emerges from the room, a portly sorry-looking Indio in tow. "Just a minute," he says: "We have to settle up."

They settle in the kitchen. The portly Indio bickers, Don Juan's repost is gruff. The Indio is silent. Apparently money changes hands and then the tall blonde can be heard: 'Give it to me. I'll send Bernard to do the shopping.'

Don Juan comes back. He looks like an old thin elfin with a white beard and wisps of hair on his head. He is gregarious, garrulous and wants me to stay for the night in the company of his two weedy male assistants and his three wives, all three from different nations, all three of different skin. A flock of vivacious children run through the room, playing chase.

"All of them are mine," Don Juan says proudly, making a sweeping gesture towards the running kids with one arm while the other holds a half-rolled joint: "Except one," he adds.

He won't say which one but I suspect it's the little red headed girl; she resembles the taciturn ginger-haired German Don Juan is now introducing as his 'botanical engineer.' Her mother, Taree, stroking the girl's hair, can't be more than twenty. Don Juan must be in his seventies. Why does he remind me of someone I knew or should have known?

"Thirty-five years ago when I finally settled for good in Utla the town had six cars. Today Utla has one hundred and fifty taxis. One of the taxi drivers is my thirteen-year-old son … A license? Bro, you must be joking. You can get a certificate to practice medicine here for a few thousand pesos. Hey people, listen to this! This guy here, Serge, he has tripped with Maria Sabina in the old days.

"Who didn't, right? I knew her well. For a while she was a kind of guru to me; she was the one who introduced me to the cult but she knew little about the rituals, its effects, its cures. She knew something. There was so much more to know, to learn but you had to find it, piece by piece from different people all over the Sierra. Bro, those who practice shamanism around here today are bullshit; they make you sicker than before you started. These days you have to walk right across the mountains to find a decent Shaman. I am the only good one left in this part of the world and that makes those charlatans hate me. Xochitl, Maria Sabina's grand-daughter tried to kill me. Competition you know. It took me forty years to learn what I know now."

Don Juan speaks the way a prayer wheel grinds on pausing only peri-odically to suck fumes from the joint he has rolled and which Taree has lit for him. The women sit and listen, in silence. The children play, noisily, unimpressed by the patriarch.

"Don't want a drag?"

I decline.

"Bro you want to try our mushies? We grow them here with official permission." He chuckles. "Sure, don't laugh, the mayor came up one day and he says to me 'Don Juan please grow more mushrooms otherwise they will become extinct.' Makes you cry, doesn't it?"

I tell Don Juan I don't wish to spoil the unique experience I enjoyed with Maria Sabina.

"Ah," he says: "Did you know her daughter, Xochitl? Dark-skinned girl with big eyes black as black as the night, always sat in on the veladas. Sat in the back corner nursing her two brats, both different fathers, not even she knew who. Then a third son came along, also sperm unknown."

He chuckles.

Of course I remembered. The sap rising in the loins during that li-bidinous phase of the velada, the vague memory of copulation or was it attempted copulation or was it only hallucination? In the light of the burning candle I still see the baby suckling one breast the piglet the other. Was that a dream too or was it reality?

"She is dead now, Xochitl," Don Juan continues, almost with glee: "Her son, Antonio, now runs the sessions and tries to live off them. He plays the Shaman. But he's useless. He mixes it all up, the wrong mushrooms with the wrong chants. His grandmother always said he was the seed of a foreign idiot. Yet the kid trailed her everywhere but she paid him no heed and Xochitl taught him even less. You know, Bro, Xochitl was never interested in curing she was only interested in casting spells. She always asked her grandmother to give her new spells? And once Maria Sabina told her Xochitl didn't want to know about the cures. When the old Curandera died her knowledge died with her and Xochitl became a witch. You understand Bro a witch casts spells a Curandera takes them away. And you know what, Xochitl put a spell on me; she pissed and shat on my land and next day I broke my leg in several places. I was running and suddenly the earth opened up and I fell into a crevasse. It took twenty-seven months to make me walk again properly and every time she saw me she laughed in my face. She hated me. I was competition because in those days fewer and fewer mushie munchers dropped in trying to live a vision they'd read in books. Today no one comes except the odd old 'ippy, nostalgic to relive a chapter in their youth. But most of the oldies have crossed the river Styx by now, cut down by heart attacks, Aids, booze, plain melancholy and sometimes a maniac's bullet, like that poor guy John Lennon who was here too."

Don Juan shrugs his shoulders. He grabs at a wooden box on the table and pulls it towards him. He opens the box and extracts several celluloid envelopes containing what looks like finely crunched herbs.

"We make our own mushroom tea now and sell it. You should try it. We worked on the right composition for years over in the laboratory. It's perfect now—a tonic for the brain and the central nervous system, the heart, the lungs and the respiratory system, the liver, the kidneys.... and it increases sexual stamina. The tea's main base is the mushroom but we've mixed in lots of other herbs. Bro, don't laugh. The ancient Chinese knew about the mushroom but only the emperor was allowed to partake of its magic powers. One day there was not a single magic mushroom left in all of China just the way it's happening in Utla. The emperor became desperate. He couldn't satisfy his concubines. His sexual strength was gone. You see, Bro, the mushroom gave him the lift he needed. Hey, Bro, I know all about that."

He cackles. The women smile.

"Well, the desperate emperor sent emissaries abroad to search for the fungus. Some of them ended up in Japan where they found the magic one. They knew it had to be eaten fresh from the soil so they dug up the soil and sent the mushrooms stuck in its own soil back to the emperor. The emissaries then settled in Japan to ensure the emperor had a steady supply of mushrooms. These Chinese in Japan did not partake of the mushroom because it was forbidden to all mortals except the emperor. But it was those Chinese that founded the Japanese race which is funny because the Japanese today are furious when you tell them their ancestors were Chinese …"

I turn over the little bags. The labels read 'Emperor's Mix, Maitake, Shiitake, Yamabushitake and perhaps—because they ran out of Japanese names—Turkey's Tail and Lion's Mane.'

Don Juan also sells oyster mushrooms, home grown in the back garden under protective netting as well as a number of concoctions billed as cures for ailments or boosters for shortcomings. A library in his living room is stacked with books, many of them about pre-Hispanic history and …

Suddenly it dawns on me, the thin man, the mad eyes, the spaced out expression … why not? Why not?

So I ask him: "What did you do before you became Don Juan, when you were still back in the Bronx?"

He is sucking on his joint, home grown he insists, better than Acapulco Gold, he says, better than the crap they sell you downtown, so he boasts.

"Bro, I was an amateur anthropologist who had the bright idea to travel to Oaxaca for his holiday. In Oaxaca I heard about a Curandera up in the Sierra who headed an ancient mushroom cult. I figured this could be a great academic paper. So I got myself the proper documents from the authorities as a researcher as well as introductions to the local authorities of Teotitlan and Utla. Then I trekked up here. Man, a great achievement in those days when the road was just a narrow track, sometimes washed away. Got up to Utla, found Maria Sabina and swallowed the damn fungus and loved it and loved Maria Sabina. Then went back to the Bronx and wrote the damn paper. Before I knew it, Bro, someone in Greenwich Village had picked it up and ran with it in print. Next thing every damn freak knew about the mushroom cult and—believe me, Bro, with no profit to yours truly—the darn paper became a little bible for the anti-Vietnam generation.

Psilocybin Mexicano was the new fad drug, Maria Sabina became the new high priestess of hippies, dropouts, draft dodgers, those looking for new kicks and those simply pissed off with the system. All of them—at least those with a sense of adventure—headed for Oaxaca while the rest tried to cultivate the fungus in hothouses. But the cultivated species was not the same, I can vouch for that. I tried it myself."

He takes another drag on the weed.

"But all this sudden attention bothered my system, Bro. Overnight I was anointed by the new wave as The Expert, the guy who'd done it all, the guy who knew it all, the guy who had tripped with Maria Sabina. Bro, I couldn't hack the attention of those damn pseudo-scientists claiming I had found the drug to solve all psychological problems when I already knew it would create more problems than it would solve. Then comes the icing on the cake. Know what? The CIA gets interested in the magic one. They tried to recruit me. But I refused. So they sent their own 007 on a mission to Utla to investigate and see if the psilocybin could become the drug to use on prisoners of war or on spies to make them talk. Bro, I tell you, that agent had all the papers from the Mexican authorities to investigate and with the full cooperation of the authorities. You know what? Maria Sabina wouldn't talk to him. She said she knew nothing and 'her little children' were only taken to cure the sick."

Don Juan passes the pouch to Taree and she begins to roll one for the women.

"I guess the CIA did some experiments and found out, just like I did, that psilocybin can turn you into a self-destructive maniac. It can also turn you into a liar because you believe certain things you saw under the influence of the drug. Bro, Jesus never existed except as a mythological creation of the early Christians under the influence of psychoactive mushroom extracts such as psilocybin, the same drug the Mazotecs and the Aztecs employed in medico-religious practices. True, on occasions, but only on occasions, it can help overcome complexes because they might come up in your hallucinations. Bro, the mushroom can be like the psychologist who tries to make you talk on the couch about your problems. Sometimes the mushroom makes you see things and then you may understand and be cured. But other times it can make bad things blow up in your mind and when that happens, man, you're gone. I mean if you have a flash where the hang-up originated, Bro, it's now longer a hang-up, is it? But if that flash goes the other way it becomes a bomb. You can freak out, forever. Many people did."

I immediately think of Christina, a colleague working for an American magazine. Like me she worked in Mexico City and one night after we had a few drinks and made love on her office sofa she told me she wanted to go on her own trip with Maria Sabina. She did go and she did come back claiming while under the spell of the mushrooms in Maria Sabina's cabin she was raped by the pig kept in the cabin together with the other animals. I guessed it must have been the boar which was together with the sow in the cabin when I tripped. Christina freaked out so badly after she came back she had to be hospitalized in a psychiatric institution in Texas. After a few months she was released. She immediately flew to Venezuela where I was on assignment at the time. Disguised under a blonde wig she pulled from her handbag a hammer and attacked the girl I was living with at the time. Luckily our maid, a hefty Negro woman, heard the screams and fended off the final fatal blows as my girlfriend lay on the floor dazed and bleeding. After two more years back in the psychiatric ward Christine was released once again and immediately flew to London where she found out I was on assignment. She knocked at the door of my apartment one evening. She convinced me she had been cured of her obsessions and no longer blamed me for encouraging her to see Maria Sabina. I allowed her to stay the night in the spare room. For reasons I will never know I woke up in the middle of the night and looked up at a bread knife descending on me. I grabbed the blade at the last moment and still bear the scars on my hand when I fended off the mortal stab. As far as I know Christina was never again released from psychiatric care.

Then there was my friend Thad who came down the mountains with me from Maria Sabina's cabin. He was already convinced he had found his home in the Sierra. He did not jump with me into the haystack. I believe he went back to the cabin or sat on the hill waiting for daylight. When he sent me the message he would stay I did not try to dissuade him. In those days you teamed up with someone on an assignment, traveled together like brothers and in the end each went their own way. You might meet again on another assignment or you might never see one another again. That was the way of the foreign correspondent.

A few months later someone told me Thad now wore flowing white gowns, had grown a long blond beard and believed he was Jesus Christ. In the end, I thought, he was just another troubled foreigner who disappeared in the Sierra. Still one night during a drunken orgy at a hotel bar in the Middle East one hack told us he knew Thad from Vietnam and had heard that the photographer one evening celebrated his own ascension to heaven on the edge of a precipice. Witnesses, the guy said, claimed he flew off into the dusk his white gown flapping like the wings of a bird. He was never seen again.

All this goes through my mind as Don Juan waits for Taree to light a fresh joint.

"Good?" he asks as she sucks in the first drag. The girl rocks her head from side to side as if to say, 'not bad, but I've had better.' She passes the joint to Brigitte who smiles at me as she hauls in a mouthful. Then she offers the joint to me 'home-made,' she says. I decline.

"Bro, I tell you, I didn't want any part of that CIA bullshit. Not even when they tangled the carrot of big money. The whole mushroom spook was turning into a tidal wave threatening to bury me under tons and tons of swirling white water creeping up my nostrils and in my ears, down my throat and up my ass. Man, I was drowning, I was drowning in fungus shit and that's when I decided to get lost, to get lost in the Sierra, lost in mushrooms, women, shamanism and lots and lots of little children. Hey, I didn't just freak out, man, I also began tinkering with experiments on rare plants. And that is now my hobby."

Brigitte reaches across the table and tries to place the joint in my hand. "Come on," she says, "one little drag. Make you relax."

She is attractive. I take a drag and feel my head expand instantly. It's potent stuff. I can feel it fumigate my brain and through the haze I hear Don Juan ramble on, "no, no, I've never regretted dropping out, never regretted becoming Don Juan. It's peace, Bro, peace. Want some of our Emperor's Mix?"

I believe I shake my head or my head shakes me.

"Hey man," I say, feeling good about using that old hippy jargon once again, "whatever happened to the Curandera, did she practice until she died?"

Don Juan takes a sip of Emperor's Mix which one of the children had brought in and poured from a can into his cup. "No, no, in the end the old lady refused to chant any more veladas or pluck her little children from the soil. I went to see her in her tiny new cabin, the one made of plywood and corrugated iron, the one her useless grandson built after the old cabin burned down. By then Bro I had learned to speak Mazatec so I asked her why she had retired and she said to me, and |I remember this word for word because it made a big impact on me and gave me this shock guilt complex. Man this is what she said: "From the day the Longhairs came to our land the holy children lost their purity. Now they have no more force. They will not help me and they will not listen to my songs. The Longhairs have ruined them. From now on the little children will no longer work. And there is no remedy for that."

During the silence that followed Brigitte offers me another drag but I am anxious to keep my wits about me because I know any moment I will find the solution to a question that has bothered me for forty-four years.

"Don Juan, how come her cabin burned down?"

He calmly sucks at the joint then leans back in his upholstered easy chair and takes a sip of tea. He inhales deeply again and allows the smoke to billow from his nostrils.

"How come the cabin burned down?" I remind him, gently.

"Bro," he begins, "the men of Utla burned it down—and with her in it. Lovely bunch of fuckers, weren't they? She made them all wealthy. During the hippy boom over a hundred cabins in town were rented out. Every peasant had a windfall selling food to the hippies. But by Jove once the boom blew itself out the new shopkeepers and tricycle drivers turned on her. She was blamed for ruining their trade by giving too many little children to that American idiot who thought he could fly. A batch of these town morons sneaked to her cabin at night, poured diesel on it and lit it. The cabin went up like a firecracker, so I am told. But she managed to crawl out through a hole left in the wall for the dog and the cat. Lucky she was a skinny slip of an old bird, or maybe she knew the secret to minimize into the shape of a cat. Who knows, hahaha?"

He laughs at his own joke then continues: "Anyway she made it into the shrubs without being seen. And the very next day she walks through the center of Utla. Oh Bro I'd have given up sex for a year to be there and see their faces, hear their shrieks, watch them quiver in their boots and probably piss themselves. They thought she was immortal. Not even fire could do away with her. So what would be her vengeance? Would the crops rot, would the animals die? Would they all be infected by chicken pox? Man, oh man, they must've been shitting themselves for months. Hahaha!"

Judging by his bellowing laugh Don Juan is still imagining the spectacle of the town haunted by the specter of Maria Sabina walking among them and the fear of her retribution. But I am still puzzled.

"Why would they try to kill her? Wasn't she their biggest draw-card and their main healer? What made them turn against her?"

Don Juan turns to Brigitte, "baby you tell him, you got the juice directly from old Feliciano. And he should know."

Brigitte brushes back her long blonde hair and smiles at me the way women can smile at you with the tacit message "I do like you." But I am too involved with the story to catch the full significance of her signals.

"Well? I say, impatiently.

"It's a long story," Brigitte replies.

"I'm in no hurry."

"It began," says Brigitte "when a Christian Values Association in San Antonio, Texas denounced the town of Utla for selling drugs to teenagers, many of them under age. The Federal Authorities sent fifty federal policemen to turn Utla upside down. Of course, they found marijuana and they found mushrooms. So the town was placed under an embargo and twenty-two men were charged with selling narcotics. All of them were jailed for a year."

"Now what has this to do with Maria Sabina?"

"I'm coming to that," Brigitte replies. She snatches the joint from Taree and inhales. After a few moments, her eyes closed, she goes on. "Someone always has to be the scapegoat when things go wrong, isn't that right Don Juan. It's the same in town as it is in this house …"

"That's not fair," Don Juan protests.

"It is not?" Brigitte snarls and I realize the weed has elicited an old lingering grievance. She glares at Don Juan as she continues with the explanation. "Just like in this house when the whispers start so in Utla the whispers went around that it was Maria Sabina and her 'ippies who brought disgrace and disaster on the town. She was the real drug runner. She was the reason bad young foreigners, the ones without money, flocked to Utla. As always, like in this house, these comments started sotto voce, then became a murmur, then a gossip, then a din and finally ended in shouts. From that it didn't take too long to raise a 'burn-the-witch' posse. There you have it."

In the silence that follows everyone takes a puff, except me.

"Did you ever discuss the burning with Maria Sabina?" I ask Don Juan. He takes another sip of Emperor's Mix before he replies: "Of course I did. I asked her if she considered me responsible for the burning of her cabin because I had written about the mushroom cult and my writing brought all those young people to Utla."

"What was her answer?"

Everyone now leans forward, eyes glued on the little man. Apparently this subject has not been discussed before. Don Juan looks up at the solid oak rafters holding up the roof. His brows furrow as if he is trying to recall something and be exact about it.

"She looked at me with her dark bottomless eyes and said: You always respected the little children and you believed we take the little children to be cured and we only take a few. But the foreigners wanted more and more and more not to be cured but to have more power—to sing better, to play their music better, to make love better … and some wanted to see what no one else could see."

I lean back and look at Don Juan. I am sure now.

Hallelujah! I have found Haberstone, forty-four years too late.

The tall blonde insists she is taking me back down into town in the family jeep. Don Juan shrugs his shoulders: "If you want," he says and looks at her hard. "I want," Brigitte says.

I only realize later what she means.

Once we are alone she becomes talkative as if a cork is pulled from the bottle of her earlier silence. She blabbers on and on while we slip around hairpin bends on the way down into central Utla. Guests come and go, she says. Some stay a few weeks, some months; others have stayed years. Some women have bred children with Him, taken them away or left them behind for Don Juan; he is happy rearing them if they are his own. He has nearly twenty sons and daughters. Once old enough the majority leave to see the world, make their own way. Few ever come back. Don Juan encourages them to leave. He needs the space for new arrivals. She has no children of her own. She cannot have children. But she loves being around them, looking after the little ones, counseling the older ones. The women sleep with whoever they want but all of them sleep with Don Juan. He insists on that if they want to stay. Oh yes, he is an expert lover, with magic hands and infinite lotions and pills; it is fun making love with him, always under the influence of the mushroom; he can bring you on and on and she has never heard complaints he failed to rise to the occasion when required. And that's amazing; after all he is seventy-five years old. But yes, there are rifts, jealousies, infighting and blow-ups with the two men.

We park the jeep in front of the church, opposite my hotel. In the colonnade below the shopping arcade men with holstered guns sit behind tables, grim-faced, not unlike a scene from a Spaghetti Western where the gunslingers wait for high noon. On the church steps stand blackboards pinned with posters hailing the Oaxaca teachers strike. The strike has already bloodied Oaxaca City where paramilitaries shot dead a number of demonstrators igniting nation-wide protests and gestures of solidarity from around the world.

Brigitte tells me the stand-off has become bloody in this remote Sierra town which had no schools when I was last here. During the years of military rule, it seems, the colonels running the town awarded a concession to build schools and appoint teachers. No one knows what the Colonels received in return for this concession.

The men with the holstered guns are staring at a school off the church square. A black police van is parked outside the school. Two policemen in black uniforms stand on the school balcony staring back at the gunmen standing at the edge of the colonnade. The scene is surreal. All it needs is Ennio Morricone's music in *The Good, the Bad and the Ugly*.

"Why are the police in the school?" I ask one of the gunmen. He does not take his eyes off the policemen on the balcony when he answers: "Protecting scab teachers."

"But all the teachers are on strike?"

"Not the scab," the gunman mutters.

I want to know more. But the gunmen have become reticent and eye me with suspicion. Don't I know what's going on? Why is this foreigner with that blonde bitch asking questions? Whose side are they on?

Brigitte drags me away. The atmosphere is volatile. She says people in Utla shoot at each other these days over control of education. She says it began years ago when salesmen, outsiders, came to convince the Indios the future of their children depended on education. Unless their children were educated the rest of the country would continue to consider them stupid chamuli. But if the parents wanted the children to escape the humiliation of being considered end-of-the-line citizen the children had to be sent off for an education.

The sales pitch worked wonders. No decent Indio wished on his children the indignities and deprivations suffered by their elders. In no time Utla was converted into the Sierra capital of education. Over twenty private schools were built within ten years. Every morning and every afternoon the town teemed with Indio children, all spic and span in clean school uniforms, all ferried to and from school from every nook of the Sierra by collective taxis, motor scooters, vans and even private cars. No Indio wants their child to miss out on schooling. Parents sold land, took up loans, sold livestock, all to pay the school uniforms and the school fees. And the fees went up and up as the school proprietors became greedier. The education system became an octopus with tentacles sponging up people's resources.

Needless to mention the curriculum did not teach Indio culture but western culture. Today the Indio children no longer speak Mazateco and Mixteco but Spanish; they no longer wear native costumes and huaraches but western dress and western shoes; the girls cut their braids, beauty salons fix them with modish hairdos right out of the fashion magazines on the salon tables; accessories soon followed, bras, cosmetics, nylons, handbags, satchels, football boots, shorts, T-shirts, Coca-Cola, hamburgers, fast food and then, finally, the latest fad—the internet and mobile phones.

The Indio culture vanished, wiped out in less than a generation.

Western consumer culture took over, starting in the schools.

Utla went commercial with hole in the wall shops run by cosmeticians, tailors, hairdressers, grocers, soft drink vendors, shoemakers. Internet cafes mushroomed where students who could not afford a computer and a connection could practice, communicate and most of all play computer games—for a fee. Then came the mobile telephone fad and soon every Indio kid pestered their parents for a mobile phone. Mobile phone shops became the new fad and if people couldn't afford their own they could use, for a fee, a mobile available in digital shops or on rigged up street-side benches equipped with a WiFi. Parents went in debt in the quest to keep up appearances. No one could afford to have their children look poor. The race was on to keep up with the Gonzales and the Sanchez. Land changed hands. Real estate agents made killings. Bank loans soared. Foreclosures and forced auctions became regular events. Soon hole in the wall shops were replaced by modern structures.

And then the teachers went on strike.

That, so Brigitte tells me, was not unusual. The teachers went on strike every year, always in May, when the renewal of their contracts came up. The government and private school owners usually bickered and bartered for a few days, even a week, then made an offer, generally about half the wage increases APPO, the Teachers' Union, demanded. The ritual was so ingrained school kids looked forward to a few days without classes in May.

But this time it was different. The State governor and the private school owners decided not to cave in. After the stand-off had lasted five months the governor proclaimed children had a right to education. He announced the Education Authorities would hire non-Union teachers to ensure classes were reopened. Not sure of his control in the capital Governor Ulises Ruiz tested the employment of scab teachers first in the rural areas.

Already a chronic shortage of teachers had existed and demand out-stripped supply. So the governor offered anyone interested, literate with or without experience, the job of teaching in those schools where teachers were on strike.

In Utla, Brigitte says, the strike was a windfall for those who had watched with envy for years as the teaching fraternity and sorority was elevated into the bourgeoisie, a town-elite with permanent salaries, intellectual status, in short superior beings. Teachers could buy cars on hire-purchase. They could buy retail businesses on credit, furniture and kitchens on credit. And they closed ranks. Anointed teachers ensured only members of their own families or close friends were selected for new teaching jobs as these became available as more and more schools opened to accommodate the tidal wave of indigenous students from villages and small towns all over the Sierra.

Anyone who could read (and some who hardly could) rushed to fill the profitable teaching vacancies in Utla. Seeing their income imperiled by scab labor the Utla Teachers Union broke ranks with the state union and terminated its strike. Their sudden surrender was in vain. The Governor decreed teachers who had been on strike had forfeited their jobs. These jobs now belonged to those who had filled them during the strike, the scab labor. State police were ordered to guard the schools against irate teachers mobbing their schools and demanding back their jobs.

All that was the reason, so Brigitte explains, why there was now a standoff threatening to become a war between those under the colonnade of the church clamoring to have their jobs back and the police on the balcony of the schools protecting 'scab' teachers, now permanent.

"Education has been a gold mine in Utla," Brigitte explains as we walk away, "it's far more profitable then was the mushroom bonanza in its days. Thousands of children from all over the Sierra come to Utla. They live with relatives or board here. These children go home at the weekend or once a month. The sad part is their parents are being exploited by the education craze just like their parents were exploited by the big landlords in the past."

She smiles at me, head crooked to one side: "Nothing ever changes in this world, does it? Everything goes round and comes around just like a carousel."

After we make love in my hotel room we talk, naked under the sheets.

One of her legs is slung over my belly, possessive-like. That irritates me. I don't want to waste any more time with love-making when I know soon she will look at her watch and announce she has to go back to Don Juan because the children expect her at a certain hour—or something to that effect. I have only borrowed her.

I ask her if she has ever heard of a man called El Tiburon. She shakes her head and I know she is telling the truth by the calm reaction to the question. I tell her El Tiburon launched a revolution in this town, a revolt against the abuse of the authorities and the landowners.

"Did he?" she says and nuzzles against my chest.

"He started his revolt with one rifle, a rifle he traded for a concession to build schools if his revolution succeeded.

"But it didn't, did it?" she says huskily, rubbing my thigh with the palm of her hand.

"He was executed for trying but I wonder what happened to the man who gave him the rifle in return for the right to build schools?"

Brigitte stops rubbing my thigh, either tired of my lack of reaction or in admiration of the man who gained a monopoly on education. "That guy had a good nose for business," she says. He couldn't bribe the military with rifles, could he, so he went into partnership with them. The Colonels got the urban plots for him. He built the schools and hired the staff and they split the spoils. I think that's how it works, so I am told," she says then starts rubbing my thigh again, this time using her fingernails. It's not unpleasant. I wonder does she do it also to Don Juan?

"How do you know all this?"

"Gossip, Town Talk. Everyone knows."

"Well if it's true," I say, "that guy converted an ancient and functional society into a capitalist consumer hub and he did it within one generation."

"Not a bad achievement" she murmurs nuzzling into my arms, "it confirms how easily it is to sell dreams and that's why we are all doomed. We always want more just like the hippies wanted to gorge on more mushrooms to get higher and higher, to reach the Nirvana of all mushroom trips. So let's you and I have another joint and make more and more love while the world chokes on its own pollution, sinks deeper into its own garbage dump and all because we want more, more, more."

She rolls over to kiss me, not exempt it seems from the 'want more' curse. Besides she must like older men though in my case I did not bring a ration of Viagra nor do I have my libido stimulated by Maria Sabina's little children or Don Juan's home-brewed potions. Brigitte is comfortably plump and I do wish I had imbibed some of Don Juan's special tea. But I haven't. So I must divert her mind into another direction.

"This rebel, El Tiburon was a friend of mine," I say, placing a casual arm between my abdomen and her wandering hand. When she frowns I continue: "He intended to restore Mazatec culture, as it was before modern materialism and technology arrived. You sure his name was never mentioned?"

She shakes her head then, after a pause she says: "Maybe you should talk to some of the old-timers, the ones sitting outside shops in chairs all day long. A couple of times I heard them mention a name, someone they called the Axeman.

As her hand begins to wander again (though I doubt she will be rewarded for her efforts) I am saved by a volley of shots below the hotel. This is followed by another volley from what I guess is the school balcony on the other side. Brigitte jumps out of bed and hurriedly begins to pull on her slip and bra.

"Get dressed," she urges, "sometimes these cowboys burst into people's homes or into hotel rooms claiming they are looking for scab labor that's been shooting at them."

The main street in Utla is not how I remember. Today it is asphalted and resembles a fourth-rate shopping mall a far cry from the muddy thoroughfare of my youth with its hand written signs announcing 'Hotel.' The shops in those days had no front walls. That's how I remembered this street on which El Tiburon walked me up and down to sober me up from the lingering nausea and flashbacks of the magic one. But those shabby hotels are no longer available. They have been replaced by proper shops with front doors. Before she drove home Brigitte explained the new hotels have moved higher up to locations with a view. The modern shops or so numerous all are squeezed together like Siamese twins, sharing walls in a street mall where anything is for sale from mobile telephones to Nike shoes, Lacoste shirts and Sony PCs though nearly all these brand names are duds from China or the labels are printed in backstreet basements and stuck on cheap duplicates or hybrids. The clientele is mostly teenage, hip gear, browsing in gangs, followed by the wary eyes of shopkeepers. It seems Indio honesty went out the window together with the old culture.

Old men are seated on wicker chairs outside shops, keeping additional vigil for shoplifters.

Utla has become a graphic example progress does not stop, even in the most remote of places where people, just as anywhere else, desire what others have and if possible what no one yet has.

I recall the East Germans after the wall came down and how they lusted for the luxuries of their cousins in the West. East Germans sold their land, their apartments, their jewelry and antiques at ridiculous prices just to have a Volkswagen, an old Mercedes or BMW instead of the two-stroke Trabi that had served them just as well, though at a far more leisurely pace.

I approach one of these wrinkled old men sitting outside a shop and ask him if he knows the Axeman. He does not take his eyes off two young boys with long hair and a girl with short hair. The girl functions as a decoy squealing, fingering goods, dancing about in a coquettish way while the boys wait until the old man's eyes are riveted to the girl. When the trio sees me eyeballing them they move on and I have the old man to myself.

"Excuse me," I say again, "I am looking for an old timer known as The Axeman. Do you know where I can find him?"

The old man looks passed me. He says nothing and when I repeat the question he mumbles, "Never heard the name."

Other old men on chairs outside shops in Utla also have no knowledge of the Axeman as if he simply does not exist. Yet what makes me suspicious is that no one asks who told me about this Axeman who does not exist. So they know and this does not surprise me. The Axeman was El Tiburon's right hand man some forty years ago. He vanished into the wilds of a Sierra in which pumas, ocelots and bears still roamed in those days undisturbed by civilization. Today, of course, wealthy trophy hunters have made those species all but extinct.

I was certain these old-timers know about the Axeman yet I wonder who gave Brigitte that name? In the end I have no choice. I hail a tricycle and on its backseat cover my nose and mouth while its two-stroke motor bellows exhaust fumes as we huff and puff our way up the terrace road, back to Don Juan.

This time George Haberstone alias Don Juan is not happy to see me. He looks even unhappier when I ask for Brigitte.

"Didn't have enough?" he asks sarcastically, adding after a pause "hoping for a second helping?"

Before I have time to think of a ripping retort Brigitte emerges from the kitchen, apron tied, and takes me away by the arm. "Vhat-a you vant?" she says gruffly, her Teutonic accent suddenly apparent. She is nervous. Obviously Don Juan does not like the occasional lovers of his harem to return for them.

"You told me to go and see the Axeman but no one has heard the name. Who gave you his name?"

She looks at me for a moment as if she is about to strangle me. "Me and my big mouth," she mumbles, then turns and walks away. But before she enters the kitchen she shouts over her shoulder, "Go and see Feliciano. He lives near the municipal hall in a brick-red house. He used to be the Mayor in the old, old days, so I am told."

Then she is gone.

Don Juan shrugs his shoulders and points to the door; a tacit signal of 'What are you waiting for? Buzz off, Bro.'

It is not difficult to find the brick red house and it is not difficult to enter even if the young man by the door gives me a hard glance.

"Who are you?" asks a shriveled old man, squinting at me from myopic eyes. He is thin, frail and looks nothing like the Mayor of Utla I remember. The grandfather chair envelopes him shell-like.

"Who are you?" he repeats, his voice brittle as his body.

"My name is Serge Dunlov. Maybe you remember me from the days of El Tiburon. I was the guy who jumped into the haystack after visiting Maria Sabina. You remember? I was a friend of El Tiburon. We met at your office when you were mayor."

The old man's face gradually comes alive as if someone had pumped air into his cheeks and fire into his eyes. He points a bony index finger at me and both the finger and his voice quiver with indignation: "You were the idiot, the idiot who told El Hombre he could run the Sierra with a few guns. You told him to go back to the old days, without documents, without money. You made a fool of him."

He pauses to brush off the spittle gathered in the corners of his mouth and I take the opportunity to voice my objection: "I did not tell him to use guns and I did not tell him to go back to the way things were in the past. That was his idea. I tried to talk him out of it, you must know that."

The old man brushes his hand across his face as if brushing away a molesting fly. "Talk him out of it, nothing," he squawks, "you ran away just like the rest, just like the ippies and those men jabbering about liberty, freedom and our rights. Like you they only talked. Then they took off, as soon as the military arrived. And we were left alone. The result was a tragedy, a real tragedy. Twenty-five people dead. But we lost more than that."

His bony finger points again in my direction and he cries, "and you were one of those bastards. You too will rot in hell."

I am beginning to sweat under my T-shirt.

He stares at me with those disconcerting gimlet eyes and snivels like someone who has a cold before he begins, though this time in more consolatory tones: "You know, of course how it all ended or don't you? I believe you don't know. If you did know you would not dare show your face around here, would he," says Feliciano addressing two middle aged men who have quietly slipped into the room. Both nod their heads loyally though their faces remain blank. Most likely both have no idea what we are talking about.

"Well," the old man says, "did you or did you not know they shot El Tiburon in the Square in front of all the people?"

I pretend I am shocked.

"Yes," Feliciano adds, "all his men were killed when they tried to fight the army."

When he stares down at his lap I ask: "I believe the Axeman is still alive."

Feliciano burps. Was it surprise I knew?

"Always the wrong people die," he says, looking at me as if to say 'you know what I mean?' Then as if collecting his wits: "Who told you he is alive?

"Someone told me, many years ago. Is it true?"

"Why don't you find out?" he snaps. "Go and see Don Efren. He will decide whether to tell your or not, or whether to kill you or not," he adds with that disconcerting cackle of his.

"Where can I find this Don Efren?"

"Look out the window," he shouts, shrilly, pointing at the large window with a view of the hills. "See that white shack on top of the hill? It's called La Casa. It's the home of Don Efren Cientofuegos. Take my word, go nowhere near La Casa. Go away instead, quick as you can."

"Why? Would this Don Efren blame me for what happened to El Tiburon and take revenge on me?"

The shriveled old man cackles: "Why would he? He believes revenge is a waste of time. Guns are far more valuable when used for your own benefit. Besides, why seek revenge when you are officially dead? The military was told he was killed with the others. Did you know," he says, not waiting for an answer, "not one of the dead was ever identified. Too many little pieces, scattered all over the place. They could never fit them together, could they?"

"El Tiburon and I were in jail in Teotitlan," I offer, hoping to ease the old man's resentment.

"You were in jail with him?"

"Yes."

Feliciano shakes his head this way and that way, slowly. "It might save your ass. He's got a soft spot for his old jail mates. If you want to see the man I'll send you up with one of the boys. He has to go up any way to take the accounts, which I do for him."

My curiosity is pricked beyond caution now. Who is this Don Efren, is he the Axeman or one of the inmates from the jail? And why is he giving accounts to Feliciano (who was always good at accounting and documenting I recall). How did he survive the failed revolt?

"Does Don Efren own property now?" I ask.

Feliciano breaks into a hysterical cackle, like a donkey baying:

"Property? He owns almost all of it, the shops, the stands, the schools, the banks and nearly every other commercial business in and around town. I mean he owns it all de facto," he adds proudly pronouncing the strange word 'de facto' then adding as if this required an explanation "it's all owned by his lieutenants, the gang he put together. One runs the bank, another runs the loan business, one the electronic stores, another the schools, another is the boss of the massage parlors and so it goes on, my friend. It's a big business empire and nearly all the money goes into his pockets."

He pauses for a moment to catch his breath or, perhaps, he ponders whether he should continue revealing Don Efren's rackets. He suddenly looks up at me and grins.

"But it has all fallen apart. People are bankrupt. They can't pay back the loans. There is not enough work to make them pay what they own by working for Don Efren's lieutenants. There is no need for new schools. Only a few families can still pay for the education or the new gadgets. There are not even customers for the schoolgirls who sell their pussies so they can buy the new fashion rags. Everything has slowed down because Utla and the entire region is broke."

How do you know all this?" I ask.

"I do his accounts," Feliciano snaps, then adds: "He trusts me. Did you know he's illiterate, just as El Hombre was?"

"Hmm! If the revenue is drying up, if everyone is broke, what's he going to do now?"

The old man bobs his head a few times before he replies: "He has so much land. He confiscated land and animals as payment for loans people could not repay his bank, understand? But land does not make enough money unless you do something with it and cows are no use if people cannot pay for milk or meat."

He cackles.

"That's the end of his business then?" I prompt.

"Oh no, he's come up with a new idea: He wants to build a golf course to attract rich people from all over the world. He wants to build discos and luxury massage parlors and have young girls working in hotels. He wants to build gambling houses, I think they call them casinos, for the big spending foreigners. That's going to be his new empire—and he'll probably do it—one way or the other. Of course the military will get their cut. In return they have already promised to run a helicopter service to fly in the money men. Now do tell me, amigo, what would our dear dead friend say to all that?"

Near the Tiber in Rome and opposite the Temple of Minerva is La Boca de Verita, the Mouth of Truth, a demon's head in marble, open-mouthed with carnivorous teeth. If your wife complains you have cheated on her and you deny her accusation the wife will demand you put your hand into the Mouth of Truth. If you have lied the demon will bite off your hand. If you spoke the truth your hand can be withdrawn unscathed. Italians are superstitious people. Few liars dare put their hand into the Mouth of Truth.

I think of the Mouth while one of Feliciano's men drives me up the hill on the back of his scooter. Innocent of the charge of running away I felt I could brave the Mouth, in my case this Don Efren. Yet for a moment I hesitate. Would it be safer if I took the bus right now back to Utla and Oaxaca City, just as I did the last time? I have already gathered a good story and I have satisfied my curiosity, so why take a risk?"

No, I decide, the story is incomplete. Was I going to miss out once again, like the last time when I left before the fatal battle with the army and then also missed the execution? The story is not complete. The key is this Don Efren who has metamorphosed into the Godfather of Utla. Who is he. How did he manage this takeover?

Out of nowhere I feel the same excitement as I felt in the past when I stalked stories with the zeal of a sleuth convinced my exposes would punish the culprits and stop others from committing the same crimes. It took me years to realize they stopped nothing. For every scoundrel I exposed ten fresh ones mushroomed. Worse, was I doing it for the common good or for my own reputation as the hack famous for digging down to the roots? And what good did my fine reputation do me? When it was opportune the management crucified me all the same in public for a minor peccadillo, in reality very much their own peccadillo for which they atoned by serving me up to public indignation as a rogue. I became their scapegoat.

Yet old habits never die. So I head up to the lion's den.

On the way Feliciano promised me his man would show me 'something' I would appreciate.

The driver, whose name is Beppe (a short name for José) has not spoken a word before we come to a stop in a small clearing. I suddenly turn weak at the knees. Have I been condemned already? I consider jumping José before he pulls his gun from wherever he hides it below his poncho.

"We need to walk through the forest for a bit," he says pointing to a narrow gravel footpath leading into the forest. For a moment cold fear grips me. Has he been ordered to take me into the forest and do it there? Do I already know too much?

"It's not far," Beppe says as if to placate my anxiety, "we don't take many people up there. You're privileged."

This does not sound like an execution.

After some five minutes walking between towering trees and thick brush we burst into a small cove surrounded by white-barked elm trees and a number of flower beds. Someone must be taking good care of this spot.

In the center of this cove is a roughly hewn granite block, shaped like a natural tombstone. Chiseled into the stone in deep grooves are the words 'El HOMBRE'.

Next to this man-sized tombstone stands an identical granite block though this one a third in size. It bears the name 'EL AMIGO'.

In front of the tombstone on a short pedestal fresh flowers of the meadows are arrayed in simple earthenware vases.

"Don Efren followed the soldiers and knew where they had buried them," Beppe explains out of the blue. "Once settled he had their skeletons dug up and had both of them buried here," he adds, matter of fact, the same way he must be making his report about the state of Don Efren's affairs.

"Then he still admires what El Tiburon did?" I ask.

"El Tiburon was his friend."

"But his friend made a wrong decision didn't he?"

"I was not there," Beppe says gruffly "nor was my grand-father" he adds beginning to walk back down the path. Suddenly I realize why he is named José or Beppe.

I remain facing the tombstone of EL HOMBRE, allowing my guilt feelings free rein as they bubble from the depth of a conscience where they had been buried in a dark niche. Only later do I become aware tears have been running down my cheeks. But by then I feel already lighter, as if I had paid a tribute long overdue.

After a while I amble around the block under which El Tiburon is buried. That is when I spot the blade of a common but rusty axe attached to the stone, held fast by four iron clips. Is this the signature of the man who had this memorial built for his friend and the loyal Teodimo?

'La Casa,' named in gilded letters over the wrought iron gates, squats at the end of a ridge above Utla. Part of the building juts over a precipice like a tongue poked out at those below. A red brick wall with a barbed wire fence on the parapet surrounds the property. Beppe has simply vanished inside while the two thugs block me at the door and look me up and down as if to measure me for a coffin or more likely the worth of my purse. One of them finally barks: "What you want?"

"I've come to see Don Efren."

"Who are you?" the thug asks, raising his nose. He is built like a wardrobe, only shorter.

"I was a friend of El Tiburon—and the Axeman" I add in the hope one of the two names might get me in. The two thugs exchange looks then the wardrobe snaps: "Wait here!" and vanishes into the house. He comes back a couple of minutes later and beckons with a nod to follow him. We walk down a dark corridor and suddenly out of the wall two strong hands grab me by the waist from behind and begin to frisk me expertly the way I haven't been frisked since Calcutta, prior to interviewing Mother Theresa. The person running hands down my body in Calcutta was no Sister of Mercy but a rather powerfully build monk. This fellow doing the job now is a bit like that monk.

In the end I am ordered to proceed. The corridor opens into a large room dominated by huge travel posters on the wall, all of iconic sites around the world—the Statue of Liberty, Buckingham Palace, St Peter's

Dome, London Bridge, Neuschwanstein Castle. I am told to wait and when I sit down in one of the wicker chairs one of the thugs tells me to stand up. I realize La Casa looks just like another shack from outside but inside it is lavishly furnished and far more spacious then one expects by its humble exterior. Between the travel posters are portraits of famous Mexican folk heroes. A piano occupies one niche. Does Don Efren play?

Behind the piano nailed to the wall hangs an axe.

While I wait for the master of the house to make his appearance, if he deigns to see me, a handsome young Indio woman enters from what I figure is the kitchen and pantry. She casts a curious glance my way then lowers her eyes and climbs down a spiral stairway leading to a basement or underground living quarters, so I presume. The stairway is of dark wood, probably mahogany. I am stunned by the opulence of the place, its elegance and good taste neither of which I would have associated with someone from Utla. One can acquire fortunes but rarely good taste. Maybe the decorator is the Indian woman.

The man who comes up the spiral wooden staircase is about my age. He is evenly suntanned, the kind of tan achieved by those artificial suntan coffins. He is definitely in better physical shape then I am and he is good looking in a rugged older man way. Yet for the world of me I cannot reconcile this figure—this man casually dressed in blue designer jeans, open neck blue shirt and expensive leather sandals—with the ragged and decrepit young man cradling an assault rifle in Utla or chopping at a piece of wood in the jail of Teotitlan four decades ago. Obviously he too has no recollection of me because he immediately goes on the offensive, barking: "Why should I care you used to know El Tiburon? If you're after a loan go to my bank."

He points a thumb towards the town, the kind of signal from someone in a bar pointing you to the toilet.

Peeved by his aggressive tone, though I could hardly expect the embrace of an old buddy, I snap: "You were El Tiburon's right hand. All of us sat with him in the jail of Teotitlan. But maybe you don't want to remember now that you're a big man living in a big house."

He squints at me, then a nasty grin spreads across his face and he looks at the two thugs who materialized from nowhere to stand on each side of me. "Boys, look at this fellow. He is that fancy smartarse jabbering about human rights and revolution when we all know human rights and revolution has been invented by dickheads who need help to jerk off."

He laughs uproariously at his definition. The two thugs join in the laughter, loyally.

"Sit down," he orders.

I plunk myself into one of the wicker chairs.

He turns to me with anger written all over his face: "Hombre you've got cojones coming here. What do you want? Are you trying to sell me another fairytale? Let's all go back to the good old days of mules if you are lucky, dragging your own plow if you're not? Back to berries and nettles for lunch, always scared of the Patrone's whip and your daughter being fucked by his sons? Yes, now and then we had fun, we gobbled a few of Si-tho's magic children, always to forget, always to cure us. Hombre, did you come here to tell me to go back to those good old days?' Are you trying to make a sucker out of me too?"

Maybe I made a mistake. My mother's oft repeated warning sounds in my ears 'its curiosity what killed the cat.' But I am stubborn and years of similar situations taught me to be quick, like the mouse that always finds a hole.

"Well, look at you now," I say, smiling engagingly, "if it hadn't been for me and my fairytale you'd still be sitting in jail in Teotitlan or you would be dead from malnutrition or a disease like Tonin and the other ghosts. I did you a favor. My talk got you out of there. Would you be living in style like this if I had not given El Tiburon the money to buy himself out of jail?"

He stares at me, making up his mind whether to strangle me or hug me. I notice by his wrinkled forehead he is trying to digest what I said. So I dash into the silence. "Whatever advice I gave El Tiburon you also followed because you too believed in what I told him. But then you changed your mind when you found out he did not want to use the gun. He believed in a pacific solution while you decided there was no such thing as a peaceful solution. For you the only solution was the gun. Wasn't that the way it was?"

Don Efren walks over to a bar and half fills a cognac glass with a brown liquid I cannot identify. He swivels the liquid in the glass and swallows it in one gulp.

"What do you want?" he asks.

That is a good question. What do I want, apart from satisfying my oc-casional pangs of conscience, pangs I quickly suffocate with the argument it wasn't my fault my Indio friend was executed for wanting a better life for his people. Emilio Zapata, El Tiburon's great idol, was killed for that same basic reason as was Che Guevara, Trotsky, Rosa Luxemburg, Abraham Lincoln, Malcolm X, Martin Luther King and a whole army of like-minded reformers, rebels and people with good intentions, though their methods may not have always been kosher.

"What do you want?" Don Efren repeats.

I must find a quick credible lie to please him.

As always when cornered during my reporter days I pander to human vanity. "I want to write a book about a man like you who has changed a primitive society into a bustling commercial community. In this community education has become the most important commodity."

He waves a dismissive hand at the two thugs and they disappear. I have struck the right nerve—again.

"I think we should have lunch together," he says and shepherds me, one arm behind my back, towards a dining room with a wooden table long enough to accommodate King Arthur and his Knights of the Round Table.

I really do recall all of our conversation because it was to fill much of what was left of my life with a sense of foreboding, the foreboding something terrible was about to happen—either to me or someone close to me. I have never believed one is born with evil but I believe evil is like a cancer that invades a person's being and grows gradually. Unless fiercely contested it ends up taking you over and destroying you.

By the time the lunch is over, after I consumed an excellent Pinot Noir and a crème caramel, I regret my curiosity had driven me to La Casa and he probably regrets he has not ordered me shot on sight.

Our conversation, as we sip the wine, begins innocently enough when the man now known as Don Efren argued El Tiburon's basic flaw was his belief human beings are good at heart, desire to be good and wish to live in peace and equality with one another.

"This is stupid poppycock," he shouts, "human beings are greedy and only want to live in peace when peace makes them richer. But it is war that usually brings wealth, wealth you take by the gun. Since all humans are greedy all governments are crooked and all their leaders are corrupt. It is their nature. So you make up your own mini-government and you run it for your own profit."

"But that means you might have to kill people to have your way. Did you?" I ask.

He stares at me, eyes narrowed: "Who told you that?"

"Just people, people in town."

"Who. I want to know who?"

"So it's not true?"

"Who?"

I am sweating and have to wipe my face to brush off the droplets.

"We'll get back to that," he says then tells me, "I learned that one kills only to gain something. Killing for revenge or because you are angry is stupid. It only brings trouble. You kill when it brings you a profit because in this world of good and bad the bad always win and the good always lose, sooner or later. Amigo, goodness is only an illusion that bad people invented to cover their badness. You agree?"

When I shake my head, non-committal, he continues: "Only fools want to be famous. It's better to work from the shadows then to sit in the lamp light for everyone to see. Yes, I live well but not in an open way because envy is people's greatest curse. I could have built a hacienda as big if not much bigger then Don Alfonso's but that would attract everyone's attention. Attention is bad for business and bad for my personal safety, entiendes, cabrón? So I live in this humble house. People don't think I am very rich and they do not know I own almost all of Utla. Haha! But why I am telling you all this, hombre, only because without you and your wild words to El Tiburon—and I was listening too—I would still be sitting threading beads in the prison of Teotitlan."

He measures me with his dark eyes, up and down.

"That's why you are still alive," he says, then leaning into my face and fletching his teeth he adds: "But if you talk or write about any of what I told you or if you write anything about me and Utla I will send my men to cut off your cojones, wherever you are in the world. And I'll have them kill your family and all your friends and believe me I will do this even if it is the last order I ever give and even if it brings me no profit."

I am stunned but I keep my mouth shut because he is about to pronounce his final verdict. He has stood up and is pointing towards the door where his thugs have magically materialized, apparently activated by the rising tone of his voice.

"Now take your skinny ass out of here," he shouts, "and don't ever come back and don't ever write about me and Utla and don't ever talk to anyone about this place or about me, entiendes cabrón?"

Of course I nod, not once but thrice. I know I am skating on wafer thin ice and one wrong move and I could end up buried in the woods near El Tiburon, though with no memorial.

"Adios!" the Axeman yells. The two thugs take one arm each, police style, and steer me out the door where a dark SUV waits for me. In the back seat, where I am deposited with a final shove, my rucksack contains all my belongings, obviously fetched from the hotel. I only glance at them. The continued presence of the two thugs unnerves me. If the two climb in I am done for. But the two remain outside, only glaring at me.

Slowly the car moves down the driveway and out onto the road.

The clouds still drift over my beach and the rip still pulls the weak swimmers out to sea. But I no longer run along the beach and tell the daring to swim with the current because drifting with the prevailing forces is easier than fighting the undertow. Nowadays I sit quietly on the beach because I don't want to be conspicuous even in this small northern seaside town to which I have removed myself, a town where I am known as Harry Robertson, a common name, perfect for an incognito.

These days I spread my towel on the crowded public beach near the flagpoles the lifesavers put up every morning. It is safe to swim between the poles where the current is weak or absent. Yet at times we all yearn to swim outside the flags, in defiance, to prick the system, to challenge the authorities, to be daring, to expose or to impress someone. I believe bucking the rules now and then is justified to precipitate change, expose the crooks, the oligarchs, the ogres and the tyrants who go to church or synagogues at the weekend yet during the rest of the week demand blow jobs from female underlings desperate to keep their jobs or from young children convinced they are serving the needs of a holy man.

Most of us dream about bucking the system, the politicians, the rich guy living down the road who made his fortune sending two pyramid schemes bankrupt yet still drives a Rolls and a Porsche. I met a guy in Italy who owns the world's biggest Prosecco label though his popular private bank went belly up wiping out the savings of thousands of people in the Veneto area. Nor he or his managers were ever charged. His Prosecco still dominates the world market.

We would like to expose them all, yet most people have loans to pay off, monthly alimony to disperse, children to educate and all of us want to look forward to financial stability during old age. So we conform and only watch when some of our fellow citizen stubbornly fight the rip. In public we call them idiots and irresponsible but privately and deep down we envy their courage.

These days I sit on the sand wedged between the multitude and watch the lifesavers with their oiled-up muscles pull the daring from the wild waves outside the 'swim safely' flagpoles. The lifesavers are efficient, determined no one strays. To the rescued they offer sermons why one must never swim outside the flagpoles and why one must always obey the rules.

Yes, I do feel smug these days because in my own way I have dared to swim outside the flagpoles and have survived—so far.

However ever since my book was published I prefer the crowded beach. It makes it more difficult for his killers to cut off my cojones.

—

ULI SCHMETZER

Born in Germany and educated in Australia, Uli Schmetzer was a well-known foreign correspondent for almost forty years until he retired to write books. For ten years he reported for Reuters news agency from Latin America and for twenty-five years for the *Chicago Tribune* from Europe, the Middle East and Asia. During his colorful career Schmetzer covered the world's major news stories—among them periodic spells reporting the Israel-Palestinian conflict between 1988 and 2004.

Uli lives part of the year in Venice, Italy, in Noosa, Australia and in Puerto Princessa, Philippines. He is the author of five other books all available on amazon.com and Kindle.

"Schmetzer's scope and detail deliver deep and practical truths ..."
DR JACK DEMPSEY
Historian, Bentley University, USA

ALSO BY THE AUTHOR

Purchase online as printed books and eBooks.

TIMES OF TERROR: NOTEBOOKS OF A FOREIGN CORRESPONDENT

A startling memoir, spiced with revealing anecdotes and disturbing insights. Schmetzer pulls no punches about how news is manipulated and massaged and how executives bow to profits, politics and lobby groups.

GAZA

A novel that follows the journey of three friends through Israel and Gaza. Through them we see the suffering and the manipulation of public opinion during the 60-year-old Israel-Palestine conflict.

THE CHINESE JUGGERNAUGHT: HOW THE CHINESE CONQUERED SOUTHEAST ASIA

The story of the Chinese diaspora in Southeast Asia and Australia, and how each country has been economically and sometimes politically dominated by a minority. A fascinating insight into the most successful and sometimes feared settlers and investors in the world today.

THE LAMA'S LOVER AND OTHER STORIES

A collection of ten short stories in which we meet a range of extraordinary individuals. Each carries their own cross in societies marred by religious, political and social injustices. The protagonists are often a composite of people the author met during his career travelling the world as a foreign correspondent.

THE HONORABLE HACK

Foreign Correspondent Serge Dunlov is deep in Latin America's Dirty Wars. Assignments take him from Mexico's Tlatelolco massacre to Castro's Havana, and then a posting to Chile for the election and the bloody fall of Salvador Allende. There he also lives a turbulent romance. Returning 35 years later, he is soon caught in the anti-terrorism witch-hunt and interned in a U.S. military camp.

www.ingramcontent.com/pod-product-compliance
Lightning Source LLC
Chambersburg PA
CBHW050400030726
47503CB00006B/1950